BECAUSE OF YOU

What Reviewers Say About Julie Cannon's Work

In *Smoke and Fire*…"Cannon skillfully draws out the honest emotion and growing chemistry between her heroines, a slow burn that feels like constant foreplay leading to a spectacular climax. Though Brady is almost too good to be true, she's the perfect match for Nicole. Every scene they share leaps off the page, making this a sweet, hot, memorable read."—*Publishers Weekly*

Breaker's Passion is…"an exceptionally hot romance in an exceptionally romantic setting. …Cannon has become known for her well-drawn characters and well-written love scenes."—*Just About Write*

In *Power Play*…"Cannon gives her readers a high stakes game full of passion, humor, and incredible sex."—*Just About Write*

About *Heartland*…"There's nothing coy about the passion of these unalike dykes—it ignites at first encounter and never abates. …Cannon's well-constructed novel conveys more complexity of character and less overwrought melodrama than most stories in the crowded genre of lesbian-love-against-all-odds—a definite plus."—Richard Labonte, *Book Marks*

"Cannon has given her readers a novel rich in plot and rich in character development. Her vivid scenes touch our imaginations as her hot sex scenes touch us in many other areas. *Uncharted Passage* is a great read."—*Just About Write*

About *Just Business*…"Julie Cannon's novels just keep getting better and better! This is a delightful tale that completely engages the reader. It's a must read romance!"—*Just About Write*

"Great plot, unusual twist and wonderful women. …[*I Remember*] is an inspired romance with extremely hot sex scenes and delightful passion."—*Lesbian Reading Room*

Visit us at www.boldstrokesbooks.com

By the Author

Come and Get Me

Heart 2 Heart

Heartland

Uncharted Passage

Just Business

Power Play

Descent

Breakers Passion

Rescuc Me

I Remember

Smoke and Fire

Because of You

BECAUSE OF YOU

by
Julie Cannon

2014

BECAUSE OF YOU

ISBN 13: 978-1-62639-199-4

This Trade Paperback Original Is Published By
Bold Strokes Books, Inc.
P.O. Box 249
Valley Falls, NY 12185

First Edition: October 2014

CREDITS
EDITOR: SHELLEY THRASHER
PRODUCTION DESIGN: SUSAN RAMUNDO
COVER DESIGN BY SHERI (GRAPHICARTIST2020@HOTMAIL.COM)

Author's Note

I worked for an oil and gas company for a few years and one of my co-workers was a man who had been kidnapped by the FARC. He was on a fishing trip when he was abducted and he was held captive for nine months and a few odd days. He could tell you the exact number of days and hours. He was not a young man but in his mid-sixties when he was taken and it took a toll on him mentally and physically. This is not his story, it was started many years ago, but his tales over coffee and bagels sounded exactly like my research. We're not perfect so any misinformation about the FARC, Columbia, or hostage reintegration is my responsibility alone. This is a work of fiction but it happens more times than we could ever imagine.

Dedication

To all the men and women who are waiting
to come home and those who never did.

PROLOGUE

I'm not leaving without her!"

She fought the hands that held her arms tight against her sides. The man was well over six feet tall and so strong she knew she'd have several bruises from his fingers gripping her arms. His buddy was equally built, and his crooked nose said that he too was used to physical violence to get what he wanted.

"We're here to get you, lady. Nobody else," Broken Nose said through clenched teeth.

"I don't care. I'm not leaving her," she shouted, accentuating her last few words.

The men had come in the middle of the night under the cover of darkness that the flares and grenades they'd lobbed at her home had obliterated. She was swept off her feet before she was able to stand and hustled into the jungle. She managed to twist around and find the dark eyes of the woman who had shared the terror with her and who was now quickly disappearing out of view.

She fought with every ounce of strength in her, kicking and scratching the man that held her. Her foot made contact with his shin, causing a muffled obscenity to escape his lips.

"Let me go." She jerked free on those words and had taken two steps in the direction of the woman before he grabbed her again. Their eyes locked, panic and desperation filling the smoky space between them. A sharp pain pierced her shoulder, and her knees buckled. Shouting voices and the sound of gunfire faded into blackness, along with the image of the desperate woman reaching out to her.

CHAPTER ONE

Bogota, Columbia

A lone bead of sweat snaked a crooked path between her breasts on its way to her navel. It was hotter than hell, even with the air-conditioning blasting on high. She'd lived in hot places before so she was used to the heat, but the humidity was killing her. Glancing around the room she couldn't help but sigh in exasperation. She shouldn't be here. She could have sent one of her staff to these meetings, but they'd insisted on her.

She had better things to do. She was way beyond this mundane jabber about contract extensions, working hours, and local versus U.S. suppliers. She was the owner of this company, for God's sake. She paid people to put up with this shit. That's what Debra and James were here for.

Debra Packer, however, her vice president for Global Digital, had barely broken a sweat. How did she do that? In the nine years she'd known Debra, Barrett had never seen her sweat. Or in Debra's case, the correct word would be perspire. Debra always said, "Ladies don't sweat, they perspire." Debra was impeccable, always perfectly put together, coiffed and fragrant. Every necklace matched her earrings, every bracelet a complement to her equally stylish accessories. It irritated the hell out of Barrett that she always had to wait for Debra who, if she played on their team, would be the poster girl for a lipstick lesbian.

How they had come to be business partners was still a mystery to her. Barrett was working on building her own software company when Debra had practically fallen into her lap. She was the granddaughter of her neighbor, a woman who'd lived next door to her for years, and Debra had knocked on her door one day and extended an invitation to dinner. After a plate of lasagna and several glasses of wine, Barrett had discovered that Debra had money to invest and she had all the brains to make Global Digital a reality. Over the years Debra had learned the business and become quite adept at landing big accounts, all the while never getting wrinkled. It didn't hurt that the men in the room obviously would rather look at Debra than her. Debra could probably get them to buy central heating simply by batting her eyelashes.

Barrett, however, was miserable. They'd been sitting in this stuffy room for three days with five men, and she desperately needed a change of scenery and fresh air. Bogota Electric was negotiating with Global Digital for a new electric-power grid system to better manage their electrical-power distribution that, in the past dozen years, had provided only sporadic electricity to the growing city. Global Digital had been chosen over a handful of companies in the world that could fix their problem, and they'd had to get special permission from the U.S. State Department to do business with Bogota Electric. What a pain in the ass that process had been.

She couldn't sit still any longer. She pushed her chair away from the large teak conference table. "Gentlemen, we're to a point where Debra and James can answer any additional questions you may have," she said, standing and nodding in the direction of Debra and her chief information officer. "If you'll excuse me." Even if they didn't, she was out of here.

Barrett knew her departure was abrupt but she didn't care. The discussions were routine and boring, at least to her, and she was, after all, the president of the company. She could do as she pleased and often did. Her reputation as a shark in business preceded her, and it was clear early on that this entire week was just a macho power play. They'd discussed nothing of substance and were basically at the same place as when they'd started. What crap.

Her car waited at the curb, and she didn't spare the panhandlers a second glance as she got in, snapped her seat belt, and told the driver to return to the hotel. At least there the air-conditioning worked. The Hotel De La Opera was a five-star establishment located in the center of the country's capital city. It was a quaint hotel from the outside, but once through the front door and into the expansive marble-filled lobby, she had immediately been able to tell that no expense had been spared. Her shoes tapped an angry cadence as she crossed the atrium, the sounds of muffled voices in the background.

Her room was large, at least by Columbian standards, with a king-size bed surrounded by soft lights, double sinks in the bath, a sitting room, and a well-stocked bar. She stripped and pulled on her swimsuit. The hotel amenities included a pool that Barrett considered barely above sub-standard, but she needed to burn off her irritation. She needed a few dozen laps and was determined to glide through the water for at least an hour. Fifteen pounds had snuck up on her while she sat behind her desk, and she was doggedly chasing each one away.

The water was tepid at best as she swam back and forth, her breathing even with each stroke. Her mind always cleared when she was in the water, but today it took longer than usual. She hadn't wanted to come to Columbia. She knew very little about the country other than what she had Googled in preparation for this contract.

The fourth-largest country in South America, located southeast of the Panama Canal, Columbia was most recognized as a danger zone rife with drugs, violence, and poverty. The phrase Medellin drug cartel was a staple on the nightly news. She had consulted the best security experts before allowing any of her staff to enter the country, and the hotel provided exceptional security as well. They traveled to and from their client's office in reserved, armor-plated cars.

Breathing hard, arms feeling rubbery, Barrett climbed out of the pool and slid the thick terry-cloth robe over her suit. She grabbed a towel and rubbed her hair, squeezing the excess water from her long locks. She'd been toying with the idea of cutting it much shorter but hadn't yet made an appointment. A waiter brought her a bottle of water, and she didn't bother to thank him before lying back on the chase lounge, dark sunglasses covering her eyes.

If Aaron could see her now he'd call her wasteful, decadent, spoiled, and a variety of other adjectives she was confident he'd have no trouble coming up with. Her brother was the greenest greenie she'd ever met. He didn't own a car, lived in a two-bedroom house with his wife and daughter, and faithfully and meticulously recycled everything according to the pamphlet that came with the blue bin. He was a strict vegan, washed his clothes in cold water, and abhorred excess of any kind. He frowned at her flying first class, thinking she should at least fly coach. He even went so far as to suggest she conduct the meeting by video conference to save on jet-fuel consumption.

The fact that she made a hundred times the money he did didn't bother him at all. She worked hard and earned every fucking penny. She could do whatever in the hell she wanted with it. So she flew first class. So what? So she ate at the best restaurants, big deal. And the outfit she wore today now lying in a heap on the floor in her room probably cost more than the waiter made in a year. Who cared? She didn't. She was all about work as well as play, with more than an occasional sleepover. Her personal relationships were superficial and fleeting. Other than her family, she'd never had any feelings one way or the other about anyone in her life.

Aaron had warned her against coming to Columbia. Based on the info he'd dumped on her over dinner last week, he must have trolled the Web for days for scary information on the country.

How could they be so different yet still be a product of the same parents? He was tall and skinny, well over six feet, whereas she was an average five foot six inches and, excluding the additional weight, had managed to keep her college weight of a hundred twenty-five pounds. The only thing about her similar to her older brother, other than the fact that they both liked to have sex with girls, was their hair. Her blond locks were long, naturally wavy and thick. He kept his equally curly hair cropped short and efficient.

Finally relaxed, Barrett strolled back to her room. It was only a little after four in the afternoon and she was restless. She showered, then pulled on a pair of loose khakis, a worn T-shirt, and sandals. She put her cash in her front pocket, her passport in the other, and her sunglasses on top of her head. She knew enough to dress inconspicuously while in the country. Any show of bling or money would be like a beacon to thugs or other street riff-raff. Jesus, couldn't these people at least take care of the tourists that brought money into their country? Without a glance at herself in the mirror she opened the door and stepped into the hall.

The elevator took her to the ground floor, and the doors silently swept open. The lobby was crowded with guests checking in, and she weaved her way through the crowd and out the front door.

Her guide was waiting for her and she fell into step beside him, pulling her sunglasses off her head and covering her eyes. She wasn't about to walk around this city without a guide. She'd studied a local map and knew where they were going, but no way would she be on the streets without some type of protection.

The sun was hot and the air thick. What in the hell am I doing, she asked herself. She could care less about the local trinkets and trash, as she called the typical tourist wares, but she would only be doing this for her family.

They walked for a few minutes, then turned left on the second street past what looked like a post office. An unpleasant scent filled her nostrils. God, what was that smell? She tried not to gag and definitely didn't want to know. The crowds thickened the closer they got to the outdoor market, until she was rubbing elbows with complete strangers.

She browsed up and down the aisles, picking up a trinket here, a souvenir there. Even with her opinion of tourist crap, she had a bookcase in her office filled with authentic items that were native to the countries where she traveled. One shelf contained a Japanese Geisha doll, a beer stein from Germany, a piece of the Great Wall, an Italian-leather letter opener, and a gold nugget from Africa.

She juggled her packages and the bottle of water she'd just bought and approached the last stall in the row. The bright colors caught her attention, and she knew she could find just the right thing for Aaron. Two men crowded into the space with her.

❖

More times than not, Barrett thanked her mother for insisting she take Spanish in high school. Granted, it had been years almost twenty years ago, but only for the sheer advantage she would have in business and in her personal life she kept fluent by occasionally watching the financial reports on the Spanish-speaking television station Telemundo.

The street vendors here in Bogota seemed to respect her and treat her differently than the tourists that didn't even make an attempt to speak their language. Their dialect was a little different than what she was used to. The difference was akin to variation in tone and pronunciation between a hard New York accent and a soft Southern drawl. More than once this afternoon she shook her head at an idiot American who thought if they just spoke louder or slower, the vendor would somehow miraculously understand English.

The contents of the last booth on the street didn't disappoint her. It was larger and better constructed than most of the others. Its three walls and roof were made of corrugated metal instead of rotting plywood. The tables displaying the vendors' wares were made of heavy plastic and didn't bow under the weight of the goods that jammed every square inch of the surface.

Barrett thumbed through the items on a table in the rear of the shanty, settling on a table runner made of natural fabric that Aaron insisted on. The pattern was simple, but the bold colors would match his kitchen décor perfectly. Hanging from a thin chain over her head was a mobile of butterflies that her niece Erin would enjoy. While the owner of the shop wrapped it up she wandered to the front of the shop and selected a paperweight for her administrative assistant Lori.

As she was putting her purchases in a bag, someone bumped her from behind. Some help her guide was in keeping people away from her. In addition to taking her where she wanted to go, he was supposed to look out for her. When she got back to the office she'd call the agency that had recommended him and drill them a second asshole. She stumbled, and before she had a chance to catch herself, strong hands grasped her arms. She started to say something but a hand covered her mouth.

What the fuck? The hand was rough and tight against her mouth, effectively shutting off any sound she might make, as well as her breath. She was lifted off her feet and scuttled away behind the booth. She managed to twist around, searching for her guide for help. She met his eyes, but he immediately looked away, turning his back to her and the man holding her.

Her heart raced as she struggled against the man and his firm grip. What in the hell was going on? The more she fought against the man, the tighter his grip, and the hand across her mouth muffled her scream of pain. Bile welled up in her throat, threatening to choke her. She forced herself not to panic, but the longer she couldn't breathe, the more difficult it became.

Think, think, she told herself. Instinct kicked in, overriding her brain, and she fought against her captor. This petty thug was not going to rob her. She kicked and scratched and finally made progress in her escape when she bit the hand that was over her mouth. The man screamed and loosened his grip. She had an instant to run and she took off. After only a few steps someone grabbed her hair from behind, jerking her head back and effectively stopping her. She let out a scream as she was dragged backward. Though she dug her heels into the dirt trying to stop, the pain in her head was almost overwhelming. She felt large chunks of hair being ripped out at the roots. Then she realized what was happening and froze. She was being kidnapped.

❖

Dozens of thoughts flashed through her brain. Kidnappings were common in Columbia. Victims were often never released, or if they were, it was sometimes after several years in captivity. Hostages were held for ransom or simply killed as a show of force, power, terror, or all three. Would she be killed? Did they know who she was, or was she just a random choice? Who would pay her ransom? Debra? Aaron? Her parents? Where were they taking her?

Another hand went over her mouth, this time trapping her tongue between her teeth. She tasted blood, knowing it was her own, her adrenaline masking any additional pain. Her arms were jerked behind her back, and she felt something being slipped over her hands and onto her wrists. Immediately the object tightened, successfully linking her hands together. They didn't feel like handcuffs, but they accomplished the same thing.

The hand left her mouth for an instant before someone stuffed a rag into it. Barrett gagged on the disgusting taste and fought down the urge to vomit. A second rag was wrapped around her head, trapping the gag in her mouth. One man held her arms while the other tied the gag tightly around her head.

Both men were behind her so she couldn't see her attackers. Hands rough with calluses handled her, and the stench from her assailants reeked of bad breath and terrible body odor. She swallowed and tried to calm down.

Someone kicked her legs out from under her, and she hit the ground with a groan. With her hands secured behind her back, Barrett had nothing to stop her face from hitting solidly on the hard dirt. Lights flashed behind her eyes, darkness threatening to overtake her. Sharp pain in her nose and her forehead forced its way through her shock and took center stage for her attention. She blinked several times to clear her head but got little relief.

Someone grabbed her feet, and she started to panic again. She was on her stomach kicking and squirming, still trying to get free. One of the men grabbed her hair again and forced her head backward, effectively cutting off her air supply. He put his knees into her back, and she started to black out when the man holding her hair released it. Her face fell into the dirt again. She struggled to get enough air into her lungs through her bloody nose. Instead, she aspirated blood and dirt before the threatening blackness won.

❖

Barrett felt like she was deep underwater and slowly rising to the surface. She was lying on her side in the mud, leaves, and other shit she couldn't identify. Without moving she surveyed her limbs, starting with the toes on her left foot up her leg, torso, each arm, and ending with the toes on her right. Her mental inventory and the lack of any substantial pain told her that nothing major appeared to be broken. Her hands were behind her back, her feet secured with what looked like zip ties, thick plastic bands used by law enforcement as a backup to regular handcuffs. Her fingers were numb, but she was still able to move them.

The gag had been removed from her mouth, and a pool of vomit and blood lay an inch from her open lips. At least she could breathe, barely. She didn't need a mirror to tell her the familiar pain in the center of her face was a broken nose. Judging by the amount of blood on the ground and the accompanying pain on the left side of her forehead, she probably had a gash there as well.

Two men were sitting on a log about six feet away, smoking a cigarette. The larger man, she guessed, was well over six feet tall and had to weigh at least two hundred fifty pounds. His hair was long and his scruffy beard even longer. He was dressed in army fatigues, an effective camouflage in the dense jungle. His partner was similarly dressed but clean-shaven and half his size. At this moment they weren't paying any attention to her.

Barrett lay still, in part to stop her head from exploding and also to eavesdrop on their conversation. Their voices were muffled, but what she was able to decipher scared the crap out of her. They were talking about how long it would take to get her back to the main camp. One man said three days, the other four or five, depending on how fast they could make her travel.

She caught snippets of names—Manuel, Santiago, and The Colonel. She was able to figure out that they'd been sent to get another one, whatever that meant, and something about a girlfriend for Liberty. Most of what they said didn't make sense, but she learned enough to know she was in deep shit.

The man with the beard, who looked just like Blue Beard, laughed when he said something about the prize that awaited him when they returned. He rubbed his crotch for effect, and his lascivious cackle made her stomach turn. The other man looked more like a young Desi Arnez and, of the two, was definitely the order-taker. He was wiry and very dark, his hair tied behind his head in a ponytail.

That thought made the back of Barrett's head hurt. Her long hair had been pulled at least twice, and she cursed its length, which had provided the two thugs she named Blue and Desi the perfect way to restrain her. When she got out of this mess she intended to cut it all off.

She closed her good eye and took a deep breath. Her ribs hurt where she'd either fallen or had been kicked, but each breath helped clear her head. She was amazingly composed. She'd been beaten, kidnapped, and hog-tied, and she was almost as calm as when she'd found herself buried under fifteen feet of snow on Mount Hood. The circumstances were very different, but like that experience, she could very well die before the day was over.

Blue moved toward her, telling his buddy it was time to go. Barrett thought it wise not to let on that she understood most of what they said, so she stayed still. He nudged her in the back, indicating she was to wake up. She debated for a moment whether to move but decided he'd probably kick her harder if she didn't.

She rolled her head and opened her eyes to find his scuffed boot inches from her face. One wrong move on her part, and he could easily knock out a few teeth. She moaned as a new pain shot through her shoulder.

"Jesus, enough, give me a minute," Barrett said without thinking. It probably wasn't a good idea to say exactly what was on her mind.

Blue reached down and cut off the zip ties, then dragged her to her feet. Her knees buckled, the darkness threatening to drape over her again. Cold water was splashed on her face and someone slapped her cheek. She screamed, her voice raspy and unhindered by the gag. Blue told her to shut up, and another splash of water hit her in the face again. Her nose hurt, and her forehead stung from the force of the water. She forced her legs to work.

Blue's face was in front of her, his decaying teeth showing proudly through a leer. He squeezed her arm tighter and told her in his native tongue just exactly what he would do to her when they got back to camp. He finished his statement with a sloppy kiss that made her retch. Both he and Desi laughed. The gag was back, this time secured with duct tape. Desi pushed her forward, Blue leading the way.

Chapter Two

Rebel Camp, somewhere in Columbia

She got to her feet before they came and hauled her to her feet. It was one of the few things she had control over, at least this morning she did. She'd learned to relish and hold on to the things that others would find inconsequential—like walking where she wanted to when she wanted to and brushing her hair when she wanted to. Even going to the bathroom when she needed to versus when they let her had become a treat.

For the past eight months, or at least Kelly Ryan thought it was that long but wasn't sure, someone else had controlled her movements every minute of every day. She moved when they told her, stood where they told her, and ate whatever they gave her. If she didn't, and sometimes even when she did, she was stripped, beaten, starved, tied to a tree, or worse.

She hadn't been held hostage the longest, or the shortest. Juan Cordoba, a Cuban diplomat, held the dubious honor of the longest at two years, and Francois LeCroix, a French banker, had been dragged into the camp four months ago barely alive. She would stop by and look in on him later after she checked on her other patients—the rebels that held her and seven other people hostage somewhere in the jungle.

Her back hurt from lying on the hard ground, but at least she didn't have any nightmares while she slept—none that she remembered. When she'd first arrived, and for months afterward, her dreams, when she was allowed to sleep, were filled with images of masked men, shouts, gunfire, and blood. So much blood.

Kelly was on her third visit to Bogota, along with five other nurses and two physicians volunteering in a rural clinic just east of the war-torn city. Her first trip to Columbia had been four years ago with a fellow nurse, and she'd immediately fallen in love with the country and its people. Their patients had nothing, and health care of any kind was virtually nonexistent. If not treated properly, something as simple as a minor cut could result in death.

Her team had been two days away from going home when the rebels struck their camp. Kelly knew the risks of simply being in Columbia, but her work and seeing just how much these people needed them had pushed any thoughts of danger out of her mind. The Fuerzas Armadas Revolucionarios de Colombia, or FARC, was established in the early 1960s by the Colombian Communist Party to defend Communist-controlled rural areas. She'd read that it was Latin America's oldest, largest, most capable, and best-equipped insurgency, with over ten thousand armed combatants and several thousand supporters. Like during most civil wars, the civilians her team treated were often caught in the middle.

Slowly she stretched her arms above her head. Her left shoulder ached, a remnant of her encounter with one of the guards she and her fellow hostages had nicknamed Hercules. He was big and burly and reminded them of the mythical Greek hero. Several months ago she hadn't moved fast enough to suit him, and when he grabbed her by the arm, she heard a pop. He silenced the resulting scream with a backhand across her face. Suffering unbearable pain, she had to talk her fellow prisoners through what to do to slip her shoulder back into its socket.

At five foot eight inches, Kelly was taller than some of her captors and, before she lost the extra fifty pounds she came in with, had outweighed them as well. She kept her brown hair as short as she could, the length necessary to keep it clean and not get caught on low-hanging branches when they were forced to march through the jungle. Scabs from insects feasting on her the night before were red and raw and itched terribly, but she'd learned how to block the constant stinging from her mind, along with many other things. She ran her crooked finger over the fading scar on her right thigh. The first hadn't healed correctly after it was broken when she was first kidnapped, and the second had resulted from a fall against a sharp rock a few months ago. Her feet were bare. The shoes she'd had on when she was captured had disintegrated under the harsh Columbian jungle conditions, and she hadn't received another pair.

She quickly and quietly followed her morning routine of thanking God she was still alive, making the next move on the chessboard in her head, and doing isometric exercises. She always started at her feet and worked her way up through the major muscles in her body to her head, then reversed the path.

Other hostages had taught her that routine was one of the most important elements to her mental survival, and it was true. Filling her days with activities that could be repeated, even if they were only in her mind, gave Kelly a sense of control in a life that was completely out of her control.

She missed her early morning walks. She used to rise at dawn, toss on her sweats, grab Needle's leash, and be out the door in ten minutes. Thinking of her dog and what might have happened to him still caused pain. Her best friend Ariel always watched him whenever she went out of town and couldn't take her two-year-old, four-legged friend along. She missed his constant presence in her life and, on more than one occasion, the rangy mutt licked her tears when she lost a patient.

The sun was filtering through the thick canopy of trees, the sounds of the camp slowly coming to life as she finished her routine. When they had arrived at this spot several days ago, she and her fellow hostages had been forced to clear away much of the heavy vegetation in and around their new camp. She found it ironic that they had to do the work that would prevent someone from raiding their camp and rescuing them. Currently twenty-eight rebels were in camp. The number varied from as few as eight to sometimes as many as fifty crowding their little settlement. She worried about Juan, the Cuban diplomat. The extreme physical labor of the last few days had sapped more of his already weakened strength. She was hoping today would be a day of rest, but she'd learned to never take anything for granted, even waking up.

Kelly heard voices in the distance, someone blowing his nose, another coughing not far away. She needed to pee and wondered how long it would be before someone came and unlocked her or if she would have to squat out here in the open. Her current situation as a hostage of the FARC living in the jungle had eliminated any sense of modesty. Of course the other issue was the fact that she had five feet of chain secured to her left ankle.

They still chained her to a tree every night, the clanking of the sturdy links no longer keeping her awake. The night guards were charged with detecting any infiltration of their camp by government troops, and with the hostages secured, they could remain focused on their task.

Kelly saw the guard she'd named Opie heading her way and breathed a sigh of relief. Of all the rebels, Opie was by far the kindest to her and the others. He wasn't as callous and didn't get off on humiliating his charges. She'd named him Opie because he reminded her of Opie Taylor on *The Andy Griffith Show*. He looked nothing like she'd envisioned a guerrilla terrorist. With his baby face and lack of facial hair, he couldn't have been a day over sixteen.

She started to say good morning but held her tongue when she saw his expression. He was angry, and if she spoke without being spoken to first, even though he was the nicest of the thugs, she would be punished.

Lowering her eyes, she stood silently waiting for some indication of what was expected of her. The uncertainty was the most difficult to deal with. Each day was like living with a manic-depressive family member. One minute things were calm and serene, but the next, shouts and screams and brutality would explode with very little advance notice and even less time for the victims to mentally prepare.

Opie didn't say anything as he knelt and unlocked the bracket that surrounded her ankle. The metal clanked when it hit the ground, an indication of its heavy weight. The place on her ankle where the metal rubbed was barely noticeable. Her body had compensated for the constant friction by developing a hard callus.

He grunted something that Kelly wasn't able to understand, and with a poke in her side with his rifle, she was moving. Three times a day she was forced to tend to the ill or injured rebels in the camp. She wasn't sure if the rebels had raided her clinic and kidnapped her because they needed her and their medical supplies or that she'd simply been in the wrong place at the wrong time. Either way she was a nurse, and whether she liked it or not, she had a job to do.

They had few actual medical supplies, and she was forced to make do with what she had, which wasn't much. Periodically men would appear in their camp with supplies, which sometimes included bandages, antibiotics, sutures and, antiseptic cream. Today, her patients, as she reluctantly called them, consisted of a gunshot wound to the foot that was looking more infected each time she looked at it, a nasty bout of dysentery she hoped wouldn't spread through the camp again, and a knife stabbing. But the care, or lack thereof, that she was able to provide her fellow hostages disturbed her most. Her job was to keep them alive so the rebels could ransom them off. They were worth nothing to them dead.

As a nurse, Kelly had taken an oath to heal, and it was very difficult to have to sit by helpless and watch her fellow captives suffer. It was only after her captors had been treated that she was allowed to check on the others, and only with leftover supplies. She was watched carefully to ensure she didn't skimp on treatment for the rebels and give more to their prisoners. Like it could get any worse, she thought as she crossed the compound.

If they were lucky they had shelter from the rain and incessant bugs feasting on them throughout the night. But they hadn't been lucky for months. Juan was lying on a dirty mat on the ground. Francois and one of the other hostages had been at least able to move him under a large tree, which offered some cover from the relentless midday sun.

After she tended to Juan, Opie poked her in the back again, signaling her that visiting hours were over. A wave of dizziness swam over her when she stood, a direct effect of very little to drink and absolutely nothing to eat yesterday. She and the others were fed only after the guards had their fill, and with the scarcity of rations lately, they rarely had more than a few scraps from discarded plates. This morning, however, she detected coffee and something that smelled a lot like eggs. Maybe that explained the ruckus last night when several people had arrived at their camp.

She tripped over an exposed root, stumbling to her knees. She muffled a cry when a sharp pain seared through the heel of her palm. She got to her feet, brushing off her hands on the legs of her shorts, a trail of blood leaving a path. *Shit, this is not good.* Even the smallest cut could be life threatening in these filthy conditions.

Between hand gestures and broken Spanish, she asked Opie if she could get some water to wash her hands. She hated having to ask for everything, but she knew the consequences if she didn't. He nudged her toward the water barrel with the tip of his rifle, and she gratefully crossed back across the camp. She scanned the camp and, not seeing anyone paying any attention to her, she took the opportunity to carefully survey her surroundings.

She could make a run for it; she had twice before. But the consequences when she was caught, and she would be caught again, were brutal. The first time she was found within minutes and tied to a tree for what felt like forever. The second it took them twice as long to find her, and the punishment was twice as severe. They beat her and broke the toes on both feet. Escaping from the camp was a possibility, getting caught was a certain reality, and surviving yet another punishment again was the only thing in doubt.

CHAPTER THREE

B arrett fought the exhaustion that threatened to overtake her and concentrated instead on putting one foot in front of the other—barely. Blue had slipped another set of zip ties over each foot, cinched them tight, and connected them with each other. She could move her feet, but only about eight inches. It was their third day in the jungle, and she'd been walking for hours, shuffling along trying to stay upright. Her wrists and ankles were raw from her restraints, the open sores burning from sweat and insects feasting on her. She'd lost her sandals when she was taken, so her feet were cut and bloody from walking on roots and rocks on the hard, cracked ground. She hadn't had anything to eat since lunch on the day she was taken and very little to drink. At least the gag was out of her mouth. Blue had ripped the duct tape off her face this morning, and Barrett was so grateful for a mouthful of fresh air, she barely noticed the hair that was pulled out along with it.

Her once-white shirt was filthy and torn and would never button again. With her hands secured behind her back she was unable to shield her face or body from the branches that hung over the trail. Barrett knew her face was covered with cuts, some more severe than others, judging from the amount of blood covering her shirt and almost-bare chest. When the last of her buttons surrendered to another vine peppered with sharp needles at least an inch long, both Blue and Desi leered at her.

Her mouth, already parched from the exertion and lack of water, became even dryer as the two men surveyed her flesh exposed between the open folds of her shirt. She knew what was going to happen and that she'd be helpless to stop it. With her hands behind her back and her feet still hogtied, she could do little to defend herself. She spread her feet as far as the plastic line would let her and squared her shoulders. She'd get at least one good shot at whoever came at her first.

It was Blue, the leader of the two, and the gleam in his eye and the erection pushing at his pants signaled his intentions. Before he got within touching distance, Desi spoke, and Barrett understood every word.

"What are you doing? The Colonel will skin you alive if she's harmed."

"I don't care. She's my reward for dragging my ass in and out of this goddamn jungle. You can have her after I'm through with her," Blue barked back at him.

"Lopez, don't. He'll think we both had her and will punish me as well." Desi was pleading.

"Then you might as well get something out of it." Blue stepped closer but stopped when Desi put the barrel of his rifle between him and Barrett. "And who's going to stop me, amigo?" Blue laughed. "You?"

Barrett saw Desi swallow and silently prayed he had the courage to stand his ground.

"Yes, Lopez. I will stop you. I won't be punished because you can't keep your cock in your pants."

Barrett held her breath as the two men sized up the other. If she hadn't been so scared she could have appreciated the classic good-versus-evil scenario, but as it was she was hoping they'd fight and simply kill each other.

Blue stepped back, never taking his eyes off her. She didn't know if she was relieved that she wasn't going to be raped, at least not right now, or disappointed that the two men didn't try to kill each other. Blue finally turned around, signaling the end of his threat. *This threat*, Barrett thought. She knew this was only the beginning.

❖

Shouts and whistles drew Kelly's attention from bandaging the foot with the gunshot wound. The infection was worse than when she'd seen it this morning, and gangrene had set in. She hoped she wasn't forced to amputate the limb like she'd been once before. Within the first week of her arrival, she'd had no choice but to remove the first three fingers on the left hand of one of her kidnappers. She tried to communicate that she was a nurse, not a doctor, and when one of the rebels put the tip of his rifle to the temple of another hostage, she stopped trying. Somehow Kelly had managed not to kill the man during the actual procedure, and miraculously he didn't die from complications. From that point on she was forced to treat every illness or injury that came into the camp.

Her escort again this afternoon was Opie, and he heard the commotion as well. As soon as she finished wrapping the foot, he shoved her toward the center of the camp. Excitement filled the thick air, signaling the arrival of either another group of rebels or another hostage. Opie nudged her in the back with the barrel of his gun to move along faster, and she stumbled but caught herself before she hit the rocky ground yet again.

The noise grew louder. The jungle moved, and within seconds, two of the rebels from her camp emerged, closely followed by two men she'd never seen. But it was what was between the men that made Kelly gasp.

They were dragging a woman into the camp. Kelly didn't know if she was dead, unconscious, or simply exhausted. Even if she were conscious, the bindings around her ankles wouldn't have allowed her to easily keep pace with the men. The men moved in unison, each one holding her at the elbow, indicating that the woman's hands were bound behind her back.

Long hair hung limply off the woman's head, her chin bouncing against her chest as they moved. It was obvious to Kelly that it was a woman, but the breasts exposed by the torn shirt dispelled any doubt for anyone else. Her pants were equally torn, her feet bare and bloody.

Shocked at another female hostage entering the camp, Kelly shivered. Women didn't fare well in these circumstances. If the lack of food, harsh living conditions, torture, brutality, or the constant threat of rape didn't kill them, the disease, heat, bugs, or any of a thousand other things could.

Kelly forced herself to remain where she was when everything inside her was telling her to go to the woman to help her. She was a nurse, a woman, and a fellow hostage, and the order didn't matter. She tried to close her eyes, get the image out of her mind, but couldn't.

She tried not to pay too much attention to the woman. She'd learned, the hard way, that their captors often used the hostages against each other for sport, revenge, or simply cruelty. Too much concern over a fellow prisoner could and would be used against them in the future.

Several months after her arrival, she'd developed a friendship of sorts with a fellow captive. Jean Paul had been in his mid-sixties and reminded Kelly of her father, and he often told her that she looked just like his daughter. Jean Paul had a weak immune system and was often ill. Their captors couldn't care less and forced him to work alongside the others when they needed to break camp, carve a new camp out of the jungle, or walk for miles through the thick, hot, humid jungle. When he wasn't sick they spent as much time as they could talking about books, history, and their families. Anything to get their mind off where they were.

One day when Kelly refused to treat the wounds of a rebel who'd just the day before raped a fellow captive, Jean Paul was hauled out of his sick bed and strung up to a tree. His wrists were bound and pulled over his head by a thick rope that had been tossed over a high branch. The rope was pulled until he dangled from the branch with just his toes touching the ground. There he remained until Kelly finally agreed to help the man. Actually, he remained there for three more days, without food or water, Kelly forced to sit beside him when she wasn't working and sleep at his feet. Finally the rebels cut him down, but not before she learned a valuable lesson.

The men released their hold on the woman and she fell to the ground, seeming lifeless. Her two escorts were greeted with cheers, back slaps, and cigars. Someone put a canteen of water in their hands. They pointed and poked at their new guest, all the while talking on top of each other like a bunch of cackling women. Kelly had picked up a few words but didn't understand much of what was being said, but judging by the tone and body language, it wouldn't be good for the unconscious woman. It never was.

Two other guards, one of whom Francois had named Harry after the Clint Eastwood character Dirty Harry, picked up the woman and dragged her closer to a tree. Taking the chain that was secured around its base, he fastened it to the woman's ankle, effectively securing her.

Kelly calculated the distance between where she stood and the woman and judged it to be about ten yards. For a fleeting moment she thought about breaking away from Opie and running to her, but it was pointless. She wouldn't be able to do anything to help her before Opie caught her, and both she and the woman would suffer for her spontaneous actions. Before she had a chance to do anything stupid, the man they all called The Colonel stepped out of his tent.

The Colonel was the leader of this gang of rebels, and he was strict and didn't tolerate laziness or insubordination. If the men didn't jump when he spoke, he punished them almost as severely as the hostages. Kelly suspected he had some type of military training by the way he issued orders and expected them to be obeyed without hesitation.

He was the tallest of all the men Kelly had seen during her captivity. He stood well over six feet and must have weighed at least two hundred sixty pounds. She would know. He'd been on top of her more than once. Pushing that thought from her mind she watched as he approached the crumpled woman.

He spoke with one of the men who'd brought the woman in, glancing back and forth between her and the man talking. The Colonel stood with his feet shoulder-width apart, and by his posture Kelly was sure he'd strike either one or both men.

She'd studied The Colonel—his walk, his mannerisms, speech patterns—and found him very transparent if you knew what to look for. And she did. She found people fascinating and would often sit in a busy mall watching them go by. It was a game her cousin Sam and she had played when their mother dragged them out shopping. They'd sit and guess the occupation of each person as they walked by, judging them by their clothes, their walk, and their companions. They had no way of knowing if they were correct, but it killed time and was fun.

The two men's heads snapped back, one right after the other, and all Kelly saw was The Colonel's arm moving back to his side. For a big man he was fast, very fast, and more than once she'd been on the receiving side of that quickness. Something the men had done or not done had displeased the leader, and he made no secret of it.

Both men wiped the smirk off their faces, blood from their noses, and snapped to attention. Even though it was all said in Spanish, Kelly knew the two men were getting their asses kicked, figuratively and probably literally as well later on. The Colonel never raised his voice, but the message was clear as the two men saluted, spun around, and marched away.

The Colonel turned and locked eyes with Kelly and she fought not to look away. She hated being a coward but had learned which battle to fight and which not to. Most were the not-to-fight variety.

"Miss Ryan, please come here." The Colonel spoke fluent English, although with a harsh Spanish accent.

Kelly kept her eyes on the ground as she walked across the dirt and stopped in front of the man. Another one of her lessons was to not speak until spoken to.

"See to this woman. She is very valuable to us." He didn't say anything else to her but issued a few stark commands to both Opie and another one of the guards standing nearby. The guard ran in the direction of the commissary, and The Colonel returned to his tent.

"Yes, sir," Kelly mumbled to his retreating back, and dropped quickly to her knees. She moved the hair that had fallen across the woman's face and felt for a pulse on her neck. It was weak but steady. Carefully Kelly rolled the woman onto her back and began a cursory check of her body for any outward signs of significant injury. Other than dozens of cuts and scrapes on her torso and extremities, and hundreds of bug bites covering her skin, the only serious wound she could see other than an obviously broken nose was a nasty cut on her forehead.

The guard returned with a meager supply of bandages and antiseptic and dropped the bag at her feet. "Water, please," she asked in Spanish.

The water in the camp was relatively clean, and she needed a lot to clean the wounds. Opie moved a few feet away and sat on a dead tree, his rifle trained in their direction. The guard returned and tossed a canteen on the ground beside her.

"It's going to be all right," Kelly whispered as she ran the cool cloth over the woman's torn skin. "My name is Kelly. I'm a nurse, and I'm going to help you the best I can. Can you open your eyes?" Kelly pressed her hand to the woman's forehead. She was warm but not burning with fever, like her other patients often were.

"Come on, open your eyes and look at me," Kelly said. "I've got to make sure you're all right." She reached into the kit and took out the antiseptic bottle. The cut on the woman's head was deep and ran almost in a straight line from her hairline down through her left eyebrow. She had no way to stitch it closed and knew it would leave a very ugly scar. She dipped the corner of a rag into the red liquid and, knowing the cut would hurt like hell, was almost glad the woman was unconscious.

It took several seconds for the liquid to penetrate the dried blood and the woman's consciousness. When it did it was like a light had been switched on. She immediately opened her eyes, shouted, and fought against her restraints.

"Ssh, it's okay. I'm trying to help you," Kelly said quietly.

If the woman continued to fight she could injure herself more than she already was. Kelly lowered her head so she could look more squarely into the woman's eyes, and what she saw took her breath away.

Chapter Four

Searing pain. That was the only way Barrett could describe it. A thousand needles poked into her skin, one at a time, and they weren't stopping. The pain pulled her out of the darkness that had mercifully covered her like a blanket. A soft voice in a language she recognized seeped into her brain. What were they saying? Barrett fought to open her eyes.

"Come on now. That's it. Open your eyes." The voice had a melodious drawl that reminded Barrett of the way her cousin Kim spoke. Gentle, rhythmic, Southern. She couldn't help but obey the request.

A tanned, gaunt face looked down at her. A frown creased the forehead, causing the expression to be severe. Deep-blue eyes peered at her from under short brown hair. *A woman?* Barrett blinked a few more times to clear her vision and drive away the cobwebs in her head. It *was* a woman.

"Good," the woman said, a small smile tipping the ends of her mouth upward. Out of the corner of her left eye, Barrett saw the woman's hand move. "This is going to hurt a little. I need to clean your cuts and set your nose."

Little wasn't the way Barrett would describe it. It was a repeat of the pain that had brought her out of the dark earlier, and the second time was no less severe than the first. She hissed and tears formed behind her closed eyes when she heard the distinctive snap of cartilage being put back in place.

"Fuck, goddamn, get your hands off me," she shouted through the pain.

"Sorry, but you'd never breathe right if I didn't straighten it. You've also got a nasty cut on your forehead. I have to clean it or it'll get infected. And trust me, that's the last thing you want."

Barrett concentrated on the sound of the woman's voice and tried to block out the pain. Slowly the stinging dissipated and she could see again. The woman could certainly pass for Florence Nightingale, or at least what Barrett thought a caring nurse would look like.

"There, if we can keep this clean, I think you'll be all right," the woman said.

But who was she and where in the hell was *she*?

Barrett suddenly remembered. Well, she didn't know *exactly* where she was, but she was somewhere in the middle of the fucking jungle. And she remembered how she got here. She tried to sit up, but her hands behind her back made it next to impossible.

"Here let me help you." The woman with the soft Southern drawl eased her into a sitting position. "That's it. Are you dizzy? Are you nauseous? Any double vision?"

Barrett couldn't answer, the movement and questions making her head pound even more. Blackness threatened to overtake her again, and she fought it. As much as she wanted to disappear into oblivion, she had to stay awake and figure a way out of the mess she'd gotten herself into. She tried to move her hands and stifled a cry.

"I said get your fucking hands off me. I don't need *your* help." That was an understatement. What she needed was about a dozen Navy Seals to crash this party right now.

"We have to clean your cut. If it gets infected, there's very little I can do."

The woman was looking at her with kind eyes. Kind eyes, my ass. She was obviously part of this gang, and no way was Barrett going to let her touch her again. Even if it killed her.

"No, you don't want me to die, do you? I'm worthless to you dead and a bundle if I'm not. Well, amigo, don't bother," Barrett said defiantly, as her head pounded.

"Let me look at your hands," the woman said, moving to crouch behind her.

Barrett barely held in the scream that shot up her arms and out her parched throat. A wave of nausea threatened to empty her already-empty stomach, but somehow she managed to swallow the bile that hadn't yet reached her mouth. Sweat broke out across her brow and slid into her eyes. She was suddenly hot, very hot.

"I said don't touch me," Barrett said through gritted teeth.

The woman came back around to face her, and Barrett detected a flicker of something she couldn't identify in her tired eyes. Now that Barrett was more focused, she felt an overwhelming need to kill her and every fucking person involved in this.

The woman didn't have a chance to reply before she was hauled to her feet and pushed in the opposite direction. Barrett understood that the guard was shouting at her to stop talking. The woman didn't look back but instead stumbled forward each time the guard pushed her. A sick feeling fell over Barrett when she realized the woman was a prisoner like herself.

❖

Kelly practically fell onto her bedroll. Opie wasn't usually this rough, but she suspected The Colonel was watching and would dole out the discipline he thought appropriate. The Colonel saw everything and his men feared him. Whereas most men followed their leaders out of respect and a shared cause, The Colonel's men knew they would be killed if they didn't. He often made an example of one of them when they broke one of his rules. The punishment was severe, quick, and unforgettable.

Opie secured the chain to her ankle, and she watched The Colonel walk slowly back across the camp toward the woman. A guard hauled her to her feet. The woman looked him squarely in the eye as he approached. Even though Kelly knew what was going to happen next, she jumped when he slapped the woman's face. Her head snapped back and she crumpled to the ground.

The guard standing next to the woman pulled her up again. Her head rolled and her knees buckled, but the guard held her upright.

"Wake up," The Colonel shouted. "I said wake up!" This time the guard tossed a cup of water in the woman's face. She sputtered and blinked several times.

"You, Miss Taylor, are a prisoner of the Fuerzas Armadas Revolucionarios de Colombia. I am Colonel Suarez and this is my camp. You will do what I say, when I say it, and as many times as I tell you to. If you try to escape we will hunt you down and catch you. No one has ever escaped from me, and you," he pointed a finger at the woman, "will not be the first."

The Colonel slowly walked around the woman as if inspecting her like a side of beef. Or like a man inspecting his next piece of ass. Kelly shuddered at the thought.

"You will be with us until your ransom is paid. That may be weeks, it may be years, but if it is not paid you will never leave." He stopped in front of the woman and looked her directly in her eyes.

"You are a wonderful catch, Miss Taylor," The Colonel said in perfect English. "You are very wealthy, your company has a lot of money, and you have family that loves you. You will fetch a nice bounty. I hope it doesn't come too soon. You are a very beautiful woman." The Colonel traced the woman's breasts with the butt of his ever-present whip.

Kelly's stomach tightened, and she was shocked when the woman spit in The Colonel's face. "Fuck you," she heard her reply an instant before he punched her in the mouth. Kelly jumped up and got the few feet her tether allowed before her feet were yanked out from under her and she fell on her stomach. When the dirt settled and Kelly could see again, the woman lay motionless on the ground, blood dripping from her mouth.

CHAPTER FIVE

B arrett tried to open her eyes. Her left one would obey the command from her brain, but only slightly. The right refused to do anything. That side of her face throbbed, and she remembered being struck in the face before she blacked out again. The pounding in her head beat to a consistent cadence.

She listened to the sounds around her. It was almost dark, and voices were murmuring in the distance. After a few minutes she felt strong enough to sit up, which wasn't easy with her hands secured behind her back. A wave of dizziness threatened to overtake her again, and Barrett took several deep breaths. She saw that her foot was secured to the base of the tree by a chain. No guards were near, but the thickness of the links would keep her from going anywhere.

"How do you feel?" The voice she recognized from earlier drifted to her. Barrett slowly lifted her head and saw the woman sitting no farther than a few feet from her.

"Like I've been dragged through the jungle for days, kicked, punched in the face, and starved." Barrett's tone was sharp. "I'm sorry. I thought you were one of them. I know you tried to help me, or at least I think it was you. Thank you." Barrett hated admitting when she was wrong, but this time it wasn't a problem.

"I was worried. You took quite a blow from The Colonel."

"Is that what you call him? He's a pig." Barrett remembered the leer on his face when he stared at her exposed breasts. It was worth the slap to wipe it off, if just for a moment.

"You need to be careful around him." The woman didn't agree or disagree with her description of the camp leader. "He has a lightning temper and an equally fast backhand."

Barrett moved her jaw back and forth. It was sore but not broken. She wasn't sure about one of her teeth. "Was that what that was?" She hadn't seen it coming but had definitely felt it all the way to her toes. Barrett looked at the woman more closely. She was also chained to a tree, but her hands weren't bound.

"How long have you been here?"

"A long time." That was all the woman said. She looked like it. She was too thin, her dark hair was chopped off around her head, her skin tan from the sun.

"How long is a long time?" The woman hesitated. "Come on. I need to know what's in store for me. Even if I don't really want to." Barrett was the type of woman who needed to have all the information. The more she was aware of what might happen, the less mystery it held. She was a firm believer that what you didn't know you'd make up, and it was probably going to be wrong.

"I think it's been about eight months," the woman answered quietly.

Eight months? Holy fuck. Barrett tried not to show her shock but wasn't sure she succeeded. "You're not sure?"

"What's the date?" The woman seemed hopeful.

"I'm not sure about today, but the last I knew it was the fifteenth of July." She'd probably lost a day or so lately. Barrett watched as the woman's face fell. For a moment, she thought she might cry, but she pulled herself together.

"One year and five days, give or take a few," the woman replied, her voice lifeless.

Barrett didn't know what to say. A year? Good God, how could anyone survive this place for that long? The huts around them, if you could call them that, were made out of sticks and pressed lumber. They were held together by rope and vines and looked as if one big wind would blow them apart. The woman was sitting on a mat of some kind, her only covering the wide leaves on the trees overhead. Why hadn't she tried to escape? That was the first thing on Barrett's mind.

"What's your name?" Barrett finally asked.

The woman hesitated as if trying to remember. Finally she said, "Kelly Ryan."

"I'm Barrett Taylor. Are there any others here?" She was referring to other hostages.

"Yes, eight of us."

"Are you the only American?" The drumming in her head showed no sign of subsiding.

Kelly glanced around. "Yes. There are two Frenchmen, one Spaniard, three Germans, and one man from Japan."

"Are you the only woman?"

Kelly nodded.

"Is everyone being held for ransom?" Barrett remembered what The Colonel had said about why she was here before he smacked her into unconsciousness.

"In one form or another, I suppose. Money and power are what they're after, and it takes money to get power and power to get money."

At the risk of upsetting Kelly, she asked, "So why does it take so long?" She saw a brief flicker of pain cross Kelly's face before she masked it.

"Money, politics, or just refusing to negotiate. Who knows? I don't speak much Spanish, even though I've been able to pick up a few words here and there. It's not as if The Colonel is going to come out and say why. It'd make him look bad in the eyes of his men." Kelly looked down at the ground, then back at her.

"In my case it's probably the lack of cash. I don't have the kind of money they're probably asking for, and my aid organization has even less."

"Why were you here, in Columbia?"

"I was doing volunteer work at a local clinic. The rebels came in and took several of us, at least those they didn't immediately kill." A wave of pain crossed her face.

"That explains the way you helped me when I first came in. Doctor?" Barrett asked.

"Nurse. But they expect me to be a doctor." Kelly nodded in the direction of the voices. "I have to treat everything from a splinter to gunshot wounds. I even had to amputate three fingers one time."

"Where are the others? Those from your clinic that were taken with you."

"I don't know. We were separated in the first few days and I haven't seen them since. They move us around a lot to different camps."

Barrett detected a note of weariness. The voices around them grew louder, and Kelly put her finger over her lips to indicate they were to be quiet. The guard she recognized as Blue was accompanied by another man she didn't know. Both men stopped in front of them, Blue casting a long look in Kelly's direction. Barrett didn't like the feeling growing in the pit of her stomach.

"Don't be stupid," the other man said in Spanish.

Blue never took his eyes off Kelly but moved closer to her, staggering the last few steps. He reached for his belt buckle.

"You are new here and do not know. The Colonel will kill you if you touch her. She is his woman," the man warned again.

Barrett's eyes moved between Blue and Kelly. Kelly was surprisingly calm, and in the fading twilight the look on her face was determined. Before Barrett had a chance to close the gap between them, Kelly stood. Her feet were braced apart as if ready for a blow, her hands at her side, the set of her jaw determined.

"Leave her alone," Barrett shouted, as she scrambled to her feet. Blue crossed the distance between them in three big strides and slapped her across the face. Barrett staggered backward and fought to remain standing as she spit blood and a tooth from her mouth.

"Shut up, stupid whore," Blue screamed in Spanish. "Watch what I do to her and know I will do the exact thing to you, twice."

Barrett didn't want to watch but couldn't drag her eyes away from the scene playing out in front of her. Kelly stood lifeless, not even trying to get away or lessen the distance between her and Blue. He reached out, but before his hand closed around Kelly's arm, a loud snap cracked the air. Blue screamed and grabbed the side of his face instead.

Kelly jumped, but not before Blue's blood splattered across her cheek. He fell to his knees screaming, and Barrett looked around for what had caused his injury. The Colonel stood to her right, a long bullwhip in his hand. The whip lay coiled at his feet, as if ready to be called upon to strike again. He walked toward Blue, who now lay on his side, blood dripping from between his fingers.

Slowly, step by step, The Colonel closed the distance with a quiet calmness that frightened Barrett. Kelly had finally moved and was as far away from the scene as her restraints allowed. The man that accompanied Blue was long gone, deserting his comrade to face his punishment alone.

The Colonel finally spoke in soft, muted Spanish. "Get up." Blue didn't move. "Don't make me repeat myself." It was several moments before Blue complied. He stood on shaking legs, anger burning in his eyes. "Drop your pants," The Colonel commanded.

Blue acted as if he didn't understand the request, but Barrett did. What was The Colonel going to do next? She shot a quick glance at Kelly and their eyes met. Silently, Kelly was telling her to stay out of it.

The Colonel shouted and, in seconds, dozens of men who Barrett assumed were other rebels came out of the jungle like ants from a disturbed anthill. He issued a series of commands and four men stepped forward. One grabbed Blue around the neck, one held his hands, another grasped his legs, yanking his pants off, while a fourth grabbed some rope. One by one Blue's wrists and ankles were tied to a tree. In the end he was splayed spread-eagle between two trees. Barrett couldn't help but notice the skin covered by Blue's clothing was much paler than his arms and face. His penis was erect from the adrenaline coursing through his body.

Everyone stood silently except Blue, who wept and begged for his life. Without raising his voice, The Colonel spoke to his men. "Your comrade has chosen to disobey one of the rules while under my command. He is being punished in a manner befitting his infraction."

Barrett held her breath when The Colonel swung the whip over his head. Once, twice, three times it cracked into the air, each time causing Blue to whimper. The Colonel turned to his men and spoke again. "My rules are few but simple. Punishment for disobeying them is severe. You," he said, pointing to Blue, "are a disgrace to the revolution. Maybe you will think the next time you cannot control your actions." With a final crack, the whip lashed Blue's penis, his scream filling the waning light.

❖

Kelly saw more than a few men instinctively grab their crotch when the whip connected two more times with the most private part of Blue's anatomy. The Colonel walked away without further comment. He'd made his point. What else was there to say? The thirty-or-so men retreated, mumbling quietly to each other. No one looked back at the man hanging unconscious between the trees.

She sat on her mat, only slightly dazed at The Colonel's brutality. For months she had seen him, whip, beat, even kill to maintain order among his troops. This evening was only another episode in a long line of what had come before. And it wouldn't be the last.

She glanced over at Barrett. She was obviously upset but didn't look too bad. Her face had that look of disbelief she saw on every new arrival in camp the first time they witnessed The Colonel's brutal temper.

"Are you all right?" she asked quietly.

"Better than he is." Barrett was shaking her head. "Jesus, I see what you mean by not crossing that guy. Other than the obvious, what did he do?" Barrett nodded in the direction of the unconscious man.

"He touched me. Or at least he was about to," Kelly said. It pained her to see how badly the man had been punished, even though she was glad he had.

"I belong to The Colonel," Kelly said, further explaining her statement. She watched as Barrett grasped the full meaning of what she'd said. First it was comprehension, then disbelief, and, finally, fear that she too would be raped.

"Don't think about it." Kelly knew exactly what Barrett was thinking. "You have to concentrate on what's happening right now, not on what might happen." She'd learned to remove herself from the here and now every time The Colonel called for her.

The first time had been shortly after she arrived in the camp. She was in a condition similar to Barrett's—filthy, exhausted, and scared shitless. She'd known that sooner or later it would happen. It was just a matter of time and by whom. At least it was The Colonel and not any or all of the other guards. He bathed regularly and wasn't overly brutal, and he usually used her body as a means to an end. All the men in the camp knew that she was his and that no one else was to touch her. Kelly thought it was more a case of The Colonel not wanting to contract syphilis or some other disease rather than some sense of sparing her.

"Have you—?"

"I said don't think about it." Kelly snapped because she certainly didn't want to discuss it. Just then Opie arrived with their dinner, or at least what the guards considered their dinner.

He tossed a chunk of bread in her direction, along with a canteen that sounded more hollow than full, and it landed on the ground in front of her. Repeating his action in front of Barrett, he walked back the way he'd come.

Kelly snatched the bread and tore it into smaller pieces. "You'd better eat. You may not get anything else for days." She bit into the familiar hard bread.

Since Barrett's hands were still secured behind her back, she couldn't hold her bread, and Kelly watched her look at it but not move toward it.

"Look, I know it's hard, but trust me. At least try to eat it. You're hungry, and you need to keep your strength up." She took another bite. "It was months before they let me have my hands in front of me. They were still secured, but at least I could feed myself." Kelly remembered how she'd been so hungry she ate whatever the guards tossed her way, regardless of where it landed. She often had more dirt and leaves in her stomach than food. They wouldn't let her starve to death, but they weren't going to go out of their way to help her eat either.

"Months?" No way would she be here that long. Debra would pay.

"'Fraid so. At least it was for me and several others. Right now they don't trust you, and since you're worth quite a bit to them, or at least they think you are, they won't risk letting you get away. I'm surprised they're not standing right next to you now." In the beginning, she'd been forced to endure the humiliation of a guard, sometimes two, observing her every move.

"Well, they're right. I'm out of here the first chance I get." Barrett looked around, clearly surveying her potential escape route.

"They'll find you." Kelly didn't want her to experience the same punishment she had when she was found.

"I don't need to run. The Colonel was right. I have money, lots of it. All he has to do is name his price, and I'm on the next flight out of this piece-of-shit country." Barrett spoke brazenly.

"Don't let them hear you say that."

"Why not? That's what they want, isn't it?"

"Because if they think you can get it, they'll take the ransom, keep you, and ask for more. They'll keep asking every time your people pay, and you'll never get out of here." Kelly hated being so blunt, but the sooner Barrett knew the rules of the game the sooner she'd settle down and not get herself, or anyone else, hurt.

"Fuck," Barrett said simply.

"Yes, you are fucked." Kelly hated the word. "We all are, and if you believe in God, now would be a good time to pray."

Barrett's head shot up and she looked at Kelly with defiance in her eyes.

Two guards came their way. She'd named one of them Bruce, after actor Bruce Lee, because he constantly practiced karate moves. The other she called Little Boy, because he couldn't keep his hands off his dick.

She and her fellow captives had taken to naming the guards so they could refer to them when they talked. They weren't often allowed to converse, and when they did they managed to share as much information as they could with each other. Each hostage shared their experiences with the guards to help the others from having to undergo the same.

The rebels didn't care what condition the hostages were in. They didn't get any additional points for returning healthy hostages versus sick ones, so they provided only the minimum for them to survive. Food was scarce, shelter even more so, and they provided free labor for the guards, who were pissed to be glorified babysitters instead of fighting for the freedom of Columbia. The soldiers and The Colonel often took their anger out on them for no apparent reason. They'd learned hard and painful lessons and banded together when they could.

Bruce said something to Barrett that Kelly had learned meant he was taking her to the bathroom. Barrett tried to get up too fast and ended up face-first in the dirt. Bruce laughed and, grabbing her arm, dragged her about five feet into the jungle.

"He won't hurt you. Don't try to get away," Kelly called. As soon as the words were out of her mouth she wished she hadn't spoken them.

Kelly waited anxiously for Bruce to return with Barrett. She knew she'd be punished for speaking, but she wanted to offer Barrett support, however little it was. The look on Bruce's face when he returned confirmed her suspicions.

After securing Barrett to the tree, Bruce approached Kelly and pulled her to her feet. Barrett couldn't hear what was being said, but within minutes both men had her tied so she was face-to-face with the unconscious man between the trees. They tied a rope around Kelly's waist, effectively lashing her to the other man. Her pelvis was pressed against the man's bloody penis, and Barrett felt sick to her stomach. They wrapped another rope around their necks, pinning her face to his.

Kelly had hardly struggled and was now silent and not moving. This time when the men spoke, Barrett heard and understood every word.

"That will teach you to talk out of line, you bitch. How does it feel to have your cunt next to Lopez's bloody dick? You're to blame for all of this." The man screamed in Kelly's face, his English broken but understandable.

"Hey, asshole," Barrett yelled, grateful she'd remembered to say it in English and not give away the fact that she spoke Spanish. He spun around, obviously not expecting Barrett to talk to him.

"Barrett, shut up," Kelly said, her voice muffled.

"No, I won't shut up." She kept her eyes on the man. "Yeah, you asshole. Do you think that makes you a big man? You're nothing but a piece of shit and can only get your rocks off with a woman who's tied up."

"Shut up, Barrett."

"Yeah, that's right, big boy. I'm talking to you." Even though her hands were still behind her back, she used her head to point to him. The pain of moving suddenly caught up with her, and she stifled a groan. Was it possible her ribs had been broken? She gritted her teeth. "You can't understand a word I'm saying, you dumb shit, but you know exactly what I mean. Your kind always does."

She expected the blow when it came.

Chapter Six

K elly could hardly breathe. It didn't matter if she turned her face to the left or right; it was still inches from the man's dirty, greasy hair. The smell of body odor, blood, and bodily fluids she didn't care to think about drifted into her nostrils. The man's blood was starting to seep into her clothes. She wanted to gag but willed herself not to. She hadn't fought against Bruce and his fellow thug. Fighting would only make it worse.

Barrett groaned.

"Barrett?" When she didn't answer, Kelly repeated her name. This time she answered with a moan.

"Barrett, please talk to me. Are you all right?"

Another moan. "My head hurts."

"Of course it does. Bruce packs a mean punch."

"No shit."

Kelly felt Barrett move, then say, "Oh, my God."

"I told you to shut up. You were too stubborn to listen to me, and look where it got you." She was tied up exactly like Kelly, with Blue sandwiched between them. Barrett gagged and threw up. She had very little in her stomach so it was mostly the dry heaves.

"Why did they do this?" Barrett asked quietly.

Kelly turned her head the best she could to make sure no one was listening. "Because I talked to you without their permission."

"What?"

Kelly couldn't see Barrett but heard the shock in her voice. "We can't speak unless spoken to first. One of The Colonel's rules."

"Then why did you do it?"

"Because I needed you to know so you didn't try to run. Don't try it, Barrett. They'll find you and punish you severely. Make an example out of you like they did this guy." She knew it was true, all the captives knew.

"Goddamn it." Barrett said.

"Yeah, him too."

"I've got to get out of here. I can get out of here. I'm in pretty good shape, have a good sense of direction, and—"

"Are you out of your mind? You can barely see, you probably have a concussion, you haven't eaten in days, and, in case you've forgotten, you're strung up in a tree like a trophy kill. I won't even mention that you can barely walk."

"Don't talk to me like I'm stupid. And don't tell me what I can or can't do."

"This isn't all about you."

"Yes, this is all about me. You can sit on your hands and let these people control your destiny, but I'm not going to rot and die in this godforsaken place."

"If you try to escape, not only will you be punished, but we will too."

"Let me guess, another of The Colonel's rules." There was more than a little sarcasm in her tone.

"Barrett, I'm just telling you what will happen and asking you not to do it."

"I don't care. I'm not going to jeopardize my chance at freedom for anyone else." It could have been minutes or it could have been hours before either of them spoke again.

"How long are they going to keep us here?" Barrett asked. "My arms are getting numb."

"Probably all night."

❖

"How do you do it?" Barrett asked.

Kelly had no idea how long they'd been lashed to this guy. Time had lost all meaning. The darkness had crept in, and she guessed that several hours had passed.

"You learn to block it out. Not think about it. You disassociate from what's going on. It's a coping mechanism. You'll learn. You'll have to or you won't make it."

"Where do you go?"

"Anywhere but here. Sometimes it's a dinner with friends, and it's as if I'm actually there sitting at the table with them."

"What do you talk about?"

The sound of Barrett's voice was oddly comforting.

"Nothing, really. You know, just girl stuff."

"Like what?"

"Work, boyfriends, girlfriends, husbands. We bitch, commiserate, laugh, and sometimes cry. It's either pizza, beer, and ice cream or wings, beer, and ice cream. One time we had lasagna, beer, and ice cream, but it just wasn't the same."

"I see a pattern," Barrett said flatly. "Tell me about your job. I think you said you're a nurse?"

"Yes, at Brookhaven Hospital in Denver. I'm in pediatrics."

"Denver? You don't sound like you're from Denver."

"I'm not," Kelly replied. "Born and raised in Alabama."

"How did you end up in Denver?"

"Long story."

"It's not like we're pressed for time here." This is really bizarre, Barrett thought. Here they were in the middle of what could only be described as a nightmare, and they were talking about things like two people did on a first date.

"Another time," Kelly said, effectively shutting down that subject.

"Okay." Barrett shifted back to the original topic. "How long have you been at...I'm sorry, where was it again?"

"Brookhaven. I've been there six years. But before that I was nine years at St. Michaels, across town."

"Why the move?"

Kelly knew this conversation was ludicrous, but it kept her mind off the dead guy in front of her. "I moved," she said simply. "I bought a house on the other side of town, and the commute was killing me. There's more to life than driving more than an hour to get to work. Luckily I can pretty much get a job just about anywhere."

"Even in the middle of the jungle," Barrett said. "Sorry," Barrett said quickly. "So at your ladies' night, who's sitting to your left?"

"Ariel. She's my best friend and my worst enemy."

"How so?"

"She holds my hand when I'm down, bails me out when I'm in trouble, and kicks my butt when I'm a bitch."

"Tell me a time when she did each of those."

"I know what you're doing, Barrett." Kelly kept her voice low.

"Then keep talking. I need something to take my mind off this, so please go on."

"My fiancé dumped me at the altar. The church was packed, the reception hall decorated, and a sit-down dinner for eighty was waiting. I was in the back of the church with my four bridesmaids cooling my heels while the best man looked for the man who'd promised to love me for the rest of his life. When he came back alone he had a message from Charles that said he was sorry and I could keep the ring."

"What an asshole."

"Ariel was right there beside me for weeks. She took a leave of absence from her job and came to stay with me. I don't know what I'd have done without her." It used to hurt to think about it, now it was just a bad memory. Good riddance, he was a jerk, she thought.

"When did she bail you out?"

"When I was almost arrested."

"Arrested? You really do mean bail you out. That you've got to tell me," Barrett said, and Kelly told her the rest of the story.

"It was when we were in college. I was young, dumb, and naïve, and I found myself at a rather rambunctious party in a park. Things kind of got out of hand and one thing led to another and… well…let's just say the moon was shining in more places than just in the sky."

"Do tell."

"No, I've said enough, thank you very much. Ariel has never let me forget it."

"As a best friend should."

"Funny, she subscribes to the same philosophy."

"And I suppose you didn't think you needed to have your butt kicked."

"No. I definitely did," Kelly said confidently.

"I'm patiently waiting for this one, which is hard because I'm not normally a patient person."

"And you have quite the potty mouth."

"Sorry, force of habit."

"Ever get you in trouble?"

"Nope."

"Bullshit."

Barrett managed to squeak out a little laugh. This entire situation was too bizarre for words. They were literally strung up with a dead Columbian rebel between them, and they were bantering like a couple of women without a care in the world. It was interesting, Kelly thought, how the mind reacted to stressful situations. Gallows humor, she thought it was called.

"Touché. Someone once told me it was a defense mechanism. That I'm over-compensating for lack of confidence or self-esteem."

"Wow, didn't see that one coming."

"Well, like you said, bullshit. Now about the ass-kicking."

❖

Barrett couldn't feel her hands or feet when she woke. Her side ached, and the dull throb in her head reminded her it was still there. She jolted awake and immediately remembered where she was. Her stomach threatened to heave again, but she willed it not to. She had to get out of here.

"Kelly?" she whispered. "Kelly," she repeated, when the woman didn't move. "Kelly, wake up. Jesus, don't be dead." Barrett choked on the last word.

"I'm not, but this guy is."

An overwhelming sense of relief mixed with repulsion flooded Barrett. "How are you?" What a stupid question, she thought.

"I'm okay. Did you get any sleep?"

"Some," Barrett replied.

Kelly must have heard the guilt in her voice because she said, "I'm not surprised. You've been through a lot."

"I don't need your pity."

"It's not pity. It's concern and caring for another human being, an action that obviously you're not familiar with."

"I've been taking care of myself for more years than I can count, and I don't intend to stop now."

Before Kelly could say anything else, a guard Barrett didn't recognize came out of the jungle toward them with a very large knife in his hand. Her stomach tightened. Was he going to cut them down or do something else with it?

The guard stopped in front of them, reached up, and cut the rope around her waist and the one holding Kelly's arms above her head. She fell to the ground in a heap. He repeated the same move on the dead man, who landed on top of Kelly. Finally he cut her ropes, and she somehow managed to miss both of them and landed hard on the ground.

Bright lights sparkled in her eyes, and it took a few moments for her head to clear. When it did she saw Kelly struggling to roll the dead man off her. When she finally succeeded, she scrambled as far away from him as she could and vomited.

Kelly retched until her stomach threatened to come out, along with last night's meager dinner. Wiping her mouth with the back of her shaking hand, she crawled over to her mat and collapsed. She was exhausted both mentally and physically. There was no way she could have slept in the position she was in. Covered in the guard's blood and urine, she'd had to endure the bugs feasting on her sticky skin all night. She'd felt every breath he took and knew the moment he took his last. She closed her eyes.

Water splashed across her face, and Kelly raised her hand to shield the sun from her eyes. Bruce was standing over her. She struggled to sit up and managed to before he lost his patience.

"Yes, sir?" Kelly asked in the way she'd been taught. Not that she'd have completely understood whatever he said to her, but usually she got the general gist pretty quickly. Bruce motioned for her to grab the dead guard and follow him.

The man's eyes were open, staring into the air, and Kelly kept her focus anyplace but on what remained of his penis. Holding him by the wrists she walked, dragging the man with her inch by agonizing inch. He was heavy, and the heat and humidity had already started the rapid decay of his body.

Crazy thoughts bounced in and out of her brain as she put one foot in front of the other. What happened to my car? What happened to Needles? Did Ariel take her? Is anyone making payments on my house? Who has all my stuff? Did Suzanne take all my *Star Wars* DVDs? What about the pearls my grandmother gave me? Oh, God, what did they think when they opened the middle drawer of my nightstand?

She almost ran into the back of Bruce, who'd stopped in front of her. He pointed to a shovel, and it was clear she was to dig a grave for his dead comrade. She surveyed the area, thankful for the rain they'd had a few days ago. The ground was soft, and when the first whish of the shovel blade sank into the earth, she drifted off again.

She was digging a grave for her pet turtle Clifford, who'd died last night while she was sleeping. She was eight and her cousin Sam, who was three years older, was helping her. Her mother had given Kelly a shoebox and an old dishcloth from the kitchen and was standing beside her in quiet support. Her mother had always been beside her for everything. If it wasn't holding a dead turtle in a box, it was sitting on the sidelines two evenings a week watching her play softball. She could always count on her mother.

Her job finished, she stumbled back into the camp area. She was exhausted, and it was all she could do to stagger to her mat. She didn't care where Barrett was or if she was okay. In this minute she had to take care of herself, and for the first time she could remember she didn't care about anyone else.

❖

Barrett was grateful she wasn't the one that had to drag Blue away. God knows what she would have had to do. Why had she come to this godforsaken country?

A guard Barrett had never seen before tossed a canteen, a piece of bread, and what looked suspiciously like a chicken leg a few feet in front of her. He repeated his actions, and more food landed next to the shackle Kelly had been locked to yesterday.

Her hands were free and Barrett grabbed all three pieces in front of her and immediately tore off a chunk of the bread and shoved it in her mouth. She swallowed it practically before she chewed it. Other than the bread yesterday, it was all she'd had to eat since this whole nightmare started. What was that, a week ago? Six days? Yes, it was six days. Or was it seven? Unlike Kelly, she would keep track of the number of days. Her exacting nature wouldn't allow otherwise.

She quickly finished her meager meal and eyed Kelly's. She felt a momentary pang of guilt, but in this situation it was every man for himself, so to speak. Kelly might have accepted her fate and become content to sit and wait until she was released, but Barrett certainly wasn't. She needed to stay sharp and alert for any opportunity to escape. She scooted as far as her chain would allow and stretched, but she was still several feet away from the piece of bread. She looked around for something to use to grab the food, but before she found anything she heard a noise behind her.

Kelly staggered into camp, and the sight of her made Barrett's stomach jump. Her face, arms, and legs were covered in dirt, the blood from Blue's injuries dark on her shorts. A cut on her leg looked raw, and her face was drawn. But she was alive.

The guard secured Kelly to the chain again and returned a few minutes later with a bucket of water. Kelly greedily washed her hands and face first, then her bare arms and legs. When her extremities were clean, she stripped off her clothes and dunked them in the water.

Barrett watched as Kelly, unaffected by her nakedness, scrubbed the blood off first her shorts, then her shirt. Her nipples were hard from the exertion and her breasts were perfect.

Kelly looked up and caught her staring. Barrett felt a blush creep up her neck. She felt like a voyeur but couldn't look away. When Kelly turned her back, Barrett inhaled sharply. Her back was covered in a patchwork of pale scars from a whip.

Anger rose in her throat and Barrett opened her mouth to say something. She stopped. What was she going to say? "How did you get those?" "I'm sorry you were whipped." There really was nothing she could say. She shuddered at the mistreatment Kelly must have endured. It was almost unimaginable.

CHAPTER SEVEN

K elly hadn't moved and Barrett was afraid she was dead. After eating the sparse meal, Kelly had lain down, turned on her side, curled up into the fetal position, and hadn't moved. That was hours ago. Or at least Barrett thought it was. The canopy of the jungle was so thick that not a lot of sun got through, but as best she could tell the sun had moved across the sky and the humidity had dropped a little.

Barrett studied Kelly for any signs that she was still breathing. She thought she detected a slight movement in her shoulders and back but couldn't be sure. She didn't want to wake her, as obviously she needed her sleep from the ordeal of last night and this morning. She herself had napped on and off throughout the day, but now she was wide-awake and had no idea if her cellmate, so to speak, was alive or dead.

Anxiety swept over her and Barrett quickly stood. Overcome with dizziness, she fought the blackness that was threatening to overtake her again. She bent at the waist, bracing herself with her hands on her knees, and took a few deep breaths, commanding herself not to faint. She never allowed her body to override her mind and didn't intend to start now.

The darkness subsided and Barrett slowly stood, arched her back, and stretched her arms over her head, her ribs aching. She was stiff from sitting too long in one position and needed to stay strong if she intended to escape. Sitting around all day waiting would dull her senses and weaken her body, and that might prove fatal.

She used the tree she was shackled to for support more than once during her exercises. She must be weaker than she thought and vowed to repeat this activity at least three times a day. The guards that were their constant companions eyed her warily but quickly got bored and resumed their game of cards.

Breathing heavily she looked up and into Kelly's open eyes. Barrett didn't know how long she'd been watching her, and a flush of relief that Kelly was alive flooded her.

"Good afternoon," Barrett said, moving as close to Kelly as her restraint allowed.

"How long did I sleep?" Kelly slowly sat up, bracing her arms behind her for support. She blinked several times and ran one hand over her face.

"Most of the day."

Kelly stretched her legs, leaned forward, and massaged her calves, then her thighs, and finally the small of her back. "God, I feel like shit. Which is surprising because I didn't think I could feel worse than…" Her words died. She obviously didn't need to verbalize what they'd gone through. "How are you?"

"I'm okay. Just bored and tired of Mutt and Jeff over there leering at me," Barrett said, referring to the two guards that sat a dozen yards away.

"The big one in the blue shirt we call Bruce, the other one Little Boy." She told Barrett why they'd named their guards and where they came from.

"I did the same thing. The guy that we were…" Barrett hesitated, not wanting to reference exactly how they knew the guy. "I called him Blue after Bluebeard the pirate. The other one that dragged me here reminds me of a young Desi Arnez from the *I Love Lucy* show."

"I can see that," Kelly said, nodding.

"Who else do we have as our new best friends?" Barrett asked, referencing the other guards.

"Most of them are in and out, but the ones that are constant are Hercules, for apparent reasons when you see him; Jack Sparrow, because he braids his scruffy beard; and Dirty Harry, because he has the biggest gun. We think he took it from one of the camps they must have raided because everyone else has rifles or machine guns."

"Machine guns?" Barrett asked. Blue and Desi each had an AR-15 slung over their shoulder with extra clips tucked into the pockets of their camo pants.

"Yeah. You know, the kind that can shoot a dozen bullets with one pull of the trigger."

"My guys had AR-15s, and one of them had a 9 millimeter."

"You know your guns," Kelly said, a combination of statement and question.

"I have a few." Actually Barrett had more than a few, but they didn't do her any good at home locked in her custom gun cabinet.

Several minutes passed before Barrett had the unfamiliar itch to fill the void. She'd always been comfortable with silence and often used it to advantage in business dealings. Most people couldn't keep their mouth shut and often tipped their hand during that time.

"So what do you do all day? I'm bored to death." Actually she was still on edge and disoriented but would never admit it. She never admitted any weakness or the fact that she wasn't completely on top of her game.

"They usually have us working around the camp. Free labor, you know?" Barrett nodded and she continued. "I check on anyone who needs it, we gather firewood for the fire, wash the dishes, the clothes, that sort of thing."

"What about the others? Where are they?" Barrett hadn't seen any of the other hostages Kelly spoke about.

"If they're still here, they're probably on the other side of the camp. Sometimes they let us be together, but most of the time they separate us."

"Why?"

"For sport, because they're bored, to fuck with our minds, and because they can," Kelly said dully. "We had a sociology professor here for a few months, and he told us that isolation was one of the best forms of psychological tortures. Long periods of being alone make you lose hope and your will to fight. It makes you much more controllable. We're humans and need human contact, especially in a situation like this. When we're all together we don't feel so alone. Kind of like we're all in this together and together we can survive."

"You said if they're still here? If not, was their ransom paid?"

"Maybe for some, I guess. Some are sold to other factions."

"Sold?" Barrett tried to keep her voice steady. "Sold for what?"

"Guns, ammunition, even another hostage, who knows. We're a commodity. Something to be bought and sold."

Barrett woke to sounds of shouts and commands. It was still dark, and their guards were scrambling around waking the others. From what she could gather they were getting ready to move and were expected to break down the camp. It was only then that Barrett saw the other hostages. The seven men reminded her of pictures showing the Nazi camps when they were liberated. They were so thin, Barrett didn't know how they were able to stand, let alone carry the heavy cases of ammunition on their shoulders. They never glanced up, never looked her way, but silently followed the commands of the guards.

"What's happening?" she asked Kelly, who stood and picked up the dirty mat she'd been sleeping on.

"We're moving."

"Where?"

"Does it matter?"

"Won't that make it harder for anyone to find us?"

Kelly stopped moving and looked at her with sad, hopeless eyes. "Isn't that the point?"

They hiked through jungle so thick they were forced to walk single file. The guard Kelly called Hercules swung his machete through the brush with very little effort. Even with Hercules's clearing, branches and vines still hung across their path. Barrett's hands were tied behind her back again, and she had to hold on to the heavy chain attached to the shackle still around her left ankle.

They stopped once during the morning and again in the afternoon, and Barrett quickly realized it wasn't for the wellbeing of the hostages. Little Boy offered each of them a drink from a shared canteen, and because her hands were still tied most of it missed her mouth and slid down her neck.

When they started again, if the hostages couldn't keep up they were poked with knives or the barrel of guns and forced to continue. Blood on the trail told Barrett that someone had been injured, more than just a scratch or two from the low-hanging branches. When the blood was still there after hours of walking she knew it was serious. Kelly was in front of her, but due to the thick jungle Barrett could barely see her, let alone tell if she was the one injured.

On the third and fourth day it rained, a hard, driving rain that beat down on them like slaps. The guards had ponchos, but Barrett and the other hostages didn't and were instantly soaked to the skin. They slogged through mud sometimes knee-deep, stopping more frequently. They didn't have any cover from the rain when they ate or slept, but Barrett was too tired to care.

At night they were gathered collectively and secured together so tight they could barely move. They were tied either back-to-back or face-to-face, their arms around each other as if hugging. Escape was impossible. The only bright spot was on the several occasions Barrett was secured near Kelly. It was on the fifth night since they broke camp when they finally were able to speak to each other.

"Are you okay?" Kelly asked, the rain effectively drowning out their voices.

"I have no idea. I'm just putting one foot in front of the other and hoping I don't fall down." Barrett had never been so exhausted. "How long does this go on?"

"It varies. Sometimes it's only a day or two and sometimes it's longer. Once we were on the move for two weeks." Kelly yawned.

"Two weeks!" She couldn't do this for two weeks, and she doubted the man tied against her back could either.

"Have you been able to hear where we're going?" Sometime in the past few days, Kelly had figured out that she understood Spanish better than she did.

"No. They're bitching about the weather, the food, and The Colonel," Barrett said sarcastically. Kelly didn't reply for several minutes, and Barrett thought she'd fallen asleep. They were lying face-to-face, and she was the closest she'd ever been to Kelly's face.

A sprinkling of freckles was evenly scattered across her nose and over her cheeks. A small scar just below her lip and lines of fatigue around her eyes and mouth were the only imperfections on an otherwise smooth face. Kelly must have felt her looking and opened her eyes.

They were dark and piercing, but clear. This close she could see lighter flecks of color forming a ring just outside her pupils. Eyebrows naturally formed into a perfect arch lay just above long, thick eyelashes. Kelly's nose was perfectly straight, in direct contrast to her own, which had been broken once in high school and again when she was taken. Lush, full lips lay open no more than a few inches from hers, soft breath caressing her.

There it was again! That spark she'd felt when Kelly had been allowed to treat her wrists. The one that made her pulse race, only this time the flame wasn't going away. Barrett felt Kelly's breathing hitch. *My God, what is going on?*

"What?" Kelly asked.

"Here I am, lying next to a beautiful woman for the night, and I can't do a thing with it. Go figure." She was amazed her humor hadn't completely deserted her.

"Go to sleep," Kelly said, seemingly not bothered by her outing herself. "We need to be rested in the morning."

The next morning and every morning for the next four days they woke and slogged through the jungle. Not since that evening in the rain had Kelly had a moment alone with Barrett. The guards must have sensed something because they kept them apart whenever they could and punished them if they even thought they were trying to communicate with each other. Barrett still hadn't learned to keep her mouth shut, and the guards seemed to enjoy pushing her buttons and then doling out whatever retribution amused them.

This move was agony for Kelly, but she'd developed the ability to go somewhere else in her head almost automatically. It was a matter of survival, and she was all about that. Finally, after what she thought was nine days of hiking, they carved a clearing out of the jungle and set up camp.

One day not long after that, The Colonel came for her. They were clearing an area to store additional supplies when Kelly saw him heading in her direction. She knew what he wanted. She always knew.

It wasn't the first time he'd come for her since Barrett arrived, but it was the first time Barrett would see it. Slowly she moved closer, hoping to get to Barrett before she said anything.

"Don't do anything stupid," Kelly said, her voice barely above a whisper. "I can handle this."

Barrett turned to look at her and saw The Colonel over her left shoulder. Defiance filled her eyes. Kelly knew Barrett wouldn't listen. "Barrett, please, don't."

Barrett squared and put herself between Kelly and The Colonel. Kelly saw his face fill with rage, and she silently prayed.

"Don't," Barrett said calmly.

The Colonel coolly surveyed Barrett as if weighing the capabilities of an opponent. Four of his men were within five yards of them and could be at his side within seconds. Kelly knew he didn't need the help. His whip was in his right hand, and to the casual observer it looked like he wasn't ready to use it. But Kelly knew otherwise.

"Really?" he replied in a smooth voice. "Are you volunteering to take her place?"

Barrett didn't answer.

"Why are you so interested in her welfare?" He nodded toward Kelly.

"Just leave her alone."

"Interesting." The Colonel rubbed his chin. "Funny, you didn't say anything the other times I had her. Oh yes, that's right, you were chained to a tree," he added, as if just remembering it. Whereas his men only knew how to inflict physical punishment, The Colonel obviously had experience in psychological abuse as well.

Kelly stood behind Barrett, and even though she couldn't see her face, she did see her back stiffen and her fists clench. "Barrett, please."

"Yes, Barrett, please." The Colonel mimicked her sarcastically.

Barrett was on him before Kelly knew what was happening. Barrett's wrists were still banded together, but she was able to head-butt him before the guards pulled her off.

"You bitch!" The Colonel shouted, raising his whip. Blood poured from a cut above his right eye, and he wiped it away with the back of his hand.

"No," Kelly screamed, and stepped in front of him. "She doesn't know what she's doing. She's only been here a few weeks. Please, Colonel, I'll do anything." Kelly begged, wanting to retch.

"I don't care how long she's been here or how much she's worth, for that matter." With Barrett subdued he turned his attention to Kelly and leered at her. "And yes, you will do anything for me." He barked several commands and Barrett was dragged away.

"Kelly! Kelly!" Barrett screamed before Hercules hit her on the side of the head with his rifle.

Kelly didn't look back when the screaming stopped and didn't look up when The Colonel reached for her.

CHAPTER EIGHT

It was dark, very dark, and Barrett couldn't breathe. She tried to move, but her feet were wedged against something hard. The same was true for her elbows and the top of her head. She was completely disoriented. She couldn't see anything but touched everything around her and was able to figure out she was in some kind of a wooden box smaller than she was. Thinking she was buried alive, she started to panic.

She clawed and pounded at the wood in front of her face. It was solid and didn't give at all. She kicked, but with her body so tightly jammed into the space she didn't have any force behind her efforts. She gasped for air, dizzy, and thought her heart would pound out of her chest. She had to get out. Everything was closing in on her, and her body's fight-or-flight reflex had kicked in full-force.

She tried to scream, but no sound came out of her mouth. It was as if she'd gone blind and mute. That thought raised her level of panic, and she fought harder against her coffin. She heard a snap and then an excruciating pain in her left hand, but not enough to stop her from flailing to escape.

Barrett didn't know if it was minutes, hours, or days when she finally collapsed in exhaustion. Every bone and muscle in her body ached, but her mind refused to shut down. She gulped down another wave of panic and forced herself to think of anything except where she was and the pain in her hand. She remembered what Kelly said about going away to somewhere else.

She thought of her house. It was her dream house that she'd designed herself and painstakingly put together over the course of three years. Someone else had done most of the actual work, but she had put in hundreds of hours of sweat in the place as well. She calmed as she pictured the view out her living-room window.

Barrett lived just north of San Francisco in a little town called Princetown. The small town—quaint, with a few tourist shops, restaurants, and boat-rental places—was nothing special, but it was home.

Her house sat on an acre of pristine beachfront property, the Pacific Ocean her backyard. It was all glass and chrome and absolutely stunning. She'd immediately fallen in love with the floor plan when her architect presented it to her. On the ground floor the master suite was separated from an office and two other bedrooms by the kitchen, dining room, and laundry. The interior was bright, decorated in sleek modern lines that matched the frame of the house. Fifteen feet separated the ceilings from the floor, giving the room additional height that added to the open feeling. She could see the ocean from every room and access it from the ground floor.

Barrett imagined the feel of the breeze and the smell of the ocean when she opened the French doors leading out to the patio. Down a small flight of steps and she stood on the soft, white sand, mere feet from the rolling waves.

In her mind she walked through every room, looked in every closet, and opened every door. She itemized what was in her kitchen cabinets and her garage and rearranged the deck chairs around the pool. She polished the handrails on the stairs, dusted the blinds on the windows, swept the front porch, and rebuilt the back deck board by board.

When she opened her eyes, she detected a sliver of light coming from somewhere around her knees. She focused on it and slowly it grew brighter. At the same time the familiar sounds of the camp coming to life drifted in. *Morning! It must be morning!* This time when her heart began to race, it wasn't due to panic but anticipation that she would be released soon.

❖

Kelly was already awake when the first shafts of the new day lightened the sky. She hadn't slept all night, worried about Barrett being still in the box for the sixth day.

When she moved about the camp performing her assigned duties she tried to get close to it, but every time she started in that direction one of the guards stopped her. The thought of Barrett's tall body in that hot, tight space made Kelly dizzy.

Why did she do it? Kelly wondered more times than she could count. Why would an almost-complete stranger risk her life to protect her, especially knowing the consequences? Would she do the same if the roles were reversed?

But it was the isolation that was the hardest. Even though she understood some of what the guards said, days would go by without anyone talking to her. She was left alone for hours, sometimes days at a time with nothing to do and nothing to occupy her mind. She'd learned to pray, meditate, and take her mind anywhere she wanted it to go. It was painful when she came back to the present, but for those few moments, that simple trip somewhere else, she was at peace.

She'd just finished her breakfast when a scuffling sound behind her made her turn around. Her stomach lurched and seemed to stop in her throat. Barrett was between Hercules and Bruce, staggering under the weight of her own footsteps. Kelly scrambled to her feet and then sat back down just as quickly. She wouldn't have been able to run to Barrett anyway, her tether only fifteen feet long. But she was alive. "Thank you, God," she muttered.

The two guards walked in front of Kelly, and when they did, Barrett opened her eyes and looked at her. Her eyes were glazed, her skin yellow, and she'd obviously lost weight. She was naked, one of the guard's favorite forms of torture. Take away your clothes and you're completely vulnerable. You're nothing.

Barrett held Kelly's eyes for as long as she could before the guard's path took her away from Kelly. In that time Kelly tried to convey to Barrett her strength and reassure her that she was okay.

It wasn't until two weeks later that she saw Barrett again. She was stacking logs by the fire pit. Kelly inhaled sharply. Barrett was thin and gaunt, and she held her left hand against her chest. Her hair was tangled and limp, her clothes dirty and hanging off her body. Her feet were bare and her pants were torn. Back and forth she went from one pile to another, carefully stacking the wood in neat little rows. When she didn't move fast enough or stack the wood exactly like her guard wanted it, he slapped her across her back with a switch. She never raised her head or lifted her gaze to see what was around her, her strength sapped, her spirit beaten away.

Finally Kelly was permitted to check on Barrett once each day, under the careful watch of a guard. She didn't risk more punishment and only asked questions relating to her condition. She hoped the expression in her eyes conveyed her concern and support.

A few days later they were allowed to construct a small shelter, consisting of branches and leaves and held together with a whole lot of prayer. The structure would keep them somewhat sheltered from the fall rains that were coming more frequently now. That night they finally had a chance to talk. They were secured, as usual, to some immovable object but were less than four feet away from each other.

"Barrett," Kelly whispered after they were alone. "Are you all right?"

"I've been better."

"Open your eyes, let me look at them." Kelly needed to see if they were clear or still hazy.

"In a minute. I'm in a king-size bed on the fifteenth floor of the Ritz, the Arc de Triumph outside my window. Can't you see the Do Not Disturb sign on the doorknob?"

Kelly was relieved that Barrett's head was clear and she hadn't suffered any significant brain damage due to her time in that box. "Sorry, I don't speak French." She closed her eyes and willed herself to imagine the sight. She'd never stayed in any Ritz Hotel, even in the States, let alone been to Paris. "What else do you see?"

"It's lit up like a Christmas tree with twinkling lights." She chuckled. "But I doubt the French would appreciate the reference."

Kelly smiled. "Probably not. What else?" she asked, both to help herself go there in her head and because she liked the sound of Barrett's voice.

"It's a mild night and the window's open. There's a breeze blowing the curtains a little, and the sky's clear. I hear the traffic but not too much. You know how it is in Paris, drivers honking their horns and cussing each other. They use both hands as a communication tool when they really should be on the steering wheel."

Kelly's eyes were closed, but she heard the smile in Barrett's voice. "Why are you there?"

"Business. It's always business."

This time she heard resignation in Barrett's statement. "Have you ever gone there for pleasure?"

"No."

"Why not?"

"Because I work."

Kelly thought that an odd answer but was reluctant to dislodge their virtual fantasy. "What are you thinking about as you look at the Arc?"

"That I was lucky I got out of the bed of the woman I'd spent a few hours with without her waking up."

Kelly wasn't surprised at Barrett's comment. She knew Barrett was a lesbian, and even though she didn't play for that team, it didn't bother her. "Do you do that often?" Kelly opened her eyes wanting to see Barrett's face as she answered.

"What? Sleep with women? As often as I can."

"No, sneak out," Kelly asked, seemingly unflushed by her comment.

"I don't invite a woman to my room," Barrett said, matter-of-factly.

"So you can escape?"

"Yep." Barrett didn't even hesitate.

"Escape doesn't sound like a word that should be used after spending the night with someone. Unless it wasn't a very good time."

"It was fine. I just don't do morning-afters."

"Never?"

"Never."

"So what else do you see outside your window?" Kelly asked, suddenly uncomfortable with a conversation about Barrett's sex life.

But Barrett was already asleep.

CHAPTER NINE

Two weeks later The Colonel approached Barrett. "Stand up," he commanded her.

She took her time and eventually was almost eye-to-eye with him. He tossed a rolled-up newspaper at her, and Barrett caught it with her good hand just before it fell to the ground.

"Open it."

She did and saw it was in Spanish. "What do you want me to do, read it to you?"

The Colonel's eyes blazed with fury, and he took a step toward her. He was so close Barrett felt his breath on her face. He smelled like Old Spice.

"Hold it up," he barked. "Under your chin facing out."

He stepped back, and as she did she was able to read the date. November the twelfth. Oh my God, she'd been captive for four months. Trying not to give away the fact that she could read Spanish, she did as she was told and looked back at him, noticing the camera in his hand. He took several pictures, then stepped closer and backhanded her hard across her face. She staggered back several feet, grasping the paper as if it were a lifeline. She tasted blood.

The Colonel took one more picture, tore the paper from her hands, then walked away.

Barrett's legs finally gave way and she slid to the ground, a piece of the paper still in her hand. "What the fuck was that?" she asked through her already-swelling lip.

"Proof of life."

"What does that mean?"

"Proof of life. The picture shows you're still alive on the date of the paper. They'll release it somehow, and it'll get back to your family or whoever will be doing the negotiating for you."

Negotiating for me. The words rang in Barrett's ears. Or was it The Colonel's backhand? It made her sound like a piece of property, and she said as much to Kelly.

"But that's what you are. They own you and will sell you to the highest bidder."

"Jesus, Kelly, thanks for the words of encouragement." Her head was starting to pound and she felt nauseous.

"You know what, Barrett? You need to get over yourself. You're not the only one here, you know. We've all been here much longer than you and suffered a lot more than you have, and we aren't wallowing in self-pity. It's not all about you."

Kelly's words surprised Barrett. They'd come out of nowhere, but she was smart enough to know to keep her mouth shut this time.

The weeks dragged by and Barrett was bored out of her mind. She was used to being in constant motion, either attending meetings, negotiating deals, or reading research her staff had pulled together. Nothing had prepared her for hours upon hours with absolutely nothing to do. The only difference between today, yesterday, and eighteen days ago was who had the latest bout of malaria, foot fungus, or a variety of other debilitating parasitical diseases. Her hand hadn't healed correctly and hurt like hell. With limited medical supplies, whatever ailment one of them had, it was just a matter of time before they all did.

The mosquitoes were the worst. Nothing held them at bay, and they had no protection from the constant bites from the little bastards. Barrett had a harsh reaction and was often unable to stop scratching. She'd have scars if and when she got out of here.

Conversation with the hostages was limited, but they were able to play cards. Kelly had managed to create a complete deck of cards out of discarded cigarette boxes. Little Boy had given her a pen, and she'd meticulously inked in the number and suits of every card in the deck. She even went so far as to draw kings, queens, and jacks in minute detail.

Barrett studied Kelly across the game. She held her cards as if they were the winning lottery tickets, the look of concentration and ruthlessness on her face one Barrett didn't see often.

Over the months she'd found Kelly to be the most concerned, caring person she'd ever met. It was obvious that she cared more about their fellow hostages than she did about herself. On more than one occasion Barrett saw her slip a portion or all of her meal to one of them that needed it more. When she had the chance to sleep under a canopy, she put it over someone else. She sacrificed her own much-needed sleep to watch over someone with a fever.

Why would anyone do that? Through careful planning, bold moves, and seizing opportunities, she'd built a life that she controlled and would never give up. But wasn't that true for most people? Their safe, carefully constructed lives kept them away from the seedier side of life. But people like Kelly and the organization that she worked with voluntarily ventured into this other life. She couldn't understand how they could risk everything—for what? For Barrett nothing was worth it.

"Barrett?"

"Yes, I'm sorry. What did you say?" Kelly looked at her expectantly.

"I said it's your turn."

"Oh yeah, right," Barrett replied, and dragged her focus back to the game in front of her.

Opie and Kong stepped into their circle and motioned for her to follow them. "Deal me out, fellas," Barrett quipped, and laid the makeshift cards on the ground.

Barrett followed Kong across the camp with Opie trailing behind them. When it became clear they were headed for The Colonel's tent, Barrett tensed.

"Colonel," Opie called out in Spanish.

"Enter." Opie lifted the flap and shoved Barrett inside.

It was dark inside the tent, the dark fabric designed to conceal from a distance. Barrett blinked several times as her eyes adjusted to the low light.

"Sit," The Colonel commanded her, and pointed to the floor.

He fiddled with something on a box near them, and Barrett recognized it as a shortwave radio. *What the hell?* He shoved the microphone in front of Barrett's mouth.

"You will be asked four questions that only you know the answer to. Answer only the question and nothing more. If you do anything other than exactly what I say, Miss Ryan will be punished. Do you understand?"

Barrett nodded. "This is Barrett Taylor." The radio crackled a few seconds before she heard a voice.

"Ms. Taylor, you don't know me but I'm Robert Graves, and I represent your family. To verify my identity and that I'm on your side I am going to say two things that only you and your family know. First, when you were eight you left a note for the tooth fairy apologizing to her that you accidentally swallowed your tooth and didn't have it to put under your pillow. Second, when you were thirteen you would sit in your bedroom and pretend you were an executive. You drew numbers on the shoebox that you used as a telephone. Ms. Taylor," the radio crackled, "do you understand what I said?"

The Colonel pushed the key on the side of the microphone and nodded to her to speak.

"Yes." Her voice quivered. What in the hell was going on here? Who was this guy on the other end of the line? Her lifeline.

"I have four questions to ask you." The Colonel nodded again.

"Okay, go ahead." This must be another proof-of-life exercise. This guy, what was his name again, Graves? He must be the one negotiating her release, and he had to establish that it actually was her on the radio and not someone else pretending to be her. She would be rescued soon!

"Number one. What did you and your best friend do on the sidewalk in front of your house?"

"We had a lemonade stand." She could see herself and Suzy sitting patiently behind a card table with a pitcher of lemonade her mother had made for them.

"Number two. What did you and your brother do on the way to school that if your parents ever found out you would be in trouble for?"

"We crossed 43rd Avenue in the middle of the street instead of going down to the light and the crosswalk." She still had dreams about not being able to get across that street.

"Number three. What happened on a rainy afternoon that made your mother call your teacher?"

"I dropped a report I'd been working on in the water and it got ruined." She remembered being so distraught that she'd cried in her mother's arms.

"Number four. What did your family occasionally do on Sunday afternoons?"

"We went to the airport, to the roof of the terminal, and watched the planes take off and land."

"Thank you, Miss Taylor. Your family sends their love and—"

The Colonel turned off the radio and stared at her with cold, calculating eyes. "If you said anything that would lead them to us, I will know, and Miss Ryan will pay the price."

"I didn't. You heard me. I answered the questions they asked me. I had no idea what they were going to ask. There was no way I could say anything in some type of code. Besides, I have no idea where we are." Even though she would do what she needed to get out of here, she didn't want anything to happen to Kelly.

The Colonel glared at her, and Barrett forced herself to keep her expression neutral and her eyes on his. It seemed like forever before he gestured to Opie and she was allowed to leave.

Barrett's mind was racing. It had been forty-one days since her photo was taken holding the newspaper. What did this mean? Was this the first radio contact? The second? The eighth? Was it the final one before the money was paid and she was released? She hated not knowing what was going on. The feeling of helplessness was overwhelming and very, very discouraging.

Later that night Barrett and Kelly were finally alone, she told Kelly about the radio contact.

"That's a good sign, Barrett. It means that they're talking."

"And what happens when they stop talking?"

Kelly didn't answer and Barrett didn't need her to.

Barrett picked up her walking stick. One hundred and thirty-two. That's how many notches were carved into a walking stick she'd found while gathering firewood in their last camp. She carved each one with a sharp stone to signify the end of another long day in captivity.

❖

Barrett woke to the sounds of screams, gunfire, and explosions. Flashes of light blinded her as they lit up the night sky. They were under some kind of attack. Two men rushed toward her, both carrying large semiautomatic rifles and wearing night-vision goggles. She staggered to her feet, prepared to fight if she had to.

"Barrett Taylor?" one of the men asked.

Barrett was stunned. The man had called her by name. For a moment she wasn't sure if she'd heard correctly. He repeated it. Finally she nodded. "Your brother Aaron sent us. He said to tell you Windjammer is buried in the backyard, the third fence post from the gate. We've got to hurry."

This couldn't be. She was being rescued. The rescuer was real. He'd told her something only three people in the world knew. Aaron was with her when she buried her parakeet, and this was his signal to her to go with the men. The other man cut the chain at her feet, shaking her out of her shock of being rescued. They started to move. Barrett heard Kelly scream her name.

"Kelly, it's okay, they're for real. My brother sent them." She was thrilled yet terrified at the same time. She was being rescued and the nightmare was over. She was going home. But it wasn't over yet. They still needed to get out of here, and that wouldn't be easy.

"Cut her loose," Barrett said, pointing to Kelly.

"We're only here for you, Miss Taylor. Let's go."

Barrett froze, the man pulling her arm to get her to move. "What?"

"Our mission is to get you, nobody else. Let's go," he repeated.

This couldn't be happening, Barrett thought. She was the only one they were going to rescue? There were a half a dozen other prisoners in this camp. They couldn't simply leave them. They would be tortured, or worse.

"What about the others? You have to take them too." Barrett was too puzzled to try to figure out why they'd come only for her.

"Let's go." The voice was strong and the command was firm. Barrett fought through the burning pain, looked over, and pointed to Kelly.

"I'm not leaving without her!"

She fought the hands that held her arms tight against her sides. The man was well over six feet tall and so strong she knew she'd have several bruises from his fingers gripping her arms. His buddy was equally built, and his crooked nose said that he too was used to physical violence to get what he wanted.

"We're here to get you, lady. Nobody else," Broken Nose said through clenched teeth.

"I don't care. I'm not leaving her," she shouted, accentuating her last few words.

The men had come in the middle of the night under the cover of darkness that the flares and grenades they'd lobbed at her home had obliterated. She was swept off her feet before she was able to stand and hustled into the jungle. She managed to twist around and find the dark eyes of the woman who had shared the terror with her and who was now quickly disappearing out of view.

She fought with every ounce of strength in her, kicking and scratching the man that held her. Her foot made contact with his shin, causing a muffled obscenity to escape his lips.

"Let me go." She jerked free on those words and had taken two steps in the direction of the woman before he grabbed her again. Their eyes locked, panic and desperation filling the smoky space between them. A sharp pain pierced her shoulder, and her knees buckled. Shouting voices and the sound of gunfire faded into blackness, along with the image of the desperate woman reaching out to her.

❖

Kelly coughed as the smoke and chemicals burned her throat. The guards were firing wildly, even though Barrett and her rescuers were no longer in sight. Barrett and her rescuers. The four words echoed in her brain as the commotion and confusion continued. The Colonel shouted orders, and he and eight men disappeared into the jungle in the direction she'd last seen Barrett.

The guards gathered the remaining hostages and brought them to the center of the camp. Kelly quickly did a head count, and except for Barrett everyone was accounted for. They all looked a little shell-shocked and confused, but thankfully none had been injured. Several of the guards weren't so lucky, and Little Boy dragged her across the camp to the first injured man.

"Sit," Little Boy barked, and kicked her legs out from under her. Little Boy's boots were inches from her face and Kelly expected him to kick her. Instead she felt the tip of his rifle pressed hard against her temple. She prayed he would pull the trigger.

❖

They moved fast. Very fast. Even with one of her rescuers supporting her and pulling her along, Barrett struggled to keep up. There were three of them, dressed in camo fatigues, with packs and very large guns. One man was in front, one behind, and one was practically dragging her through the jungle.

She knew without being told that they had to be quiet, and she bit her lip to keep from crying out when she stumbled, which was just about every step. The man beside her ripped open what was left of her shirt. The pain in her shoulder was like a hot poker, almost bringing her to her knees.

"Sorry, Ms. Taylor," he whispered. "We don't have time to stop right now, but I've got to get something on this."

Using his teeth he ripped the corner of a white package, quickly stuffing the corner in one of his many pockets. He dumped the white powder on a gauze pad he'd pulled from his pack.

"This is going to sting," he said an instant before he pressed it to the wound on her shoulder. This time her knees did buckle, and the man caught her before she fell.

"Breathe, breathe," he said a few times quietly in her left ear.

Barrett did as she was told, and the darkness that threatened to overtake her subsided along with some of the pain. She barely felt the needle stick from the shot in her arm. He expertly wrapped a field dressing around her shoulder, effectively trapping her arm against her chest. She tried not to think about how close she'd come to being killed. Now if only the infection from the slug in her shoulder didn't kill her.

Barrett was about to say she couldn't go any farther when they stopped. One of the men stood watch and one consulted his map and compass, while the medic handed her an energy bar and told her to eat. He rummaged in his pack and pulled out a pair of fatigues like they were wearing, a pair of socks, and sturdy boots.

"I'll help you put these on," he said, handing them to her. "They'll protect you from the elements, and you can't go much farther without decent footwear." Three minutes later they were on the move again, the man looking at his compass every few minutes.

Their travel was slow since they had to tread lightly to minimize any trail they might leave behind. More than once Barrett heard the familiar whack, whack, whack of the machetes cutting away the jungle, and she and her rescuers disappeared deeper into the jungle and stayed out of sight.

When they finally stopped to rest, her rescuers, who identified themselves as Mark, Sam, and Trevor, explained how her brother Aaron had contacted their agency to get her out. They'd been searching for her for weeks before they intercepted one of her proof-of-life radio calls and were able to track the signal.

"We have to go back," Barrett said. "I can't leave Kelly there. You don't know what they'll do to her." Barrett's voice didn't sound like her own. It was pleading and desperate. She didn't care.

"I'm sorry we can't go back," Mark said gently.

"Then why did you leave her? There were eight more hostages. Why didn't you take all of them?" She repeated the question that wouldn't leave her alone.

"Our orders were to get you."

Barrett interrupted him before he could continue. "And you're actually going to leave them all behind? You saw them. You saw Kelly. How can you do that?" She was incredulous.

"We only have supplies for you. If we took all of them it would have substantially decreased our odds of getting you out. We all might have died."

Barrett understood the words but couldn't hear them over the pounding in her head. She couldn't shake the image of Kelly calling her name, reaching out to her. The expression on Kelly's face when she was forced to leave her behind was burned into her brain.

❖

Kelly gritted her teeth as she cleaned the wounds on her feet. After Barrett was rescued they'd moved camps three times, never staying in one place for more than a few days. The constant movement had affected all of them, especially the already weakened ones.

Barrett had been gone for almost two weeks, and they'd been punished every day. Juan Cardoba had died two days ago on the way to this campsite, and Kelly had begged The Colonel to bring his body along for a proper burial. He only acquiesced when Kelly said she'd carry him. That had only lasted a few hours until she finally collapsed under the strain and was forced to leave him behind.

She was exhausted. She didn't know how long it would be before they were on the move again, and she needed to sleep when she had the chance. But she couldn't.

She thought about Barrett constantly, wondering if she'd survived. She'd been shot, and the image of Barrett's body recoiling was something she would never forget. Where was she now? Was she out of the jungle? Lost? Dead? How had those men found her? Who were they? Who hired them? Would they come back for the others? Would they come back for her?

❖

Barrett heard the whop, whop, whop of a helicopter, a big one. "That's our ride," Mark said, pointing to the sky. They'd been in the jungle for days, and Barrett was so tired she could barely lift her head. They'd stopped at the edge of a clearing, and it was all she could do to stay on her feet. Her shoulder throbbed and her vision blurred if she moved too fast, but she didn't think her wound was infected. It shouldn't be, for all the shots of penicillin Trevor had given her.

The radio in Mark's hand crackled, and he said something Barrett couldn't hear. A few minutes later a helicopter painted in varying shades of jungle green dropped out of the sky and hovered just above the ground.

"Let's go," Trevor shouted over the noise of the rotors.

Barrett's feet barely touched the ground as two of the men practically carried her across the field. The door of the helicopter was open, and another fatigue-clad man was behind a huge machine gun, swinging the barrel left and right, looking for any sign of trouble. The men lifted Barrett into the helicopter, followed her in, and within seconds they were airborne.

CHAPTER TEN

Someone kept calling her name, and she wished they'd just shut the fuck up. It was dark, her head was pounding, and she wanted to go back to sleep. She felt like her body was swimming in a thick fog and she was trying unsuccessfully to surface.

"Barrett? Barrett, can you hear me?" The voice was vaguely familiar.

"Barrett, open your eyes for me."

"Shut up." Pain shot through her head when she tried to lift her arm. It wouldn't move.

"Come on, Barrett. Open your eyes. You're in Panama. You're safe. Open your eyes."

She opened them a crack, the light piercing her head like an ice pick. "Turn off the goddamn light." Her voice was hoarse and weak. She heard a click, and the pounding behind her eyelids lessened a bit. She opened them again, this time wider.

Without moving her head, she saw the familiar decorations of a hospital room. The large lights overhead, the curtains hanging from the ceiling, the beep and hiss of machines. "Where am I?"

"Pie-tiya Medical Center in Panama. We brought you here straight from Columbia."

Finally a face to the voice moved so she could see him. It was Aaron.

"Aaron?" She felt confused and dazed and not quite all together.

"Yes, ma'am. The one and only. How do you feel?"

"Like I fell out of that helicopter. Panama?" Barrett wasn't sure she'd heard correctly.

"Yes. Panama has some of the finest medical facilities in South America. You're in good hands here. You're safe."

"What happened?"

"You were shot and in pretty bad shape when we got you here. They took you right into surgery and removed the bullet from your shoulder. They cleaned your cuts and scrapes, reset the break in your fingers, and patched you up," he said matter-of-factly.

"How long have I been here?"

"Four days."

Four days? She had to get up. Had to go back and get Kelly and the others. She tried to sit up, but stars clouded her view and blackness swam toward her.

"Hey, take it easy. Where do you think you're going?"

"I have to get Kelly and the others." She slurred the last few words.

"You're in no shape to go anywhere right now. You have to rest so we can take you home. Mom and Dad will be back in a few minutes. They went downstairs to get something to eat." Her brother looked at his watch. "We're all so happy you're okay. The doctor said your prognosis is good. It was touch-and-go for a while, but once they got the infection under control that was the turning point."

Barrett wanted to say something but couldn't remember what it was or even how to form the words. The machine to her left beeped a steady cadence, and Barrett let it take her under. The last thing she remembered before succumbing to the darkness was Kelly's face as she reached out to her.

"Just one more question, Ms. Taylor."

"You said that four questions ago," Barrett said sharply. She was tired, needed to pee, and more important, needed to get out of this room. The hospital staff was exceptional and had done everything to make her comfortable. It wasn't their fault she was going stir-crazy after three days.

The investigator from the U.S. Embassy asked his question and finally left, taking the ambassador and two others with him. Aaron sat patiently in a chair at the foot of her bed.

"What did Lori find?" Barrett asked before the door closed behind the men. She didn't need to explain. Aaron knew what she meant.

"Let's talk about this later. You need to rest."

"No. I'll rest after you tell me. I know Lori has something."

"If I tell you, do you promise to rest?"

Fine." Barrett acquiesced to his stupid terms. "What?" He appeared puzzled. "I said I'd rest, so tell me."

"Kelly Ann Ryan. Born July third, 1981. Parents Robert and Fran live in Birmingham, Alabama, where Kelly grew up." Aaron flipped to the next piece of paper in his hand. "Graduated with top grades for her MSRN from the University of Alabama, moved to Denver, and has been a nurse since 2002. She's been at Brookhaven Hospital for six years and has volunteered with Medical Missions for seven years, making eight trips to places like Guatemala, Honduras, Chile, and of course Columbia. "

Geez, Barrett thought. What kind of person intentionally puts herself in harm's way?

"Divorced from Max Thomas six years ago after eighteen months of marriage. Her credit is stellar, or at least it was before she was kidnapped and couldn't pay her bills. Her house is in foreclosure and her car has been repossessed. She was grabbed on June twenty-ninth last year and three ransom demands have been made, but no money has been paid."

"Where's my phone?"

What for?" Aaron asked.

"I need to call Lori and have her—"

"No."

"Aaron—"

"You promised, Barrett." Aaron sounded much like he did when they were kids.

"Just this one thing."

"No."

She thought about arguing with him but decided to rest, and then he'd willingly give her the phone.

"Okay, you're right." The look on Aaron's face was priceless. She rarely, if ever, gave in that easily. "Why don't you go down and get some coffee, and I'll take a nap till you get back." She was plotting before the door shut behind him.

❖

It was like a scene out of the movie *Castaway* when the main character returned to civilization. A dozen people were milling around the hotel room, and the banquet table was overflowing with food. Barrett wasn't interested in either and fought to remain calm. Didn't they realize she'd been a hostage for, how long was it—seven months? She needed all these people to get the hell out of her room and give her some peace.

They'd all come once they heard she'd been released from the hospital. In addition to her parents and Aaron, Debra had brought their entire staff, who'd cornered Mark, Trevor, and Sam for most of the afternoon and pumped them for details on other missions they'd completed. She was still in Panama, but in a room at the Trump Ocean Club International Hotel and Tower, located on the waterfront in the Punta Pacifica area of Panama City.

Her room was on the forty-third floor, adjacent to her parents and across the hall from Aaron. Her parents had insisted she come here from the hospital three days ago to continue to rest and regain her strength before the long trip back to San Francisco. Not up to arguing with them, she'd acquiesced but now wished she were back in her own house and out from under the watchful and somewhat smothering eyes of her family.

She never doubted that they loved her, especially now after what Aaron had gone through to rescue her. It had cost a small fortune, which he gleefully informed her that *her* company had paid. The fact that they'd all come out alive had made the global news wires, and between the newshounds, paparazzi, and the people in the room she'd had enough.

"A little overwhelming, isn't it?" Aaron asked as he stood beside her. "Everybody's so happy to see you."

Barrett nodded, trying to find the right words. "Get the fuck out" wouldn't do. Nor would "Yes, I got out, but I left others behind. What about them?" So she simply nodded and sipped her glass of ice water. That was one of the first things she'd wanted. A glass of ice water. She hadn't had anything cold to drink or hot to eat in months, and she'd started with the purest beverage in the world. She'd managed the hot meal a few days later.

Looking around, Barrett felt disconnected from everyone and everything. The shrink her parents had flown over from the U.S. was an expert in trauma and the mental and psychological effects of being held hostage. They'd talked briefly before Barrett realized she didn't need a shrink, just a little time for herself, by herself, to get reacquainted with her life. She told the doctor as much, who stated that was a normal reaction but that she should see him for at least another few months to help her ease back into her life. She told him that was bullshit, paid her bill, and told him to go home. Now if she could just do the same with everybody else.

Her mother glided across the room, the smile on her face never wavering. As a matter of fact it was the same smile she'd had the first time Barrett saw her in the hospital room a week ago.

"Barrett, darling, how are you holding up? You look a little tired."

Her mother always thought she looked a little tired. Her mother's constant concern for her health irritated Barrett, but she cut her some slack. It wasn't everyday a daughter was kidnapped, held for ransom, rescued by paid mercenaries, and returned home. Oh, and how could she ever forget about getting shot? As if the ugly scar on the front of her left shoulder or the scar on her forehead wouldn't remind her. Her souvenir could have been worse. She could have come back in a box.

"I am a little tired," Barrett said, obviously shocking her mother. Barrett had never admitted to being tired even when she was absolutely exhausted. It wasn't quite a lie. She was tired—tired of all these people. Her mother jumped into action like Barrett knew she would, and within minutes the room was empty except for her family.

"Come sit down, Barrett," her mother said, tapping the couch cushion next to her.

Barrett turned from her view of the Panama Canal out the window to look at her parents. Ginny and Howard were in their late sixties and today looked every bit of it. Her mother had aged significantly since Barrett had seen her last, and her father had lost most of his hair and a good twenty pounds. She herself had lost forty-three, and the strain of captivity was apparent. Her hair was cut ultra short, her skin dark from the sun, and her eyes alert and wary of everything around her. God, what a family portrait this would make, she thought.

"I'm going to lie down for a while. Wake me when it's time for dinner." After a few hugs and "do you need anythings" her family left. Finally she was alone.

She stripped out of her clothes and showered. Even after her return and being scrubbed and disinfected from head to toe, she still felt dirty and grimy. She was anemic due to poor nutrition, had a pestering fungus on her feet, her shoulder ached, and her wrist was still in a sling, but she was otherwise healthy.

The first thing she'd done when she was finally able to shower by herself was shave her legs. That simple act wasn't easy with her left arm still useless, but it made a world of difference in how she felt. She'd had a decent haircut in the salon downstairs and had bought some clothes that fit. She'd insisted on getting her hair cut the minute she was released from the hospital. She'd never again have hair long enough to be used to grab or drag her anywhere.

Wrapped in a thick terry-cloth robe with the hotel logo embroidered above her left breast, Barrett sat in a plush chair she'd pulled in front of the expansive window. After months in the hot, humid jungle, she found the air-conditioning wonderful. She sipped her iced tea and took stock of her situation.

The doctors had told her that, barring any complications, she should have a full recovery. Other than the scar from the surgery to remove the nasty bullet, a slightly crooked nose, and the scar on her forehead from the cut she'd suffered while being taken, she'd have no lasting physical effects of her ordeal. The weight loss wasn't too bad, but she could stand to put back ten of the forty she'd lost. The pins and rods that held her reconstructed hand in place looked like a child's erector construction set, but that too would be removed. All in all she considered herself pretty damn lucky.

Closing her eyes and leaning her head back to rest on the chair, she let her thoughts drift to Kelly. Actually they didn't have to drift far, as Kelly was always on her mind. What had happened to her once The Colonel returned empty-handed? Did he take out his anger and frustration on her? He'd known, as the only women in camp, that they would bond, and he'd used that fact against one of them whenever he felt like it. She was sure he'd do so now.

The *tink, tink, tink* of the ice against the glass drew her attention, and Barrett saw that her hand was shaking. It did that every time she thought about Kelly and the others. The shrink had talked to her about survivor syndrome, often called post-traumatic stress syndrome or PTSD.

He'd said she might experience symptoms of anxiety, depression, social withdrawal, difficulty sleeping, and nightmares. He cautioned her about the possibility of flashbacks and how she might feel guilty for being rescued when so many others were left behind.

She'd listened with half an ear because the words applied to someone else. She didn't have PTSD, for God's sake. She'd never let her subconscious rule her conscious mind, and she wasn't about to start now.

Sure, she felt bad that Kelly and the others weren't with her today, but she had to get back to her life. Too much had happened without her. Her business was suffering, and they'd lost several major contract renewals. She'd missed too much and needed to get a grip.

CHAPTER ELEVEN

The mere thought of food made Kelly want to retch. She'd barely eaten in a week and was sick all the time. She'd probably caught some parasite from the water, the mosquitoes, or God knew what else. It was hotter in this camp, the humidity stifling. Everyone was listless, and even the guards didn't seem to be paying as much attention to them as in the past. At least the punishment for Barrett's escape had stopped.

For the first few weeks after the daring midnight rescue, the hostages had been stripped naked and forced to stand for hours in the heat, humidity, and driving rain. When one of them finally collapsed in exhaustion, another was punished. Kelly wasn't exempted from the punishment and actually received more. She wasn't allowed to treat her fellow hostages, and when The Colonel called for her, he didn't touch her but tormented her for hours by talking about how he'd caught, tortured, and finally killed Barrett.

Kelly refused to believe his tales, and each time he started in she switched her mind into being somewhere else. She built a new house brick by brick, decorated every room, landscaped her yard, and had barbeques with new neighbors. She was back at work providing superior care to her patients and spent time with friends in the mountains.

She tried not to think about Barrett and what she was doing. She refused to believe she'd been caught and killed. Her rescue was too well executed, her rescuers too well armed and trained to have failed in the depths of the jungle.

One day, out of sheer boredom, Kelly had asked Barrett to describe her house, her office, and a typical workweek. She loved listening to Barrett talk and was fascinated by her life. It was so very different from her own. She knew Barrett was wealthy but that wasn't what made Barrett interesting; it was her view of life. As she talked, Kelly couldn't help but discover their differences.

Kelly didn't care about money or things. She was born to be a giver, to take care of others. Whereas she was selfless, Barrett looked out for herself. Kelly needed people and a connection, but Barrett preferred to be alone. Kelly would rather negotiate and acquiesce to avoid an argument or confrontation; Barrett fought for what she wanted.

Was she sitting behind her desk ruling the world of business? Was she sitting on her back patio watching the waves crash over the rocks? Was she driving down the Pacific Coast Highway, the top down on her BMW, her hair blowing in the wind? Was she having dinner in a world-class restaurant? Was she alone?

It didn't matter to her that Barrett was a lesbian. Even when they were forced to strip in front of each other she hadn't felt uncomfortable. Barrett hadn't referred to any one special woman, and Kelly surmised that Barrett was transitory in her relationships with women. One night she'd asked her about it.

"Have you ever had a steady girlfriend?"

"No. Have you?"

"Of course not." The question had surprised Kelly a little. "I'm not gay." She hoped she hadn't sounded defensive.

"That's okay," Barrett said. "I won't hold it against you."

"Thank God. I'm so relieved. We heterosexuals always worry about how people will react when we come out to them. Luckily I haven't lost any friends because of it."

"You're a real smart-ass, aren't you?"

Kelly heard the laughter in Barrett's voice. "I used to be, but I asked about you."

"And I answered you."

God, getting information out of Barrett was proving to be difficult. "Why not?"

"Why not what?"

"Barrett," Kelly said, teasing her. "You don't like to talk about yourself, do you?"

"Of course I do. I'm a successful businesswoman, or at least I hope I still am. And like anyone in my position, I've been interviewed countless times. I've always answered any question they asked."

"I doubt anyone asked why you never had a steady girlfriend."

"You're right there. But I'll save you having to ask again. I'm too busy. I've been completely dedicated to building my company for as long as I can remember. Having a steady girlfriend takes time, effort, and commitment. I have very little of the first, am too tired for the second, and I don't do the third. Thus…no steady girlfriend."

Barrett stated her position so succinctly Kelly had to think about it for a few seconds. "So you—"

"I keep it light, never stay the night, and make sure the lady knows the rules. What about you? You got a steady beau waiting for you?"

"No. I'm sort of in between, as they say." For her, however, the time between had been getting longer and longer. The more she dated the less spark she felt, until it had reached the point that she was seriously considering staying single the rest of her life.

"I can't believe a pretty girl like you doesn't have guys lined up waiting their turn."

Kelly couldn't help but laugh. "I wasn't always this beautiful," she replied. "I was quite a bit heavier and a lot nerdier. Now, however, I guess I'd be described as lean, with that fresh, outside glow, and my social skills have definitely improved," she added.

"Well, I happen to think you're pretty amazing. If you ever need a date, just give me a call. I'd be proud to be your escort."

Kelly laughed, a tickle in her stomach at the invitation. Was Barrett escorting someone else tonight? Were they sharing intimate conversation over candlelight and fine wine? Was she planning her seduction and escape? Had she gone on with her life like this nightmare never happened? Had she been changed by her experience? Did she ever think of her?

❖

"What?" Barrett asked a little too sharply. Everyone around the table was looking at her expectantly.

"Let's take a short break," Debra said to no one in particular, yet everyone immediately jumped up, practically falling over each other to get out of the room and leaving Barrett and Debra alone.

"Don't look at me like that, Debra." Barrett pushed her chair back from the conference table.

"And how am I looking at you?"

Barrett didn't answer her but asked a question of her own. "What do you want, Debra? Obviously you have something on your mind."

"I want you to tell me what's going on with you. You've been back to work for a month, and I don't think you're ready."

"Well, you're wrong."

"No, Barrett. I don't think I am. You can't sit still, you have no focus, you can't follow a conversation, and you look like shit."

"Gee, thanks, Debra. With friends like you who needs business enemies?"

"You know I'm right," Debra said, refilling her glass from the pitcher on the credenza behind her.

"I don't pay you to psychoanalyze me," Barrett snapped in irritation, even if Debra's words were pretty close to the truth. Thank goodness she didn't know about her nightmares and overwhelming sense of guilt because she was here and Kelly and the others weren't. She was safe, sleeping in a comfortable bed and had hot running water at the turn of the faucet and more than enough food to eat. Her fellow hostages on the other hand slept on the hard ground, bathed out of a cup, and had scraps of leftovers if they were lucky.

"You don't pay me at all, which is why I'm the only person who has nothing to lose by telling you the facts of life. Everyone else tiptoes around you, afraid to say the wrong thing." Debra crossed the room and sat in the chair next to her. She turned both their chairs so they were facing each other, their knees almost touching. Her voice was gentle.

"I'm worried about you. You look worse today than you did when you got home. I can't even begin to understand or imagine what you went through. It's completely okay for you to still be a little rattled by—"

Barrett shot out of her chair. "I am not a little rattled, distracted, or any other word you can dig up to describe what you think is going on. There is nothing wrong with me. Now either get everyone back in here or I've got better things to do."

Later that evening alone in her house, a tumbler half full of scotch in her hand, Barrett watched a baseball game. She had no idea who was playing and really didn't care, but the cadence of the broadcaster's monologue was somewhat soothing. She used to love the silence after a long day. She would come home after dinner or a business meeting and sip two inches of her favorite liquor and unwind. If she'd been with someone she'd strip, shower, and fall into bed and not move until her alarm went off at five. Every morning she began her day with a run on the beach, two cups of coffee, and a strawberry protein smoothie on the way to work. Now, the silence was deafening.

She couldn't get her mind to shut down. She was in a constant state of anxiety and every sound made her jump, which irritated the hell out of her. She would never admit it to her, but Debra was right. She couldn't focus and had the attention span of a two-year-old. She couldn't sit still, had absolutely no appetite, and had tried unsuccessfully to lose herself in sex. On the other hand some days she could barely drag herself out of bed, was listless, and had no interest in anything whatsoever.

But the guilt of leaving Kelly and the others behind weighed her down the most. She'd read all about survivor guilt and the theories of PTSD and refused to admit she might be suffering from it. To do so would mean she wasn't as strong as she was before, that she was no longer able to take care of herself, that she needed to be dependent on someone else to help her get through this.

As much as she refused to admit it, her captivity had changed her and she didn't like what she saw.

❖

The nightmare wouldn't end. No matter how hard she tried to wake up, her eyes wouldn't open. Barrett knew she was dreaming but couldn't stop the scene unfolding in her subconscious. It was the same one that played in a continuous loop night after night. Smoke and gunfire obliterated everything, but the one thing she could see clearly was Kelly reaching out to her.

Finally the beeping from her alarm interrupted the reel, and she staggered naked into the bathroom. It was still dark outside, and she didn't turn on the light but slid open the shower doors and stepped inside. She twisted the cold-water knob and slid to the floor as the icy spray cooled her sensitive nerve endings.

It was several minutes before Barrett pulled herself together and stood. Her legs were still weak, and her hands shook as much from the cold water as from her frayed nerves. She washed her hair and tried not to think. She bathed her body and tried even harder not to think. But being able to lift her injured shoulder only halfway constantly reminded her of her ordeal. Of course the pins and rods in the fingers of her left hand wouldn't be removed for another few months, and that very public souvenir generated more questions than not. Twenty minutes later she was dressed and out the door, her briefcase slung over her good shoulder.

Barrett avoided Debra as much as she could the next few weeks, not up to another come-to-Jesus confrontation. She busied herself with reviewing proposals, making phone calls, and setting up customer visits. At work she surrounded herself with people who challenged her mind, forcing her to concentrate. She avoided her family as much as possible.

Aaron called her on it one evening when he surprised her by picking her up at her office and taking them both to their parents' house for dinner. The evening was cool, and her mother served dinner on the patio overlooking the eighteenth green of the golf course behind their house. She and Aaron were alone on the patio.

"I'm worried about you, Barrett."

"Don't be. There's nothing to worry about. I'm fine." She recited all of her well-practiced answers.

"Bullshit."

Barrett turned and looked at her baby brother, raising her eyebrows. She couldn't remember a swear word ever coming out of his mouth.

"You heard me right. That should give you some idea how worried I am." He held his hand up. "No, don't give me the I'm-fine speech, because I know you're not. Mom and Dad may be buying it, and the people at your office, but *I am not.*

"At the risk of completely pissing you off, you need to see somebody. You look like shit. The circles under your eyes aren't due to overwork, you bark at everybody, and if I know you, you're fucking everyone trying to escape. You need professional help to work through this because you're doing a shitty job of doing it on your own. I know you're fiercely independent and refuse to let anyone help you, but this is the rest of your life we're talking about here, not some business deal. And unlike one of your famous business deals, if you fuck this up you may never recover."

Barrett was stunned. Not only had he cussed several times during his little speech, she saw fire in his normally calm eyes. She loved her brother, even when he overstepped his boundaries in her life.

He was right. She did look like hell, wasn't sleeping, and when she did go to bed it was with some nameless stranger she used to try to escape. For just a few minutes she needed to forget the image of Kelly reaching for her, to hear soft moans of passion instead of Kelly's voice calling to her. For just a few minutes.

It had worked in the beginning. She could lose herself in the moment, in the curves of a female body, the feel of a woman's soft skin, the smell of her arousal, the taste of her. But lately, the more she tried, the more it failed, and the more her life spun out of control.

"I know what I need to do," she said quietly. The idea had been forming in her mind for the past few days, and she was ready to take action.

"You know I'll do anything I can to help you." He reached over and squeezed her hand. "Just name it."

"What's the name of the agency you hired to get me out?"

"What?" A frown of confusion creased his broad forehead.

"The company you hired to get me out of Columbia. Who are they?"

Realization dawned on her brother's face. "That's not what I'm talking about, and you know it."

"I know that I have to try to get the others out. I can't sit here, eat great food, take a shower whenever I want, and go wherever I want whenever I want when the others are beaten, starved, and chained to a tree." Barrett quieted her voice so her parents wouldn't hear. "I have to do this, Aaron, and I'll either do it with the same group of guys or I'll find my own."

For the first time in months Barrett felt in control of her life. She would do everything she could, spend every penny she had to get Kelly and the others out. She had to. She couldn't be the only one to come home.

CHAPTER TWELVE

B arrett paced. She'd awoken this morning more on edge than ever before. She sensed something was happening and had been waiting all day for the phone to ring. She looked at her watch too many times to count, each time just minutes from the last.

Eighteen days ago she'd received the call informing her that Trevor and his team had finally discovered signs of the rebels. They'd been in the jungle ninety-four days.

Trevor had not been receptive to her offer when she had spoken to him a few months ago.

"I need you to go back and get them out."

"Ms. Taylor, the probability the rebels are anywhere near the location where we extracted you are zero. They probably moved out before their search party returned."

"I don't care," Barrett said forcefully. She often used this same phrase in the course of her work, negotiating contracts, making demands on her people, but that was nothing compared to her insistence on this subject.

"Ms. Taylor, this isn't a good idea."

Barrett ignored her throbbing shoulder. "What's your fee?"

"Ms. Taylor—"

"I know, Trevor. It'll take weeks, maybe months to track them down. It'll be expensive. I know all that and I don't care. I want you and your team for this job, and I'll pay whatever the cost." For the

first time in her life money didn't matter. They had settled on a fee and she'd been waiting ever since.

She couldn't help herself and looked at her watch again. Had they run into trouble? *Please God, let them have her.* She jumped as her cell phone rang.

"Taylor."

"Package secure."

Relief Barrett had never experienced flooded her body, making her knees weak. She stumbled to the chair and fell into it.

"Five boxes in route."

"Thank you." A dial tone was the reply.

She couldn't move. Her pulse was racing and she felt light-headed. It wasn't over yet, but Trevor and his team had Kelly and four others.

"Lori," she shouted, and sprang from the chair with more energy than she'd had in weeks. "I need the plane and I need it now." She'd had a private jet on standby for weeks, waiting for this call. Her bag was packed and in her trunk. She ran out the door with one thing on her mind: a silent prayer that they would all arrive safely.

The flight to Panama lasted a lifetime. The plane was large enough that Barrett could walk around, but not big enough to take more than eleven steps in either direction. Back and forth she paced, losing count of the number of times she turned and retraced her steps. The flight steward had long since given up on offering her anything to eat, drink, or read. Time seemed to stop, and Barrett fought the panic attacks that threatened to overwhelm her.

A thousand different thoughts raced through her head. Was Kelly injured? Had she been hurt in the rescue? What about the others? Trevor had said five hostages were in route. What about the others? Including Kelly, there had been eight when she left. She prayed she hadn't been too late.

Her plane touched down in Panama, and Barrett was out of her seat before it stopped at the private terminal. She fought the urge to shove the flight steward out of the way and open the door herself, and she flew down the stairs onto the tarmac. A uniformed attendant was holding a door open for her, and she barely felt the change from the wet humidity outside to the cool air-conditioning inside the private waiting area.

Kelly's plane, a medical transport, had not yet arrived, and Barrett stayed glued to the window, watching the empty landing strip reserved for private planes. Trevor was using two helicopters to fly the hostages to a small airstrip where the transport plane was waiting. It was not equipped to be an in-flight hospital, but with a doctor, two nurses, and three emergency medical technicians onboard, it was more of a mobile triage unit. The medical workers would administer any immediate care that was needed in order to stabilize the patients until they arrived at the hospital in Panama.

A plane slightly larger than the one Barrett had arrived in landed and taxied to the gate. She was so nervous she could hardly stand still. She took a few deep breaths to steady herself as the door of the plane opened and several more medical personnel boarded. She wanted to be the first one on the plane but knew her presence might delay immediate medical attention to someone who needed it. Instead she stepped outside into the blistering heat and midday sun.

Two men carried a stretcher down the stairs, and Barrett's anxiety kicked up a notch. The attendants pressed a yellow bar at the head of the stretcher, and the legs unfolded and locked in place. Barrett stepped forward as the immobile patient was wheeled closer. A sigh, mixed with relief and continuing anxiety, passed her lips, but she didn't recognize the man. He was pale but breathing, and she said a quick blessing before he was whisked away into a waiting ambulance.

One by one the other rescued hostages descended the steps. Some needed a steadying arm while others were able to negotiate the dozen steps under their own power. All of them looked to be in shock or bewildered as to what was going on and where they were. As each stepped out of the plane and into the afternoon light, Barrett held her breath until she recognized that the person wasn't Kelly. She greeted each one before he was helped into an ambulance.

My God, what was taking so long? Why wasn't Kelly the first one out? She couldn't have been badly injured or she'd have been one of the first off the plane. Was she dead? Were they waiting until all the survivors were off before they removed the bodies?

Finally, when Barrett thought she couldn't stand there a moment longer, a shadow passed behind the plane's small door. Barrett's knees began to buckle when she recognized Kelly stepping out onto the first step of the stairs. Their eyes met and locked, and Barrett started to breathe again. Even from this distance Barrett could see Kelly's eyes were clear and focused on her.

Overwhelming joy and relief flooded every nerve and limb on her body. Kelly was safe. Kelly was alive. Kelly was home. Barrett stifled a gasp. Guilt, blame, and responsibility instantly replaced her euphoria.

"Oh my God, I'm too late," Barrett whispered. Kelly was pregnant.

CHAPTER THIRTEEN

Kelly was a bit wobbly on the stairs, and before she'd taken three steps Barrett was in front of her, offering her a steadying hand. It was solid, warm, and real. Kelly still wasn't sure this wasn't all just a dream. They'd moved so many times after Barrett was rescued, and several times the guards had played a cruel trick and told them they were being released. But this wasn't another mind-fuck. Barrett stood in front of her, as solid and real as Kelly remembered, and for an instant she forgot.

Gone were the pain, the sleepless nights, and the never-ending hunger. Gone was the sense of helplessness and despair she'd felt when Barrett had disappeared into the jungle. Gone was the desolate loneliness that threatened to swallow her into the black ink of the jungle night. Gone were her doubts and fears that she would never return home. In that instant, in that moment, Barrett was here.

Kelly saw the instant Barrett knew. The single, most obvious reminder that she had been a captive—at the mercy of others, dependent on them for every scrap of food, form of shelter, and every breath she took. The reminder would be with her forever. She would never be able to forget.

Just as suddenly Barrett's strong arms were around her, and Kelly stopped thinking. Barrett was here. She was free. She was safe.

Kelly's body gave way in complete exhaustion and relief, and Barrett swept her into her arms before she fell. Kelly instinctively wrapped her arms around Barrett's shoulders and buried her face into her neck.

"It's okay. I've got you."

Barrett's voice was soft and soothing and one Kelly had thought she'd never hear again. She tightened her hold, never wanting to let go.

"It's okay," Barrett repeated. "You're safe. I won't let anything happen to you. I promise. No one will ever hurt you again."

Barrett carried her to a waiting ambulance and set her gently on the stretcher. Kelly didn't want to let go of the woman she'd thought about endlessly since she was rescued all those months ago. She'd never thought she would touch her again or hear her deep voice in anything other than her dreams.

Barrett grasped her hands and pulled her arms from around her neck. Kelly started to panic that she would disappear again, and Barrett squeezed her hands.

"I'm not going anywhere," she said, her voice calming Kelly's frayed nerves. "But you have to let go of my hand so the EMTs can take a look at you before we go to the hospital."

Kelly nodded, realizing she still hadn't said a word since stepping off the plane and seeing Barrett.

"Thank you for coming back for us." It surprised her that her voice was strong and gave no hint of the turmoil she was experiencing. She was out of the jungle for the first time in over two years. Her feet were on solid ground, so to speak, and pretty soon she would have a roof over her head.

"I'm sorry it took so long," Barrett said, her face drawn.

"We're safe. That's all that matters." Barrett was here now.

Barrett shook her head. "It took too long."

The EMT closest to Kelly spoke up. "Your blood pressure, heart rate, and pulse are good. You have a little rattle in your lungs, but nothing to worry about. Now, let's get you inside and on your way to the hospital."

Her expression must have spoken volumes because the young man looked at her, then to Barrett, then back at Kelly again. "And Ms. Taylor is coming with us."

Kelly relaxed and didn't let go of Barrett's hand during the entire ride to the hospital.

❖

"Ms. Ryan, I'm Doctor Martin. I know you've been through a lot, and we're going to take good care of you."

The doctor turned and spoke to Barrett. "Ms. Taylor, good to see you looking so well." His voice was warm. "Much better than the last time I saw you. How's the shoulder?"

"A bit stiff now and then, but pretty good."

Kelly's heartbeat sped up, and the monitor blipped in response. She'd never forget the sight of Barrett falling backward from the force of the bullet hitting her.

Dr. Martin glanced at the telltale machine. "As I was saying, we're going to take good care of you. We'll tell you everything we're going to do before we do it. Okay?"

Kelly nodded but didn't make eye contact. She'd endured too many months of following strict orders not to.

"If you're uncomfortable or frightened in the slightest, let me know and we'll stop. We won't do anything you don't want us to."

"Dr. Martin was on duty when I came in. When I heard you were on the way in, I requested he be the one to check you out." Barrett's comment explained everything.

"Jackie here," he indicated a nurse in purple scrubs standing beside him, "will get you out of those clothes. Do you think you can help, or should she just cut them off?"

It took a moment for Kelly to realize she'd been asked a question. For months she'd simply been told what to do.

"I can do it," Kelly said, remembering all the other times she'd stripped in front of complete strangers. But suddenly she was very shy in front of Barrett, which made absolutely no sense. Barrett had seen her naked dozens of times, but this was different. Kelly glanced at Barrett, grateful when she turned around, offering her privacy.

Kelly was poked, prodded, x-rayed, and had eight vials of blood drawn before Dr. Martin quietly asked, his back to Barrett, "How far along are you?"

Kelly appreciated his diplomacy and tact and answered just as quietly. "About four months, but I'm not sure."

"I've called for a female obstetrician," he said, his voice gentle and understanding. "Dr. Foster will be able to help you in whatever way you need. In the meantime, Jackie will get you cleaned up a little. I'm sure you'd like a shower, but that'll have to wait till you get upstairs to your room."

She tried not to flinch as Jackie expertly cleaned off the top layer of grime and dirt while Barrett waited outside. She kept telling herself this wasn't a dream, that she was safe. She desperately wanted to brush her teeth but knew that too would have to wait.

Kelly was finally clothed in a clean hospital gown, and Nurse Jackie slid open the door, allowing Barrett back in. Kelly smiled. "I probably smell just a little better, but I know I feel much better."

Barrett didn't move closer to the bed. "I know exactly what you mean. All I wanted to do was brush my teeth."

Barrett finally smiled, and Kelly's pulse raced and her stomach did a little flip-flop. She didn't have a chance to say anything before a woman in her forties with long jet-black hair stepped into the room. Kelly immediately reached for Barrett's hand, dropping her eyes and stiffening out of habit.

"Miss Ryan, I'm Doctor Marilyn Foster. How are you feeling?"

Barrett squeezed her hand. "A little overwhelmed," Kelly admitted, glancing back and forth from the doctor to her lap.

"I can't even imagine," she said, without pity in her voice.

The doctor stepped closer, and the blips on the heart monitor jumped and stayed high. Barrett squeezed her hand again.

"It's okay," Barrett said quietly.

She clutched Barrett's hand and tried to calm down.

"Do you want to talk privately?" Dr. Foster asked so only Kelly could hear.

"Miss Ryan?"

Kelly tried not to flinch at her name, expecting the blow.

A familiar voice eased her fear. "It's okay, Kelly. You're safe here."

Tentatively she raised her head, still not certain this was all real. Jesus, when would she stop questioning that she was safe? Barrett's face confirmed that she was. She nodded. Barrett made her feel secure. She'd hung on to her both literally and figuratively since stepping off the plane. But this was different. She knew she had nothing to be ashamed about but didn't want Barrett to be a part of this, to see her like this. At least not right now. She nodded.

"Ms. Taylor, would you please excuse us for a few minutes?"

Barrett looked at her expectantly, and Kelly nodded again. "I'll be okay."

Barrett seemed to be weighing her choices before agreeing to leave. "I'll call your parents and tell them you're safe and will talk to them as soon as you can."

For an instant Kelly was afraid Barrett would tell her parents she was pregnant but then realized Barrett knew that was for her to do.

"That would be great."

The door clicked shut behind Barrett, and Dr. Foster laid the clipboard on the table beside her.

"How far along are you?"

"Four months, I think," she answered hesitantly. "After a month or so my period was spotty at best. I never imagined I'd get pregnant."

"Would you like to tell me about it?"

She risked a glance at the doctor, whose eyes were warm and understanding. Kelly took a chance and started at the beginning.

Forty minutes later Dr. Foster said, "Before we go any further, let me see what we're dealing with." She moved the sonogram machine next to the bed and lifted Kelly's gown, exposing her rounding belly. Kelly flinched.

"I'm sorry." Dr. Martin quickly pulled her hand back, her voice full of concern.

Kelly risked another glance and said, embarrassed, "No, I'm sorry. It's just a habit I'll have to break. Go ahead." She suddenly realized this was the first time she'd given someone permission to do anything.

The gel was cold, and Dr. Foster expertly moved the wand over her stomach. She adjusted knobs and concentrated on the screen. "Pretty good guess. From what I see, I'd say you're closer to five than four months along, but I won't quibble over a week or two."

Kelly simply nodded, not quite hearing the words. Even though she knew she was pregnant, hearing it confirmed officially made it real.

"Do you want to keep this baby?"

The blunt question surprised Kelly. "I don't know," she answered honestly. "Until an hour ago I didn't think I had a choice." She frowned and counted in her head. "Is it too late?"

"If you decide to terminate I can help you with that." Dr. Foster didn't answer her question, but Kelly was a nurse and knew the difficulty of an abortion this far along.

"How long do I have to decide?" She forced out her question.

"Not long. You know as well as I do the risks and availability the further along you are." She adjusted a few more knobs and pushed a button on the screen. Paper slid out of a slot on the side of the machine. Kelly knew it was a picture of the baby. Her baby. Dr. Foster didn't show it to her but instead said, "If you want this it'll be in your chart." She clipped the photo behind a few papers on her chart and turned her full attention to Kelly.

"If you'd like, I can arrange for someone to talk with you about your options. No pressure one way or the other. Just information."

Kelly nodded again, unable to find her voice.

❖

Barrett hung up and slid her phone back in her pocket. Kelly's parents were ecstatic, to say the least, and Barrett had sent the plane she'd chartered to pick them up. They'd be here late tomorrow afternoon.

"She'll be okay?"

The question from Dr. Martin came from behind her. Barrett turned around and sighed. "I hope so. She's been through a lot."

"And faces a lot more," he replied.

Barrett knew exactly what he was referring to. No way had she expected Kelly to be pregnant, but then again she'd never really thought about those kinds of things. Since returning, Barrett had realized she'd never thought about anyone.

"Yes, she does. But she's strong," Barrett said automatically. Kelly was emotionally strong, but now that she was out from under the constant pressure of captivity, how would she adapt? And now she had a child. The Colonel's child. At least she thought it was The Colonel's. For Kelly's sake, she hoped it was.

"Come in," Kelly said when she knocked on the door. Kelly had been moved to a room on the seventh floor, and Barrett wasn't allowed in until the nurses got her settled. She pushed open the door and stepped inside.

Kelly was sitting up in the bed, an IV dripping something yellow into the needle in the top of her left hand. Her hair was wet, her cheeks flushed. The hospital bed with its white sheets and the corresponding harsh fluorescent lights made Kelly look small and frightened.

"Hi," Kelly said tentatively.

"Hi," Barrett replied, not quite sure what she should say. Thankfully Kelly did.

"This is the first chance I've had to thank you."

Barrett stepped closer. "No need for thanks. I was lucky enough to get out, and I was determined to do everything I could to do the same for you and the others. I'm just sorry it took so long." *And for me to figure out that's what I should do.* Barrett continued to beat herself up for not thinking of it earlier.

"How are the others?" Kelly asked.

The question didn't surprise Barrett. Even now, after they were safe, Kelly was concerned about others. "I'm not sure. I've kind of been focused on you." Barrett was somewhat embarrassed for not thinking of them. "I'll go find out."

"Wait," Kelly said, as she turned to leave the room. "You don't have to. I'm sure they're getting the best possible care. Sit down. You're making me nervous."

"That makes two of us." Barrett pulled the chair closer to the bed. "How are you feeling?"

"I'm not sure."

"Do you need something? Do you want me to call the nurse?" Barrett asked quickly.

"No, I don't need anything. I'm just not sure how I feel. I know I'm out of the jungle and safe, but it's almost surreal. I've dreamed about this so many times I stopped dreaming. I never thought I'd see this day."

Barrett had experienced that feeling too. It was almost like a form of disassociation—real but not certain it was really real. Kelly had been held captive much, much longer, so what she was experiencing had to be ten times worse.

"I'm pregnant."

Barrett felt worse than ever before. "I don't know what to say. God, Kelly. I'm so sorry I didn't get to you sooner."

"Don't be." Kelly shook her head emphatically. "You did what you could, and you have to believe that."

Barrett's mind knew that but her heart and soul didn't.

"The doctor said I need to decide what I want to do."

The *do* in Kelly's statement was clear, even to someone like Barrett, who didn't have the first clue about being pregnant. She didn't know if she should ask, make a comment, or say nothing at all. But she had to say something. Kelly was looking at her expectantly.

"What do you want to do?" That was the safest response she could come up with.

"I don't know. I'm afraid this child will constantly remind me of…" She didn't need to finish the statement. They both knew what she was referring to. "But it's a child," Kelly said, laying her hands over her belly. "My child. It had no say in the way it was created, so why should it be punished for it?"

"What will your parents say?" Barrett knew Kelly's family was close and ultraconservative. How would they react to the news?

Kelly's face lost all color. "I don't think they'll take it well."

Barrett wasn't sure she was taking it well. She'd had more awkward, tough conversations than she could remember, but this one was by far the worst. "How so?"

"They believe sex outside marriage is a sin and a child created outside of marriage is a bastard, regardless of the circumstances."

Barrett couldn't help but cringe and wished she could keep her opinion to herself. "Surely under the circumstances they'll think differently. You're their daughter and you were raped." Barrett even hated saying the word.

"Maybe." Kelly answered halfheartedly, as if trying to convince herself.

"They're your parents and they love you. When I met them they were worried sick about you. All they wanted was for you to come home. And now you have. How can they not be grateful for that, whatever the circumstances?" Barrett didn't expect an answer.

"You met them?"

Barrett told Kelly about her visit to her parents shortly after she'd arrived back in the States. When the taxi had stopped in front of a large ranch-style house in the center of a well-manicured lawn, Barrett had given the driver a twenty-dollar bill and told him he'd get another hundred if he waited for her.

Her hand shook as she knocked on the front door. They weren't expecting her, but she knew she'd be welcome. The door creaked open, and an older version of Kelly stood expectantly on the other side.

"Yes?"

"Mrs. Ryan? I'm Barrett Taylor. I was with your daughter in Columbia."

A frail hand shot to the woman's mouth, stifling a gasp. "You were the one that got away."

The news that she'd been rescued had caused a media frenzy. Thankfully Aaron and Debra had handled all that, and she had yet to have to face the hordes of media that wanted to talk to her. "Yes, ma'am. May I come in?"

"Oh, my goodness, where are my manners?" The storm door opened and Barrett stepped inside. "Robert! Robert, come here quickly." Mrs. Ryan motioned Barrett into the living room.

Her shoes clicked on the gleaming wood floor as Barrett crossed the large room.

"What is it, Fran?" A man with Kelly's eyes hurried into the room.

"Robert, this is...I'm sorry. I forgot your name."

Barrett stepped forward, her hand outstretched in greeting. "Mr. Ryan, I'm Barrett Taylor."

A flicker of recognition passed over his face and then was replaced with confusion. He looked at his wife then back at her.

"She was the one that was rescued. She was with Kelly."

The man's face lost all color and he started to sway.

"Maybe we should all sit down," she said, indicating a couch and two matching chairs.

She didn't wait to get settled before she said, "The last time I saw Kelly she was okay. She was a little thin, but she was healthy and strong. All things considered, she was holding up pretty good."

"Was she…" Kelly's father hesitated.

"She had all ten fingers and ten toes," Barrett said, feeling the tension in the room increase. "And everything in between." A familiar pang of pain shot through her stomach when she remembered the scars on Kelly's back.

"I won't lie to you, Mr. and Mrs. Ryan, it's rough. But your daughter is smart and strong and knows what to do." Knows what to do to survive, Barrett thought. "She helps the other captives. She helped me when I first got there. She saved the lives of a few hostages with her care." Barrett waited as Kelly's parents reached for each other and grasped hands. "They don't mistreat her as much as they do the others." Kelly's parents blanched. Oops, not the right thing to say. She never was any good at self-censure.

"We're happy for you, Ms. Taylor. That you were able to get out," Mr. Ryan said.

"Mr. and Mrs. Ryan, please believe me. I did everything I could to take her with us. I am so sorry." Barrett's voice broke on the words.

Kelly's mother reached over and laid her cool hand on Barrett's leg. "I saw your story on the news."

"The men that rescued me could only take me. I begged them to take Kelly and the others, but then I was shot and…" Barrett's explanation fizzled. What could she say? Anything just sounded like an excuse.

"We knew you did everything you could."

No, I didn't and I will never forgive myself.

"How are you doing?" Kelly's father asked.

His question surprised Barrett. This wasn't about her. This was about Kelly, their daughter. They'd been living with the fear of not knowing whether their daughter was alive or dead. They didn't know when or if she'd ever be released. And what they were imagining might be happening to her had to be unbearable.

"I'm fine, thank you. She talked about you all the time." Barrett changed the subject. She didn't want to focus on herself. She was free. What more was there?

Barrett proceeded to tell Kelly's parents some of the tales of Kelly's childhood she'd shared during the hours they spent together. Mrs. Ryan served iced tea, and after an hour or so Barrett rose to leave.

"Thank you so much for coming," Mr. Ryan said, grasping her hand in both of his. They were rough and callused from years on the assembly line. "And thank you for talking about Kelly. So many of our friends don't. I guess they're afraid to mention her name. Like not talking about her somehow will make us forget about her and where she is." His voice held anger now.

"Robert," Mrs. Ryan said, putting her hand on his arm. He immediately responded to her, and Barrett wondered how something like that happened between two people. She'd never really given it any thought—how two people could be so attuned to each other. Her parents had been married for over forty years, but she sensed more love in this house at this moment than everything she'd ever felt in her own house while growing up. Kelly's parents had something very special and had passed that caring gene on to their daughter.

"Yes, thank you, Barrett. It meant a lot to both of us. Just knowing where Kelly is and what she's doing is comforting. We can focus on what we do know, not what we're imagining."

Mrs. Ryan rose on her toes and pulled Barrett close, hugging her so tight she had trouble breathing. She guessed it was her way of being close to Kelly. Mrs. Ryan stepped back and kissed her on the cheek.

"You take care of yourself, Barrett. What you went through can't be an easy thing to recover from."

Mrs. Ryan seemed to see right through Barrett's bullshit and bravado and into her nightmares. It made her very uncomfortable.

"Yes ma'am, I will," she replied, and realized she meant it. She needed to do this for Kelly and for Kelly's parents, who needed it as well.

Kelly played with the corner of the sheet. Barrett's guilt doubled to see her so forlorn when she should be celebrating. "I called them once I got the news you were out. They were ecstatic. They'll be here tomorrow morning. They can't wait to see you." She didn't need to tell her she'd sent a plane for them.

"I suppose I need to talk to them," Kelly said, with little enthusiasm.

Barrett stood. The phone was on the table just out of Kelly's reach, and she handed it to her. "I'll give you some privacy." Kelly grabbed her hand.

"Please stay," Kelly said, a mixture of hope and fear on her face.

Barrett was surprised at the strength of Kelly's grip. "Of course I will if you want me to." Kelly only nodded as she punched in the number.

Even though she'd asked Barrett to stay, Kelly felt alone. For months she'd dreamed of hearing her parents' voices again. Her mother's soft Southern drawl and her father's good-natured teasing had kept her from going insane more than once. But she struggled to find something to say. What could she say? "Hello, Mom and Dad. I'm home and I'm pregnant." That was a bombshell she wasn't interested in dropping, especially since she hadn't decided what to do.

Maybe it would be easier if she told them over the phone. It'd give them a chance to adjust before they came tomorrow and spare her the reproachful look she knew would be on their faces. If Barrett were only right and their happiness that she was home overrode the fact that she was "with child," as they would phrase it. But she knew her parents, and this wouldn't be easy.

Her hand was shaking so bad she almost couldn't hang up the phone. She hadn't told them. She'd barely been able to say anything over their excited chatter and questions. Her father had rushed to the other phone and interrupted her mother more times than not. She didn't think either one of them realized she'd barely spoken.

"Can I get you anything?" Barrett asked.

Barrett's voice soothed her racing pulse. "No." She shook her head. "I'm fine. Just a little overwhelmed with everything today." That was an understatement. She'd refused to believe she was being rescued until she saw Barrett waiting for her on the tarmac. She and the other hostages had been transferred from camp to camp, guard to guard so many times. One time, just for the sheer fun of it, the guards had told them their ransom had been paid and they were taking them home. When it was obvious it was nothing but a cruel joke, Kelly had refused to break down and sob like the others.

"I understand."

"How did you get through it?"

"Time." Barrett answered quickly. "That, and I refused to turn the lights off, afraid I'd wake up and find it was all a dream. It's overwhelming, Kelly. Don't let anyone tell you otherwise."

Kelly liked the fact that Barrett had empowered her. It had been a long time since she'd felt control over anything in her life.

"A psychologist will be in in a few minutes to talk with you. It's all up to you. She won't force you to do anything you don't want to."

"How do you know it'll be a woman?" she asked.

"Because it's the same person who talked to me when I came out."

"And did you talk to her?"

"Not in the beginning."

Barrett's answer surprised her. Barrett had given her the impression that she was strong enough to withstand anything and that she wouldn't need any help readjusting. "What changed your mind?"

Barrett's eyes searched her face, as if she was trying to decide if she could trust Kelly with her story or the severity of the truth. She could practically feel Barrett judging her strength.

"Tell me, Barrett. I want to know. I need to know what to expect."

"The nightmares. The flashbacks. The panic attacks when I was alone. The panic attacks when I was in a crowd. The panic attacks when someone moved too close to me or bumped into me in the elevator."

Barrett's words were soft but her description sharp. Kelly was under no misconception that she'd simply fly home and go to work the next day. She wasn't coming back from a vacation or even another medical mission. She didn't know what she was coming back to. Everything was different. Everything had changed. She'd changed, and the life growing inside her was the biggest adjustment she'd have to make.

"What am I going to tell everyone? About the baby?" Kelly said at Barrett's apparent confusion.

"Everyone like who?"

"My friends, coworkers, women in the grocery store that ask." Kelly knew these were stupid questions and had no bearing on her decision whether to keep the baby.

"Your friends won't need an explanation, you probably won't be back to work for months, and as for the complete strangers that ask, tell them…" Barrett cocked her head in the way Kelly had learned she did when she was thinking something through. "Do strangers make comments and ask pregnant women questions?"

"Yes, they do. For some people, pregnant women are fair game to strike up a conversation with. Like they're now part of the club." Kelly had never felt the need to talk to a pregnant woman other than out of politeness, but she'd seen it happen to several of her friends.

Barrett nodded. "Tell them whatever you want. Tell them the truth or make something up or simply tell them it's none of their business. Because it is none of their business."

Barrett's voice was firm and strong as she said the last few words, which gave Kelly some much-needed strength.

Chapter Fourteen

The light knocking on the door startled Barrett. She'd been watching Kelly so intently she blinked a few times to get her bearings. Kelly had asked her to stay until she fell asleep, and even after her breathing had become deep Barrett couldn't make herself leave. One of the nurses had brought her a light blanket, but she didn't sleep. She couldn't.

She remembered her first few days in the hospital. Every time anyone had approached, she'd started to panic, thinking they'd shove a disgusting gag in her mouth and drag her away again. She would wake in a panic, afraid everything was a dream. Her breathing was quick and shallow, her blood pounded in her head, and the tightness in her chest was crushing. It took minutes, sometimes as long as an hour, for her system to return to normal. She hoped a familiar face would spare Kelly that fear.

The knock repeated, the door opened, and Kelly's mother appeared, followed by her father. They stood in the doorway, appearing unsure whether to come in. Barrett glanced at Kelly, who was still asleep, and hurried to the door.

"She's sleeping."

"We don't want to wake her, but we just can't wait any longer to see her," Mrs. Ryan said, rubbing her hands together nervously.

"Of course." Barrett understood. She'd had the same feeling a mere twenty-four hours ago. She couldn't even imagine what

Kelly's parents were going through. She stepped aside and they entered the room without a sound.

They tentatively approached Kelly's bed, one on each side. Mrs. Ryan reached out and took Kelly's hand, and her father quickly followed with a kiss on her forehead. Kelly woke with a start and pushed at her father leaning over her. He jumped back as if struck. Barrett stepped into her line of sight.

"Kelly, your parents are here," she said softly. Barrett saw the panic-stricken look slide away to be replaced with understanding and clarity that the people beside her were no threat. However, her reaction had clearly shaken her parents.

"Mom, Dad," Kelly said, looking between them. "I'm so glad you're here." Kelly reached up and was immediately engulfed in her parents' arms. Barrett silently slipped from the room.

The familiar fragrance of her mother's perfume and her dad's aftershave was comforting and reassuring. Kelly relaxed and simply enjoyed the moment. When her parents finally released her and stepped back, she expected to see Barrett sitting in the chair at the foot of her bed. She'd been there every time she woke several times during the night. At least she thought it had been the night but wasn't sure. She was still adjusting to the rapid change of events.

"You're so thin," her mother said, drawing Kelly's attention back to her parents.

"Not a weight-loss program I'd recommend to anyone," she quipped, suddenly nervous. Her mother was looking at her much too closely. She wasn't ready for this. She pulled the sheet and blanket a little higher on her chest.

"How are you, Dad?" she asked, hoping to change the subject. "You look tired."

"We didn't sleep a wink last night after Ms. Taylor called us. We were so excited and had so many people to call. While you were gone your friend Ariel called often to check up on us and see how we were doing, so we had to phone her first."

"And we didn't want to keep the pilot waiting," her mother added.

"The pilot?" Kelly was confused. The pilot of a commercial airplane certainly wouldn't wait for a passenger.

"Yes, the pilot of the plane. Ms. Taylor said he would be waiting for us at the airport whenever we were ready to go."

Kelly shook her head, no more clear about what her mother was talking about than before her explanation. "What are you talking about?"

"The plane Ms. Taylor sent for us," her father said, like it was the most natural thing in the world.

"She sent you a plane?"

"Yes. She said she didn't want us to have to wait for a regular flight, so she had one waiting for us."

Kelly was still a bit foggy, but it was beginning to make sense. Barrett must have chartered a plane to fly her parents here. Where was here again? Panama? When was she going home?

"Ms. Taylor told us you have some intestinal bug and a few other things I didn't understand. If the rest of the other test results come back okay, you can come home."

Kelly could only nod in relief. The doctors hadn't told them she was pregnant. "That's good to know, Mom. I'm ready to go home." She lied but knew that was what her parents wanted to hear. She didn't know what she wanted to do. Barrett had told her she'd feel disjointed, like she didn't belong anywhere for a while. She just needed a few days to get her head straight and figure out what she was going to do.

"You'll come home with us, where we can look after you properly," her mother said, cupping her cheek. You need some solid food and love, and you'll be good as new. Everybody can't wait to see you…"

As her mother's voice turned into background noise, Kelly's mind raced. She didn't want to go to her parents' house. She couldn't. Not now. Especially not now. And how was she going to tell them she was pregnant? Earlier, when she lay awake, she'd decided not to terminate this pregnancy. She hadn't yet decided if she would keep the baby or give it up for adoption. She had time to figure that out.

"Only for a few days, Mom." Kelly replied with as much strength as she could muster. "The sooner I get back to my normal life, the better I'll be." No way was she going to be able to stay under the watchful, disapproving eyes of her parents for very long.

She turned to her mother. "What happened to my things? My car? My house?" Without her income to pay her mortgage and her car loan, had they been repossessed? Where was all her stuff—her books and the antique crystal vase she'd picked up in a yard sale that had ended up being worth a fortune?

Her parents looked at each other, then quickly back at her. What was all that about?

"Mom?"

"Everything is just as you left it, Kelly. When it looked like it would be a while before you…" her mother struggled, as if trying to find the right words, "we arranged to have a service look after your house."

"But who paid for it? Who paid the mortgage every month? And my car note?" Something was going on, but she couldn't quite put her finger on it. It was as if her parents were trying to keep something from her. "Dad?"

"Don't worry about it right now, hon," her father said, taking her hand. "Your mother's right. You should spend some time with us, get back on your feet before you head home. Who's going to take care of you if you go home now?"

Something was obviously up with her house and her things, but she was suddenly very tired and didn't have the strength to push the issue. It had been a very long time since she pushed for anything, and she felt hesitant to do so. Her parents were strong willed and not a good place to start in her muddled condition.

"My friends. Sarah and her husband Steve live across the street. Sarah stays home with their kids, and we've gotten to be pretty good friends." They really weren't that close, but a little white lie to get out from under the watchful eye of her parents was worth it.

"Let's just take it day by day, shall we?" her father said, looking directly at her with that expression Kelly knew as his final word.

❖

Barrett leaned back against the cool hospital wall, her head against the hard surface, and closed her eyes. She'd stepped out a few minutes ago to give Kelly and her parents some privacy, suddenly very tired.

For a moment she was the one in that hospital bed trying to make sense of the world in front of her. She'd been captive for only a short time compared to Kelly, and she knew Kelly was in for many difficult months. Even more so because she was pregnant.

A pang of guilt almost knocked Barrett to her knees. If only she'd have figured out what she needed to do sooner, if only she'd called Trevor a few weeks earlier, if only she could have gotten her out sooner…the *what if's* tumbled through her brain.

"Barrett?"

Barrett opened her eyes and saw the familiar face of her psychologist, Dr. Grace Hinton. Barrett had called Dr. Hinton as soon as she heard Kelly was alive and had flown her here as soon as Kelly had arrived.

"How are you doing?" the doctor asked. Her expression was benign, but her eyes gave away her concern.

Barrett moved away from the wall. "I'm fine." She tried to lie convincingly.

"Are you?

Okay, maybe not so convincingly. "I will be." She corrected herself. "As soon as Kelly's cleared to go and is back home and settled."

Dr. Hinton eyed her critically, and Barrett fought the urge to squirm. From their first visit Dr. Hinton could always see right through her bullshit. Even though it went against everything she'd taught herself, Barrett had found herself opening up to the woman, unlike the man her parents had sent.

"You know she may never be settled." Dr. Hinton cautiously emphasized the last few words.

"I know. But she has family and friends that love her, and she'll have everything she needs to get well. I'll see to it," she said, determined to do so.

"You're not to blame, Barrett."

She pushed down an angry, automatic rebuttal, but not before Dr. Hinton saw her reaction.

"Don't take this on, Barrett. This is not about you. You did nothing wrong. As a matter of fact, if it weren't for you, Kelly would still be there."

"I know." Barrett didn't quite hide the frustration in her voice, wasn't even sure she wanted to.

"Do you?"

Barrett sighed, suddenly even more tired. From the day Trevor and his crew had hit the ground in Columbia, she'd constantly fought to keep her emotions off her sleeve, which wasn't like her, not at all. She needed to be careful. Barrett took a deep breath.

"Yes, I do. But I'll do everything I can to help Kelly."

Dr. Hinton looked at her for several moments. "Okay," she said finally, shifting her gaze from penetrating to concerned. "But you need to remember to take care of yourself too. This will bring up old memories, and you need to be prepared."

Too late, Barrett thought, but didn't say the words.

❖

The knock on the door was a relief. Kelly loved her parents, but they were smothering her and she needed them to just back off a bit. She felt guilty for thinking that, knowing that they must have worried themselves sick. She vowed to try to be patient with them.

"Come in." The door opened, and she felt a flush of relief when Barrett poked her head in.

"I don't mean to interrupt, but Dr. Hinton's here."

It took a moment for Kelly to recognize the name. She'd been seen by a dozen doctors since she'd been here. Then she remembered. Dr. Hinton was the psychologist Barrett had told her about.

"Have her come in."

Barrett opened the door wider, and a short, stocky woman entered. Her hair was pulled tight into a bun, and she appeared to have slept in her clothes. She looked nothing like a shrink and everything like a grandmother. Maybe that was a good thing.

Barrett introduced Dr. Hinton, and Kelly noted that Barrett omitted the type of doctor she was when she repeated the introduction to her parents. She was grateful, not wanting to go into all that with her parents right now, if ever.

"You're not what I expected," Kelly said, after Barrett took her parents to the cafeteria to get some dinner, giving her and Dr. Hinton a chance to talk privately. She was rewarded with a warm laugh and a deep, caring smile.

"And what did you expect?"

"Some uptight shrink, I guess. Either that or the touchy-feely type that talks about Zen and inner peace."

"How do you know I don't?"

"Because Barrett wouldn't put up with that," Kelly answered, even though she really had no clear idea what Barrett would put up with.

"Very astute observation." Dr. Hinton nodded as if weighing the validity of her comment. "What else did Barrett not say about me?"

"I don't think you're here to talk about what Barrett said," Kelly replied, her answer maybe a little too harsh.

"No, not specifically, but she is a very big part of why you're here and why I'm here."

"Are you going to tell me that we can talk about whatever I want?" Kelly asked.

"No."

"Are you going to ask me how I'm doing?"

"No."

"Am I going to look at ink blots and tell you what I see?"

"No, not unless you want to"

"Then why are you here?"

"Because Barrett asked me to come."

"Why?" God, this was starting to feel like twenty questions, but Kelly couldn't stop herself.

"I know what she told me. You'll have to ask her."

"Some sort of doctor-client confidentiality thing?" Kelly realized she was bordering on belligerent and forced herself to calm down.

"Not at all. You know why I'm here, Ms. Ryan. You weren't surprised when I walked in."

Kelly appreciated Dr. Hinton's honesty and forthright answers. She hadn't backed down or even moved from where she'd stopped next to her bed. She hadn't even reached out to shake her hand. Kelly pointed to the chair next to the bed. "Please sit down and call me Kelly."

❖

"I'm sorry, what did you say?" Barrett had no idea what Kelly's mother had said.

"I said I'm worried about Kelly. She doesn't look good. She's practically skin and bones, has no energy, and her skin is cold."

Barrett tempered the angry words that came to mind. "She's been through a lot. The living conditions weren't that good, and she didn't always have enough to eat. The water was always a risk, and the mosquitoes carried all kinds of diseases." Barrett knew she was probably saying too much, but it upset her that Kelly's parents seemed to expect her to look exactly the same coming out of Columbia as she had when she went in.

"Yes, I suppose you're right," Mrs. Ryan said, not too convincingly.

"Just remember that Kelly's alive and she's free." Why did she have to tell them that? "The rest will take some time to fall into place. She'll get stronger every day, and with the right food, and plenty of it, she'll gain weight."

Barrett wondered if Kelly had told her parents about the baby. They hadn't said anything, and it certainly wasn't her place to break the news. Maybe Kelly had decided not to keep it and didn't need to discuss what wouldn't be there in a few days.

"We just want her to come home with us," Mr. Ryan said. "But she doesn't want to. She said she'd stay a few days but was adamant about going back to her house and back to work." He shook his head, obviously not agreeing with his daughter's plans.

"She needs us," her mother said, and Barrett got the impression she was trying to enlist Barrett's help. No way was she getting in the middle of that.

"I know Kelly's thrilled to see you and grateful for you wanting to help, but maybe she just wants to return to her life as quickly as she can. You know, get back into the routine of going to work every day, the grocery store, seeing friends."

What a load of crap, Barrett thought. In Kelly's case it was nothing but serious crap. There was no normal after what they'd gone through. It was the new normal where your friends and co-workers tiptoed around the subject yet wanted to know every gruesome detail. Where your family never mentioned it, thinking that if they didn't put a name to it, it hadn't really happened. As if she and Kelly could ever forget.

"But she's our baby. She needs us." Her mother almost wailed, repeating herself, wringing her hands.

What it was, Barrett thought but didn't say, was that they needed Kelly, not the other way around. "Mr. and Mrs. Ryan, I'm going to make sure Kelly has everything she needs to get through this. And she will get through it." Barrett placed one of her hands over each of Kelly's parents'. "I know it's not what you want to hear, but Kelly has to do this her way, and that may not be what you think she should do, including moving back in with you. I know you only want what's best for her and want to take care of her, but in the end that might not be what's best for her."

Barrett had no idea when she became so philosophical or even where those words came from. Dr. Hinton must have channeled them through her. Barrett really didn't care, but she did care about helping Kelly get to where she needed to be, wherever that was.

Dr. Hinton entered the hospital dining room and caught Barrett's eye. "Why don't you go back and see Kelly for a few more minutes," Barrett said, returning her attention to Kelly's parents. "I'll be up a little later to take you to the hotel, and you can check in and get some rest yourselves."

Kelly's parents didn't even recognize Dr. Hinton as they passed her. Dr. Hinton sat down in the chair to her left.

"You look pretty wrung out."

"Her parents are—"

"Typical parents, wanting to take their child home and protect her from experiencing any more pain of the cruel world?"

Barrett chuckled, the tension in her body sliding away. "God damn, you're good," she said, teasing.

"That's why you dragged my butt out of bed at zero-dark-thirty this morning, put me in a tin can, and flew me what felt like halfway across the world. The least you can do is buy me a cup of coffee, and not cafeteria coffee. I saw a Pete's down the block." Dr. Hinton stood. "You're buying."

Barrett stood, knowing she'd made the right call to bring Dr. Hinton. As much as she wanted to ask how their conversation went, she knew Dr. Hinton wouldn't tell her, and most importantly, she didn't want to invade Kelly's privacy. Feeling almost normal, whatever that was, Barrett extended her arm. "With an offer like that, how's a girl to refuse?"

Two cups of coffee and an hour later, Barrett loaded Kelly's parents into one cab, and she and Dr. Hinton climbed into another for the drive to the hotel.

It took longer than normal due to the rush-hour traffic that was a staple of life in any big city. A wave of exhaustion hit Barrett as she slid her keycard into the slot in her hotel-room door. Once there, she dropped the card on the desk, emptied her pockets on top of it, and opened the minibar door. She reached for a beer, changing her mind at the last second and pulling a Coke and a cordial of Crown Royal off the neatly organized shelf.

The hotel had graciously filled the ice bucket, and she dropped three square cubes into a tumbler, emptied the cordial, and added a splash of Coke. Kicking off her shoes, she walked across the room, the thick carpet caressing her tired feet. The curtains were open, offering her a view of the Panama Canal in the distance. She sat down in a side chair and put her feet on the small table in front of her.

Barrett sipped her drink, first once, then again, then a third time, feeling the warm liquid slide down her throat. She stretched her neck side to side, then front to back, each time counting to ten in an attempt to ease the tense muscles. She needed a massage but didn't have the energy to call the front desk and schedule one.

She'd been at the hospital since Kelly arrived yesterday and all day today, dealing with her parents and Dr. Hinton, and it was now close to ten thirty. All in all she'd been up almost forty hours and was well past the point of being tired. Fatigue tugged at every muscle, yet her brain continued to run on full speed.

Barrett refilled her drink on the way to the bathroom and turned the faucets on in the tub. She tossed in a few of the scented beads she found in a container next to the tub, and the air filled with the fresh fragrance of chamomile. Maybe a warm, relaxing bath would slow her thoughts down enough that she could sleep. A few hours would work, it always had. Rarely did she get more than five or six hours of sleep a night, and lately it had been more like four than six.

Leaving her clothes in a pile by the sink, Barrett grabbed her cocktail and walked to the tub, the tile cool under her feet. Not even trying to suppress a sigh of pleasure, she slid into the warm, fragrant water. She set the jets on low and lay back, her head on a pillow thoughtfully provided by the hotel. She closed her eyes and felt the tension start to ease from her body.

Snippets of the last few days flashed through her mind like a kaleidoscope, each morphing into the other. First it was the phone call from Trevor, then the miles she'd paced in the plane to get here. The waiting was the worst, and her pulse beat a little faster as she remembered her overwhelming sense of relief when Kelly had stepped off the plane. When she saw Kelly lying on the crisp white sheets, her hair wet from a bath. When Kelly smiled at her. When Kelly took her hand and didn't let it go even when she slept. The dread in Kelly's eyes when she told her she was pregnant.

A myriad of emotions crashed through Barrett as she struggled to maintain her composure. Tears pushed at the back of her eyes and her hands started to shake. Abruptly she sat up and wrapped her arms around her knees. The water moved in tandem as Barrett rocked back and forth, tears streaming down her face.

The shrill of her phone startled her. She rubbed her hands over her face and looked around, finally remembering she'd left it on the ledge behind her.

"Barrett Taylor," she said, after clearing her throat of any remaining emotion. She tensed as she listened to the voice on the other end. "I'll be right there."

❖

Barrett ran down the hall, skidding to a stop in front of Kelly's door. A nurse in a pressed white uniform hurried out from behind a desk piled high with charts and papers. A meal tray with remnants of someone's dinner was balanced precariously on top of a nearby trashcan.

"Ms. Taylor, I'm Peggy Stone. I'm the one who called you."

Barrett needed to get into Kelly's room, and the last thing she wanted to do was chat with some nurse.

"I have to talk to you before you go in," she added, touching Barrett's arm when she didn't stop.

Barrett forced herself to take a breath and try to control herself. "Thank you for calling me," she said calmly, but still anxious to see Kelly.

The nurse nodded. "She woke up disoriented. She panicked and started pulling out her IVs, which of course caused blood to stream out of her arm, which upset her even more."

Barrett nodded in turn. "Okay."

"We couldn't get her to calm down. She was thrashing around and knocking over the equipment, and we were afraid she might hurt herself more than she already had." The nurse paled.

"What? What happened?" Barrett was fighting every urge to push the well-meaning nurse out of the way and see for herself.

"We had to restrain her."

"You what? Don't you have any idea what she's been through?" Barrett clenched her teeth in anger. "She was a hostage for months, chained to a tree and tied up like an animal. For God's sake, she must have gone out of her mind."

Barrett ran her hands through her hair, mussing it more than it already was. She ached for Kelly and what she must have gone through, what she was still going through. "Get out of my way." She was almost growling.

"She's sedated right now. Dr.—"

Barrett didn't wait to hear what else the nurse was saying but stepped around her and pushed open the door.

The light on the wall above Kelly's bed was on, the sconce diffusing the otherwise harsh hospital-room light. Kelly was lying motionless on the bed, the sheets tucked neatly around her. Barrett froze when she saw the leather restraints around Kelly's wrists and ankles.

"Oh, Kelly," she whispered, and forced her feet to move. She stopped at the side of the bed, resting her hand lightly on Kelly's. It was cool, and in a moment of panic Barrett thought she was dead. The beep of the heart monitor seeped into her brain, reminding her that Kelly was simply sedated. If the shallow rise and fall of her chest was any indication, *simply* sedated was not the case.

"Kelly. It's Barrett. I'm here," Barrett said, gently stroking Kelly's hand. "I'm here now and I'm not leaving again." The normal cadence of the heart monitor sputtered, and Barrett's own heart skipped in tandem.

"Kelly, it's okay. You're all right. You're here in Panama and I'm right beside you. Just sleep a little longer and you'll feel much better when you wake up." The monitor slowly resumed the rhythmic beeps, but another, faster set was coming from the machine below it.

Frowning, Barrett followed the leads from the machine, under the covers where they ended, taped to Kelly's stomach. She didn't know anything about pregnancy or babies, but from what she could deduce, it was monitoring the baby's heartbeat. Barrett watched the yellow line peak and recede much faster than Kelly's green one. She remembered hearing somewhere that a fetal heartbeat was almost twice the normal adult rate.

"Your baby's fine, Kelly. From what I can tell its heartbeat is strong, and since no alarm's going off, I think's it's okay. But what do I know? I barely know how to hold a baby, let alone what one's supposed to be doing in their little incubator."

Knowing she didn't have permission, Barrett still unbuckled the restraint holding Kelly's left wrist to the bed. She slid it down Kelly's hand and dropped it under the bed, the clinking of the metal buckle as it hit the floor reverberating in the room. She did the same with the other before sliding the chair closer to the bed and took Kelly's hand in both of hers as she sat. She made herself as comfortable as she could, resting her forearms on the white sheets, and settled in for a long wait.

Barrett turned when a shaft of light spilled into the room and across Kelly's bed. It was a nurse she hadn't seen before, and the seasoned veteran expression said Barrett was in for a battle to stay in Kelly's room.

"It's against the rules for you to be here. Visiting hours are over," the woman said, her tone echoing her words.

"I was called a few hours ago."

"Yes. I'm aware of Miss Ryan's episode."

Barrett could almost hear the *tsk, tsk* that this nurse was so obviously thinking.

"Episode? You call it an episode? She woke up, didn't know where she was, and her reaction after what she's been through was perfectly normal." Barrett knew the exact moment the nurse saw Kelly's unrestrained wrists, and she grabbed the advantage.

"Yes, I took them off. She does not need to be restrained. She's sedated, prettily heavily if her vitals are any indication. She certainly isn't going anywhere, and it'll be hours before she opens her eyes." Barrett refused to let this nurse or anyone else tie Kelly up again. They would have to restrain her first.

"Doctor's orders," the nurse said, looking around the room for the restraints.

Kelly's heart monitor sputtered again, but the nurse, intent on finding the restraints, didn't seem to notice. Kelly knew what was going on around her. Barrett had read that patients sedated or in a coma could sometimes hear. The calming of Kelly's heartbeat earlier proved it.

"Look, Nurse," Barrett squinted to read the nametag pinned to the puke-green smock, "Samuels. I'm not going anywhere. I'm going to sit right here next to Kelly until she wakes up. And when she does, she'll see a friendly face and not have another *episode*." Barrett frowned. "Now you can either let us be, or you and at least three very big guys will have to throw me out of this hospital because I am not leaving her."

Nurse Samuels' scowl deepened, but she didn't say anything as she checked Kelly's IV and then left the room.

Barrett squeezed Kelly's hand and the monitor slowed. She smiled. "That's right, Kelly. She's gone. You should have seen the sourpuss. By the mile-deep frown lines on her face, I don't think she's smiled in thirty years. But I told her, didn't I? She's all bark. She reminds me of Nurse Ratched in that movie with Jack Nicholson. You know, *One Flew Over the Cockoo's Nest*. She's probably scared to death of me now and telling all the other nurses there's a crazy woman in room 722." Barrett chuckled. "I'm okay with that. Whatever it takes."

Barrett thought she felt Kelly squeeze her hand but wasn't sure. It was probably wishful thinking. But then again…"I know you're scared. So many things have changed in the time you were gone. And you've changed more than anything. I know I did. Actually, it took me awhile to figure that out. I thought I could step back into my life like it was the day I was taken." And had she ever tried.

Barrett had been anxious to get back to work and had showed up at the office her second day back in the States.

The reaction on everyone's face told her that they didn't expect her. The receptionist was new and almost didn't let her past the double doors into her office. Georgia, the woman from the marketing department who occupied the first cube behind the doors, did a double-take as Barrett walked by, then hurriedly picked up her phone. Debra choked on her coffee when she stuck her head into her office to say hello.

"Shit!" she exclaimed, coughing a mouthful of coffee onto the papers on her desk in front of her. "Barrett, what are you doing here?" She busily mopped up the liquid.

Barrett was slightly annoyed. Why wouldn't they expect her? It was her company. Did they think she'd never come back? She'd been gone long enough. God only knew what shape they were in financially and what ruffled feathers she was going to have to smooth over with their customers.

Debra came around her desk and wrapped her in a bear hug. Barrett tried not to stiffen in response. Since her capture she flinched every time someone touched her and hated crowds even more than usual. Great attributes to have as a CEO of a major technology company.

"Are you sure you should be back so soon? Why don't you take some time, relax, get back into the groove of things slowly," Debra said after Barrett pried herself out of her welcoming hug.

"I've had plenty of time. I spent the last seven months doing nothing but stare at the dirt under my butt. I'm bored to death, and I have to get back to the job."

"But—"

"But nothing," Barrett said sharply. She softened her tone. "I know you're worried about me, but there's no need. I'm fine, and I'm ready to work again. Now, is my office in the same place, or did you turn it into a yoga room while I was gone?"

When she finished telling Kelly about her first day at work, her back ached and her right foot was numb. She'd exaggerated some parts, glossed over one or two, and completely lied about others. She wanted Kelly to stay calm, and telling her exactly what had happened that first day absolutely would not do it.

Barrett stood, put her hands on the lower part of her back, and arched backward. She stifled a groan as she bent at her waist for ten seconds to the left and right, repeating the movement a few times. The beeping of the fetal monitor sped up in unison with Kelly's.

"Hey, it's okay, Kelly," Barrett said, moving to the other side of the bed. "I'm still here. Just had to stretch a little and my foot went to sleep." She ran her hand up and down Kelly's forearm several times. "Remember that time when we had to sit for hours, and after we got up I fell flat on my face? Same situation, but this time I held on to the back of the chair so I wouldn't repeat that little swan dive. This time I probably would have cracked my head open instead of almost drowning in that puddle of mud." By the time she'd finished her reminiscing, the two heartbeats slowed.

Tears filled Barrett's eyes when she looked at the scars on Kelly's wrists. They were red and ugly, and calluses had formed in some places. Her stomach clenched at what Kelly had gone through. She'd been in the brutal custody of The Colonel long before Barrett had arrived, and Kelly and the others must have suffered immensely because of her escape.

Barrett was destined to feel guilt every time she thought of Kelly and the others. At times guilt and shame overwhelmed her so fully she found it hard just to look at Kelly. Not only had she been rescued and the others had not, but they'd been punished because she got away. It was almost like Barrett had two strikes against her.

Three strikes and I'm out. But out of what? Barrett didn't know.

Chapter Fifteen

K elly struggled to reach the surface. She didn't know where she was but instinctively knew she had to get to the top, break through whatever was holding her. With one last push of effort she opened her eyes.

The Styrofoam tiles in the ceiling were chipped and dingy white. Panic struck her when she realized where she was and what had happened last night. At least she thought it was last night. Her eyes darted around and fell on Barrett sitting in a chair beside the bed, her head back, eyes closed. She looked anything but peaceful. A frown creased her forehead and her lips were tight. Barrett obviously wasn't dreaming of something pleasant. Kelly shifted a little and Barrett's eyes shot open, concern replacing the frown.

"Hey," Barrett said, standing close to the bed. Barrett laid a hand on her forehead. "How are you feeling?"

"A little groggy." She noticed for the first time that Barrett's other hand was holding hers. She liked the strong and calming feeling it provided.

"What happened?" Bits and pieces of the events of last night bounced in and out of her mind like a bad flashback. She couldn't quite get a grip on what had actually happened.

"You woke up and were disoriented. You, uh…"

Barrett's eyes looked everywhere other than at her. The Barrett she knew never had any trouble looking anyone in the eye and had been punished for it on more than one occasion in the camp.

"What is it, Barrett? What happened?" Kelly felt stronger, her head clearing with each passing minute.

"From what they tell me, you must have been having a flashback of some kind. You were lashing out and fighting everyone who was trying to help you."

"I didn't hurt anyone, did I?" She'd feel terrible if she had.

"No, but they had to restrain you and…well, they had to sedate you after that." Barrett spoke almost as if she'd done it.

Kelly looked down at her hands and feet. "Who took them off?"

"I did." This time Barrett looked her directly in the eye, her voice strong.

"Why?"

"Because you didn't need them anymore." Kelly detected something else behind Barrett's statement but didn't feel up to pushing the subject right now.

"Thanks." Kelly thought that one word sounded lame, but it was all she was capable of. She looked at the bouncing green and yellow lines on the machines next to her bed.

"I think it's the baby's," Barrett said. "It's hooked up to your stomach with those sticky things."

Kelly could only stare at the yellow line as it bounced across the little screen. *My baby. That's my baby's heartbeat.* A sense of wonder filled Kelly at the same time tears burned the back of her eyes.

"Pretty awesome, isn't it?"

"Yes, it is." Kelly continued to watch the evidence of the life growing inside her. The lump in her throat was large, and several minutes went by before she could say anything.

"Why are you here?" She glanced at the clock on the wall above the foot of her bed. Not quite eight in the morning. Then she noticed the sun streaming through the curtains and heard the noises outside her door.

"Just keeping you company," Barrett replied, again barely looking at her.

"You'll go to hell for lying like that, you know." The effects of the sedation were wearing off rapidly. Kelly finally felt like she could string more than one or two sentences together.

Barrett's face finally relaxed but she didn't let go of her hand. "Then it'll be one hell of a party because all the fun people will be there."

Kelly smiled, then sobered quickly as she turned her attention back to the bouncing yellow line. Was that supposed to symbolize a bouncing baby boy? How ironic.

"What am I going to tell my parents? About the baby," she added when Barrett's expression said she had no idea what Kelly was referring to.

"What did Dr. Hinton say?"

"I asked you," Kelly said quickly. It was obviously not the answer Barrett wanted.

"Other than you're pregnant, I don't think you need to tell them anything," Barrett said cautiously.

"What do you mean?" It was her turn not to follow.

"I mean, they don't need the details. Anyone can figure it out."

Is that what everyone would think when they looked at her belly? That a baby conceived in violence grew inside her? Would they ever be able to think of anything other than imagine what had happened to her? Would she? Could she?

Barrett moved and sat on the edge of her bed, still holding her hand. "Jeez. I didn't mean to upset you. I'm not good at this stuff."

"I haven't had a lot of experience with it either." Kelly spoke with more than a touch of sarcasm.

"I mean I don't know what to say, how to offer comfort. What you want me to say or what you want me to do. I don't have many close friends, and I'm out of my element here. My brother used to tease me all the time about it. I guess I wasn't born with the caring gene."

Kelly saw the embarrassment on Barrett's face. "What does he do now?" she asked, hoping to change the mood.

"Tiptoes around everything."

"And it makes you crazy." Kelly had learned that Barrett was a straight-to-the-point kind of person.

"Yes. But I understand. Actually, it took several sessions with Dr. Hinton before I could accept that was his way of dealing with everything."

"You like Dr. Hinton, don't you?"

"No."

Barrett's answer surprised her.

"I respect her. I listen to what she says, then think about it and draw my own conclusions, which she promptly validates, by the way. I don't like her because she makes me uncomfortable, pushes me out of my comfort zone, and forces me to put my feelings into words. And not just any words. Descriptive, specific words. God, she's worse than my freshman English teacher, Miss Crowley."

Barrett smiled again, and Kelly felt the mood lighten just a little. "And you hated Miss Crowley too?"

"No. I had a great big baby-dyke crush on her. I would have done anything for her, even if it meant embarrassing myself every time I had to read one of her assignments in front of the class."

"And what do you think about her now?" Kelly was genuinely curious.

"I saw her at our ten-year class reunion, which, by the way, I swore I'd never go to and swear I'll never go to another," Barrett said adamantly. "Anyway, she was just as hot as I remembered her to be. It was her first year of teaching, and she was only eight years older than me. That's a big difference when you're fourteen and she's twenty-two, but not when you're twenty-seven and she's thirty-five." Barrett raised her eyebrows a couple of times like Groucho Marx and grinned, the sadness gone from her face.

"You didn't?" Kelly really wanted to know.

"I don't kiss and tell," Barrett replied smugly, using her fingers to mimic zipping her lips.

Kelly laughed for the first time in a long time, and it felt good. "Does she?" Before Barrett had a chance to answer, the door opened and Kelly's parents walked in.

Her mother reached her first and bent over and kissed her cheek. Her father followed, and Barrett stepped back from the bed. For some reason Kelly felt an odd sense of loss when she did.

"How are you feeling this morning?" her mother asked.

"What are all these for?" Her father pointed to the two monitors at the head of her bed.

"They're just keeping track of a few things." Kelly hoped she could deflect the conversation onto safer topics. She wasn't ready to tell her parents and to see the pain in their eyes, the pity that would be there every time they looked at her. She hadn't even decided what she was going to do with the baby. The last thing she needed was to try to respond to a dozen questions that she herself didn't have answers to. When she saw her father lean over and read the fine print on the screen, she braced herself.

❖

"What is this, Kelly?"

Her mother stopped straightening her wrinkleless sheets and looked at him. "What are you talking about, Robert?"

"What *exactly* is this keeping track of?" her father added.

He knew. She could see it in his eyes. It wasn't rocket science, for God's sake. If the words Baby Ryan (Kelly Ryan) scrolling along the bottom of the screen didn't give it away, her stomach would as soon as she stood up. She looked between her parents, then to Barrett.

"It's a fetal monitor. I'm pregnant. We think I'm about five months along."

"You think?" her father said, and Kelly detected anger in his voice.

"Yes. The doctor is basing it on the baby's size," she said quickly. She felt like she was seventeen and had gotten herself "in trouble," a phrase her father still used today. Her mother must have worked her way through the shock, because she gasped and put one hand over her mouth, the other on her chest.

"What are you going to do with it?"

The way her father said the word "it" told Kelly everything she needed to know. She knew this was going to happen. She'd hoped and prayed it wouldn't, but it had. She looked at her parents, then Barrett, then back at her parents.

"I'm keeping it."

Her mother's gasp told Kelly her opinion of her decision. Her father's scowl was just as loud. Before either one of them had a chance to say anything, she took the offensive.

"I know you're surprised by this news, but quite frankly I can't believe you are. I was held hostage for over two years by angry, bored, sadistic wanna-be soldiers. When they weren't starving us or poking at us with a sharp stick just for the fun of it or making us walk for days without stopping or stringing us up to a tree like Jesus, what did you think was going to happen?" Kelly knew she was probably overreacting, but she was angry. These were her parents, the two people in the world who should support her no matter what, especially under these circumstances.

"Don't you speak to us that way," her father bellowed, his face almost as red as his shirt. "We are your parents and you will respect us."

"And I'm your daughter, and you're supposed to love me no matter what."

"Why don't we all just take a breath for a minute." Barrett stepped toward the bed, holding her hand up as if signaling peace. "You've all been through a lot, and the past few days have been something no one should have to deal with. Everybody's on edge."

"You stay out of it," her father growled. "If you hadn't waited so long to go back for her, this never would have happened."

"Dad!" Kelly said, frightened by the anger in his tone and the look of shock on Barrett's face.

"You're right, Mr. Ryan," Barrett said, her voice calm, almost detached. "I should have gone back for Kelly sooner. As a matter of fact, I never should have left without her. And not that you care, but that will haunt me the rest of my life. I have more money than I'll ever spend in my lifetime, and I can buy whatever I want, but the one thing I can't buy is peace of mind. It's not my fault Kelly's pregnant, but it is my fault that she had to stay one more day in that hellhole longer than I did. That's something I can't change, and I'll spend the rest of my life making it up to her."

The only sound in the room was her mother's quiet weeping and the beep of two heartbeats. Kelly was stunned. She had no idea Barrett felt this way. Her parents' reaction, though expected, wasn't the end of the world. They would either accept her decision and welcome their grandchild or they wouldn't. If she and her baby weren't welcome at their table, she'd set her own. But it was Barrett's words that cut the deepest, and it was Barrett she extended her hand to when her parents left the room without another word.

❖

"It's not your fault, Barrett."

"What your father said was true. If I'd gotten to you sooner—"

"Stop it right now," Kelly said, not even trying to keep her anger in check. "My dad had no right saying that."

Barrett walked to the window, turning more than her back to Kelly. "He only said what everyone's thinking."

"Everyone is not thinking that," Kelly said desperately. Barrett was closing down, shutting her out.

"It doesn't matter."

Kelly threw the sheets back and started to climb out of bed. Barrett must have heard her because she turned around.

"What are you doing? Get back in bed." Barrett tucked the sheets around her.

"Barrett," she said, but a knock on her door was followed by Dr. Martin sticking his head in.

"May I come in?" he asked. It wasn't really a question because he was in the room before she had a chance to answer.

"How are you feeling this morning?" He looked at the dual blips on the monitor.

"Fine," Kelly lied, and the way Dr. Martin looked at her showed that he knew it too.

"I want to go home," she said, surprising herself. She wanted to stay here, where she was safe and the world was held at bay, but she wanted to go home more.

"I think you need a few more days. We have some more tests to run and you're anemic. Dr. Foster wants to see you a few more times before you leave."

"What is today?" she asked Barrett.

"Tuesday."

"I want out of here Friday morning. I need to get back to my life. I want to get my finances in order and find out if I need to find a new job."

"Kelly, you don't need to worry about any of that right now," Barrett said.

"Yes, I do. I'm not independently wealthy like you. I need to work," she said sharply.

"How about a compromise?" Barrett turned to Dr. Martin. "What if Kelly checked out tomorrow but stayed at the Trump for a few more days? She could come back for whatever tests she needed but start to get acclimated to the world."

"That might work," Dr. Martin said cautiously.

"I want to go home." She knew she sounded like a petulant child but couldn't think clearly enough to come up with any other argument for her case.

"You don't have a passport," Barrett said simply. "We can go to the embassy Monday and get things started. It'll take a few days to get it issued, and in the meantime you can have your tests and rest."

Kelly hadn't even thought about how she'd get out of the country. Jesus, she thought, she had absolutely no form of identification. And no credit cards, however meager her credit limit was. It was probably zero now.

"I can't afford that," she said sadly. A hotel sounded better than staying in this drab room, but with no way to pay for it, she had to stay here whether she liked it or not.

"I'll take care of everything. All you need to do is focus on getting well."

Kelly started to object, then thought better of it. Barrett had orchestrated her rescue, and the least she could do was be grateful. She looked between Barrett and Dr. Martin. She needed to talk with him about follow-up care when she got back home anyway. "Okay, but just until I get my passport. Then I'm going home." She held her breath, uncertain as to their reaction.

The last time she'd demanded something the results were dark and painful. Out of self-preservation her mind automatically shifted to another place. There the wind was warm, the sky clear and blue, and the laughter of friends filled the air. The touch on her arm was gentle, like that of a friend or lover, not hard and hurtful, intending to inflict pain.

"Kelly, it's Barrett." The soft voice drifted around the edges of her mind as if looking for a way in. It repeated her name again and she focused on it.

"If the docs clear you to fly we'll leave as soon as you get your passport. It shouldn't be too much longer."

Just then, Dr. Hinton came in.

Chapter Sixteen

Barrett watched Kelly struggle to maintain control. They were in the backseat of the car Barrett had hired to take them to the hotel, and Kelly's eyes were darting everywhere. Barrett remembered how she'd felt during her first venture out on a public street. She'd been terrified that she would be kidnapped again and didn't relax until she'd double-locked the hotel room door behind her. She laid her hand on top of Kelly's. They were shaking.

"It'll be all right. It just takes time."

"You sound like Dr. Hinton."

Barrett couldn't help but smile. "Just repeating what she told me at least eight dozen times."

"Does it, or is it just all bullshit?"

Barrett chuckled. "A little of both, I suppose. But it does get better."

"Does it ever go away?" Kelly kept looking straight ahead.

Barrett didn't know if she should tell Kelly the truth or lie. One would give her hope, the other hopelessness.

"It did for me." Kelly turned her attention away from the crowded street to look at Barrett. "Okay, not a hundred percent, but I'd say I'm at least ninety." Kelly's expression didn't change, and the knot in Barrett's stomach clenched a little tighter.

"Dr. Hinton said I could see her as much as I need to."

"That'll be helpful."

"When I told her I couldn't pay her, at least not right away, she said it was all paid for."

Barrett waited for the rest.

"Did you do that?"

"Does it matter?" Barrett asked, trying to evade the question.

"Yes."

"Then yes, I told her to send the bills to me. It's the least I can do." It was definitely the least, but it should be more.

"Thank you," Kelly said quietly as the car pulled into the circle drive of the hotel.

While waiting for the elevator to take them to their rooms, Barrett felt Kelly's fear grow as more people joined them. She didn't think Kelly was aware that she stepped closer to her as each new person arrived. When Kelly hesitated to get on the elevator with other people, Barrett signaled for them to go on without them. "We'll catch the next one." It took two other elevators before they were alone going to their floor.

Kelly looked at herself in the mirrored elevator doors for the first time since the day she'd left the States on her ill-fated medical mission. Her skin had an unusual pallor, which accentuated the dark circles under her eyes. She was thin, almost to the point of looking anorexic, her pregnancy accentuated by her gauntness. Her hair was dull and lifeless, and the fungus on her feet was finally beginning to clear. She needed a manicure, professional haircut, and twenty pounds. What she wanted was a hot bath, a hamburger, and a cold beer. She could have only one of the three, the burger needing to wait until her body was ready for it and the beer till after the baby. The nutritionist had cautioned her about eating anything other than bland food at first and to slowly introduce one food at a time. Her body wasn't ready to resume her normal eating habits without rebelling.

"God, I look worse than death warmed over. And please don't tell me I've been through a lot. If I hear that phrase one more time I'll choke on it."

Barrett snickered. "Good for you. I think you look great."

Barrett's reply surprised her. "Good for me?"

The doors opened and Barrett motioned for her to go down the hall to her left. "Yeah, good for you. It's great to hear you fight back."

Kelly thought about Barrett's comment. She felt safe with Barrett and trusted her. With others…well, not fighting back was a lesson she'd had to learn the hard way, and it would probably be equally hard to unlearn it.

"I feel safe with you," she said, surprising herself. Barrett must have been surprised too, because her steps faltered and Kelly almost ran into her.

"I'll never do anything to change that, Kelly. I intend to do everything in my power to make sure you never feel afraid again."

The seriousness in Barrett's eyes was overshadowed by sadness and something else she couldn't quite pinpoint. They reached a door before she figured it out. Barrett pulled a cardkey from her pocket and slid it in and out of the thin slot above the door handle. The light flashed green, and Barrett turned the lever and pushed open the door.

The room was exquisite. Kelly walked through the foyer and into the large main room. She'd never seen a hotel room so extravagant, and she certainly didn't belong in this one.

"Barrett, this is too much. I can't accept this."

"Kelly, please, let me do this for you." Barrett walked farther into the room. "All that matters is that you're safe and comfortable."

Kelly didn't protest again as Barrett showed her where everything was in the room. "This door connects to my room, and your parents are one floor down. I could try to get the one on the other side for them if you'd like."

"No, where they are is fine," she said. The last thing she needed was their judgment seeping through the crack under the door. She walked to the large window overlooking the canal. The view was breathtaking and made her a little dizzy. She grabbed the back of one of the patio chairs to steady herself.

Barrett came and stood beside her, and she immediately felt calm. "Thank you."

"You don't have to thank me, Kelly."

"Yes, I do. You rescue me, send a plane for my parents, then Dr. Hinton, and now this." She indicated the hotel room. "I don't know how I can thank you, or repay you." She'd already approached the topic of paying Barrett for everything she'd done, and Barrett had immediately shut her down. Out of the corner of her eye Kelly saw Barrett turn toward her.

"Please look at me, Kelly."

Slowly she turned too and met Barrett's concerned expression. "You don't owe me anything."

"I owe you everything," she said, and that was the crux of it. Without Barrett she'd still be in the jungle and would deliver her baby in that hellhole. She owed Barrett more than money. She owed her her life, that of her unborn child, and her sanity. She owed her the chance to breathe fresh air, control her own life, and not be chained to a tree like an animal. She owed Barrett in ways she would never be able to begin to count.

"If not me, someone else would have rescued you."

"No, Barrett. You were my only chance, and I'll never forget that fact. Because of you my baby will be born in a hospital and surrounded by people who love her."

Kelly sensed Barrett's unease when she mentioned the baby. "It's okay to talk about it. It is the elephant in the room, so to speak."

"It's a girl?" Kelly saw a spark flash through Barrett's eyes.

"Yes. Dr. Foster confirmed it this morning before I checked out." The feeling that had rushed through Kelly at the news she was carrying a girl was indescribable. Every maternal instinct had kicked in, and she was more certain than ever that she'd keep this baby and raise her in a house filled with love. Someday, somehow, she'd explain to her daughter how she came to be. But until then she had more important things to deal with.

"You've definitely decided to keep her?" Barrett asked expectantly.

"Yes, I have." She moved her hands from the chair to instinctively cover her growing belly. "I love my parents and will always want their approval, but I'm a grown woman, and I make my own decisions, whether they like them or not. And they obviously don't like this one." Her heart broke a little at the thought that her daughter might not have a relationship with her grandparents, but she'd rather have that than expose her to their misguided beliefs. A knock on the door interrupted her train of thought.

"I'll get it," Barrett said, leaving her alone on the patio. Kelly immediately felt the void her absence created. She'd come to depend on Barrett to help her through the confusing, often frightening maze of her return. Barrett had guided her through some very difficult times, and at times Kelly was almost overwhelmed by her generosity. But it was the least Kelly could do.

"Kelly, honey, Barrett told us you'd be here today," her mother said from behind her. "How are you feeling?" she asked stiffly.

"A little tired. I'll do better now that I'm out of the hospital. I don't know how they expect you to get any rest with everyone coming in and checking on you all the time." It was small talk, of no consequence whatsoever, but better to talk about nothing than not talk at all.

"I know. Aren't these rooms wonderful? Ours is a suite. I've never been in such a nice hotel, let alone one this nice." Her mother was practically gushing. Her father, on the other hand, hadn't said anything and had barely stepped into the room. It was as if he might catch something if he did.

"And Barrett is paying for everything," she added in a hushed tone.

"Yes, Mom, I know. It's very generous of her."

Now her father stepped forward. "It's the least she could do after leaving you behind with those men—"

"Dad, that's not fair. She didn't leave me. She had no choice." Why couldn't they see that? She looked for Barrett to see if she'd heard her father's cruel words. She wasn't in the room, but the door to the adjoining room was open. She must have gone to her own room when her parents arrived. At least she hoped that's how it'd happened.

"Dad, I love you very much, but I will not let you talk about Barrett like that. You seem to forget she was held by the same people I was and endured the same sadistic conditions all of us did. Eight of us were there and only five came out. I don't hear any of the other families blaming her for not coming sooner. They're grateful their loved one is alive. She did what she could, when she could. And I'm damn happy she did. If you don't have anything good to say about her, then you don't need to say anything at all. Because if you do, I'll never speak to you again."

❖

Barrett closed the connecting door. She didn't need to hear anything else after what Kelly's father said about leaving her behind. There it was again, hitting her right between the eyes. Would it ever stop ripping her guts out? Would she ever stop thinking about it every minute? Would her life ever return to normal? What in the hell was normal anymore? She had no fucking idea.

Barrett declined Kelly's invitation to join her and her parents for dinner and spent the remainder of the evening pacing her room. She wanted to be with Kelly but knew she needed time alone with her parents. After flipping through the channels for the umpteenth time, she went to bed, turned off the light, and hoped she'd get some sleep.

The scream woke Barrett. She shot out of bed and ran across the room and through the adjoining door before she remembered she was wearing only a pair of boxer shorts. With the exception of a small shaft of light coming from the bathroom, all the lights were off in Kelly's room. Barrett blinked a few times to let her eyes adjust. Kelly was thrashing around in her bed, and Barrett hurried to her.

"Kelly, it's Barrett. Wake up. You're safe." The bed dipped under her weight when she sat down and reached for Kelly, pulling her into a sitting position. Her eyes were tightly closed and Barrett grasped her hands. They were cold and shaking. "Kelly, wake up. It's just a dream. You're safe. You're in the hotel here in Panama. I'm here, wake up. You're okay." After Barrett repeated the reassuring words several times, Kelly finally stopped shaking and blinked rapidly as she opened her eyes. Even though they were open, they were glassy. Kelly's whole body started to shake again, and Barrett gathered her into her arms.

"Shh." Barrett scooted back and leaned against the headboard, pulling Kelly with her. She wrapped her arms around Kelly's shoulders and held her close. "Shh, shh, it's okay. I've got you. Nothing's going to happen to you. You're safe, and nothing will ever happen to you again." Kelly shifted and laid her head on Barrett's shoulder. Her arm draped across Barrett's stomach, and she snuggled close.

Barrett talked about nothing and everything, and the more she talked the calmer Kelly became. Barrett was aware of her nakedness but Kelly was oblivious, lost in a deep sleep. Barrett lightly stroked up and down Kelly's warm, too-thin arms and let her thoughts drift.

It had been a long time since she'd held a woman like this. She frowned when she realized she'd never actually held a woman like this. She held women as a prelude to sex, and as a post-coital requirement, but never just to comfort or chase away a bad dream. It was a new and pleasant experience. Instead of making her antsy to escape, it was oddly fulfilling.

Kelly shifted and snuggled closer, her hand brushing a bare nipple. A jolt of desire shot through Barrett's body down to her toes, and she was suddenly very warm. What the fuck? This was not a sexual situation by any stretch of the imagination, so why was she reacting like it was? It wasn't as if she hadn't had sex in a while.

The night before she got the call that Kelly and the others had been rescued she'd spent many hours in the arms of a beautiful blonde trying to forget. The orgasms had been perfunctory but the feeling was nothing compared to this. Words like *contentment* and *peace* came to mind. Words like *desire* and *passion* also came to mind, and Barrett pushed them away. They were completely inappropriate, and Barrett wouldn't do anything to risk what she had with Kelly, what she owed to Kelly.

She closed her eyes, suddenly very tired.

❖

Kelly was finally warm. She wanted to drift back into the cocoon surrounding her. She felt safe and secure. Her mind was calm, her head clear. She felt refreshed and relaxed. She didn't want to open her eyes and end the moment. She could stay in this place forever. But her bladder overruled her brain, and she had to move. She opened her eyes, blinking a few times, and came instantly awake.

Her head was resting on something soft, moving up and down in rhythmic motion. Soft air lightly caressed her face. The skin in front of her was bare, tan, and feminine. The curve of a breast started where her fingertips ended.

A vague recollection of the night before tickled the edges of her mind, then became clear. She was in the hotel room next to Barrett's and she'd had a nightmare. She remembered Barrett's voice soothing her. These must be Barrett's arms around her, comforting her. Barrett's presence calming her, saving her from herself.

"Sorry about this," Barrett said, surprising her.

Kelly didn't know she was awake. "About what?" Her voice was husky with sleep.

Barrett's breathing quickened. "I woke up and heard you and didn't stop to get dressed. I meant to go back to my room, but I must have fallen asleep instead."

"I'm the one that should be sorry—for waking you up."

"Tell you what," Barrett said, her voice rumbling under her ear. "Let's both just agree to not feel guilty about any of this."

"Deal," Kelly said, wishing Mother Nature wasn't knocking on her bladder so she and Barrett could stay in this position forever. Unfortunately she didn't have a choice and started to untangle herself from Barrett's arms. She tried not to look but couldn't help herself as her gaze drifted to Barrett's bare chest. Without thinking, she touched the scar on her shoulder. Barrett drew in a sharp breath.

"I was so afraid this had killed you." This time Kelly's voice reflected the fear she'd just mentioned.

"It almost did." Barrett's voice was thick.

"I…"

Barrett covered her hand with hers. "It didn't, and that's all that matters."

Barrett's eyes were dark and serious, and Kelly couldn't quite read what was behind them. She studied Barrett's hand covering hers. The sores from her wrists being bound were gone, replaced by smooth skin. Hers, however, were raw and callused and would probably be scarred forever. She felt self-conscious and pulled her hand out from under Barrett's, and when she did, it inadvertently slid over her breast. Barrett's nipple instantly grew hard and Kelly jerked away. "Sorry" she mumbled, as she practically ran into the bathroom but, before closing the door behind her, saw Barrett's nudity reflected in the mirror above the sink.

Kelly leaned over the sink, head dizzy from the exertion. Her heart was beating like she'd just run a mile at a full-out sprint. God, she was so tired and weak. Her hands were shaking as she stripped out of the pajamas her mother had bought for her. She stood naked in front of the mirror. If she thought seeing herself in the elevator mirror yesterday was shocking, this was much, much worse.

She was no more than skin and bones, as her grandmother would say. She'd lost all muscle tone, which was surprising since she and her fellow hostages had been little more than a manual-labor force. On her previous medical missions she'd seen the effects of starvation, and she was now one of the statistics. Turning sideways she slid her hands over the rounding of her belly. A life was growing inside her, one completely unexpected but hers nonetheless.

What would her daughter be like? Would she have soft, straight hair or dark, angry eyes? Would she be kind and gentle or cruel and heartless? Would she use her knowledge for good or evil? Would she be born healthy? Looking at her reflection in the mirror Kelly couldn't help but ask if she would be born at all. Completely overwhelmed by what she saw in front of her, she sank to the floor and cried.

Barrett quickly got off the bed, dashed into her own room, and pulled on a T-shirt. After brushing her teeth she wasn't sure if she should return to Kelly's room. If she did, was she overstepping her boundaries, butting into Kelly's life, taking advantage of the situation? Or did Kelly need her? Not sure what to do, she decided to play it in the middle and just hovered near the door separating their rooms. If Kelly needed her she'd be there, and if she didn't, it wouldn't be awkward.

After several minutes Barrett grew worried. She didn't hear either the shower or any noise coming from Kelly's room.

"Kelly?" Barrett called out as she walked farther into her room. Barrett called for her again. Standing in the middle of the room, she cocked her head and heard soft crying coming from behind the bathroom door. Barrett knocked. "Kelly, are you okay?" When she still didn't answer, Barrett tried the knob. It wasn't locked and turned easily in her hand. Kelly was slumped against the wall, arms wrapped around her legs. Her face was buried in her knees, and her shoulders moved as she sobbed. Barrett knelt down beside her.

"Kelly. What is it?" she asked quietly, wanting to reach out to her but afraid to. It was several moments before she answered.

"Nothing. I'm fine." She didn't sound very convincing.

"That's why you're sitting on the bathroom floor, buck naked and crying?" Barrett cringed. Why had she said that? This was definitely not funny. But for some reason her question made Kelly smile, and a sliver of relief trickled around her.

"No, normally I'm on the patio. But I made an exception this time."

"Isn't your butt cold?"

This time Kelly laughed. It was small and quiet, but it was a laugh. "Now that you mention it."

"Then let's get you up. Were you trying to take a shower?" Kelly nodded, and Barrett helped her stand. "Okay. I can help with that." Making sure Kelly was okay, Barrett opened the shower door and turned on the water. She adjusted the temperature and extended her hand to help Kelly inside.

"You okay?" she asked before stepping away.

"Yes, thank you."

Barrett closed the door. She wanted to give Kelly her privacy but also didn't want to leave her alone. She needed to make sure she was okay and stayed that way. Kelly's back was to her, the water sliding over her scar-laden skin. A shaft of pain sliced through Barrett when she saw how many of the scars were fresh. She could easily count her ribs.

Barrett laid the plush blue towel next to the shower door and reluctantly left the room.

CHAPTER SEVENTEEN

Six days later Kelly buckled her seat belt in the plane Barrett had chartered to fly them home. She tried to convince Barrett she was capable of flying commercial, but Barrett had insisted and she finally acquiesced. The takeoff was smooth and almost silent as the plane lifted off the ground, bound for Denver.

The entire week in the hospital and the four days in the hotel had been a blur, punctuated by more nightmares and tense visits from her parents. They didn't mention the baby or her plans when she returned home, all three of them preferring to have meaningless conversation. She confirmed her decision not to terminate her pregnancy with Dr. Foster and had several sessions with Dr. Hinton. She wasn't anywhere near where she needed to be mentally or physically, but she needed familiar surroundings to ground her. She was adamant about going home.

Barrett sat in the seat across from her, her gaze focused out the small window. She had been beside her almost every minute. Kelly had insisted on letting her buy only a few sets of clothes to get her through until she was able to go shopping on her own, with her own money. And that was another thing she had to figure out.

Did she even have a job? Would she be able to go back to work? She was too weak to do more than walk up and down the hall of her hotel. Gradually she'd progressed to eight laps, but that certainly wasn't enough for the strenuous job of nursing. Oh, and she couldn't forget about the baby that would consume her time and energy in a few short months.

Kelly recalled their conversation two days ago regarding her house. She didn't quite remember how the conversation started, but it wasn't long before Barrett confessed she'd paid off her mortgage.

"You did what?"

"Kelly, I have plenty of money, and you didn't need to worry about where you were going to live when you came home," Barrett *said matter-of-factly.*

"But that's too much."

"Don't worry about it,"

"It's not your responsibility," Kelly said, anger starting to boil. She finally gave up, knowing her arguments wouldn't change anything.

Kelly hated owing anyone, especially when it came to money. It was bad enough that she owed the bank, but no one that she knew was in a position to pay cash for a house. Except, of course, Barrett, who explained how she'd found out who held her mortgage and just how easy it was to go into the bank and write a check for the balance. She wasn't so lucky when it came to her car. The bank had taken the car back after four months, for non-payment. They didn't care that Kelly couldn't make the payment—just that she didn't.

Barrett's eyes were closed, and Kelly took the opportunity to study her. She looked a little butch, and with her hair much shorter than it was when she was in camp she pulled it off easily. She was obviously a powerfully successful businesswoman, the way she took control and just expected things to get done as she asked. She filled any room with confidence and charisma that, even in her weakened condition, Kelly found surprisingly sexy.

The scar on her forehead was noticeable, and Kelly felt bad that she hadn't been able to do more to keep it from scarring so much. It had been all she could do to keep it from getting infected. Barrett had told her about the surgery to fix her hand and repair the damage the bullet had inflicted in her shoulder.

Kelly knew Barrett blamed herself for leaving her behind. She didn't, but couldn't get Barrett to change her thinking. If their roles were reversed, she supposed she'd feel the same. As it was, she owed Barrett her life, which trumped anything and everything else. God, they were both a mess, but all things considered it could have been much worse.

Barrett opened her eyes and caught her staring at her. She watched as Barrett's eyes turned from unfocused to smoky to piercing. She wanted to drown in those eyes and let them take away all the pain of the world. Even when they were captives, Barrett had been a steadying force in her life. She hadn't connected with any of the other hostages in the camps like she had with Barrett. Like now. A certain something about Barrett had inexplicably reached out to her then, and that pull was definitely here now.

"It's my turn to ask how you're doing."

"I'm fine. I'm not the one who was just rescued."

"But you were not so long ago. Reliving this can't help but affect you."

"You sound like Dr. Hinton." Barrett frowned.

Barrett was obviously uncomfortable talking about her experience. "She didn't divulge any doctor-patient confidence. Even though I'm still not certain which way is up, I can read you pretty well. We didn't go through what we did together and not share a bond. We depended on each other, and that doesn't change now that we're out." Kelly was surprised at her words. She'd never really thought about it that way, but once the words came out of her mouth she believed them.

Barrett's eyes narrowed as if she were looking into her soul. She should have felt uncomfortable, but instead she felt confident— that she could count on Barrett for anything and she would do the same for her. She owed Barrett more than just her life, and she would forever be grateful.

"It's only been a few months since you've been home," Kelly added.

"Actually it's been closer to six, and thank you for your concern, but I'm fine." Barrett's tone said that topic was closed. "This isn't about me, Kelly, but about you."

"I'd hope we're at least friends, if not more so. After all, it's as much about you as me. Friends give and take from each other."

Barrett smiled. "You're right. I'm giving and you're taking. So get used to it."

❖

The plane circled Denver International Airport and Kelly's nerves were on overload. She was going home, a place that, on more than one occasion, she hadn't thought she'd ever see again.

The familiar Rocky Mountains were out her window, snow covering every peak. The sky was cloudless and looked just as Kelly had imagined it when she closed her eyes and envisioned herself there.

"Thank you for arranging this." They were arriving at the executive terminal, where access was tightly controlled. The last thing she wanted or needed was to deal with the throngs of well-meaning friends and story-seeking media. Barrett smiled and only nodded.

For most of the flight Barrett had been relaxed and talkative. She'd grown more quiet and introspective the closer they got to their final destination. Barrett said she intended to stay in Denver for a few days to help her get settled, and that she had some business to attend to while she was here. Kelly wasn't sure the second reason was true but didn't say anything. She'd always hated confrontations and really hated them now.

Whether it was because they were at the executive terminal or Barrett's connections, she was whisked through Customs in record time and within fifteen minutes was sitting next to Barrett in the rear of a black limo on her way home.

She must have nodded off because the next thing she knew Barrett was waking her. She was warm and comfortable, her pillow soft. As she fought to open her eyes Kelly realized that her pillow was Barrett. When had she scooted over and curled against Barrett? Every time she fell asleep with Barrett nearby, she woke either in her arms or so close to her she could have been in her lap. What was up with that?

Yesterday when she spoke with Dr. Hinton, she mentioned it to her. After talking it through, Kelly concluded that she felt safe with Barrett and her reaction was only natural. Dr. Hinton had assured her that with time she'd feel safe again on her own. Intellectually it made sense, but Kelly had always been impatient with things that took time.

She felt Barrett stiffen. And in a second she cursed.

"What is it?" Kelly sat up and Barrett pointed out the window. Now it was Kelly's turn to cuss. "God damn it. I specifically told my parents not to tell anyone I was coming home today." She knew she sounded as panicked as she felt.

Across the front of her house hung a sign that read WELCOME HOME, KELLY! The letters were at least three feet high and painted in bright-green letters on white paper. Balloons flanked either side and rose majestically from her mailbox on the curb. Cars were parked on both sides of the street in front of her house as far as she could see.

She groaned and fell against the back of the seat. "Oh, God."

"There must be a dozen cars here," Barrett commented, a frown creasing her forehead.

"At least." Kelly was both annoyed and frightened.

"Didn't Dr. Hinton caution you to ease back into your life?" Barrett told the driver to pull over and double-park a few houses before Kelly's.

"Of course she did. She told my parents that too. Obviously they don't listen to her any more than they listen to me. My mom must have called Ariel and set this all up. God damn it," Kelly said, for lack of anything better.

Barrett took her hand. "You don't have to do this, you know. I can take you to a hotel, and you can come back when everyone's gone."

Barrett was offering her an escape, and she wanted to jump at it. She didn't want to face her friends. She was barely used to being able to speak without permission and certainly wasn't capable of pleasant small talk right now. She had no idea what was going on in the world, had completely missed the presidential election, and had never heard of Barrett's phone, the iPhone 5, or the xBox One, which she'd seen in a TV commercial last night. And she definitely did not want to talk about her captivity, captors, or her baby. She was just coming to grips with it all herself.

She turned to Barrett. "Stay with me?"

"Of course," Barrett said without hesitation.

"You don't know what my friends are like."

"No, but I know you. I promise," Barrett said, smiling, making an X on her chest with her finger, "to not leave your side until you throw me out."

❖

All these people need to get the hell out of here, Barrett thought. They had no idea what they were doing to Kelly. But she did, and she struggled to find a way to get everyone to leave. Kelly was bombarded with well wishes and welcome-homes. When anyone approached, Kelly stepped closer to her. Many times Barrett deflected questions about her or their rescue and directed the conversation to safer, more non-threatening topics.

The shadows under Kelly eyes were darker than they'd been an hour ago. After three hours she was obviously exhausted.

Barrett whispered in her ear. "Do you want me to ask everyone to leave?" Kelly simply nodded. "I'll be right back." Barrett left Kelly's side for the first time since they'd arrived and hurried back with a glass of champagne and a spoon.

Tapping lightly on the glass to draw their attention, she said, "Ladies and gentlemen." Another few taps on the glass. "Ladies and gentlemen. On behalf of everyone, I'm sure we're all thrilled that Kelly's home and we know she's exhausted. So, before we all start leaving in a few minutes I propose we all raise our glasses in one final drink to celebrate that Kelly is back with us, where she belongs." Barrett held up her glass the highest and everyone followed suit. Thankfully, everyone got the hint and started saying their good-byes. She couldn't have made it any clearer that it was time for everyone to leave. Everyone except Ariel, the woman Kelly had introduced as her BFF, took the hint.

Barrett wasn't sure if she liked Ariel. On more than one occasion she caught her whispering, and Barrett didn't know if she was telling the others to go to hell or contributing to the topic of Kelly's pregnancy. She was good at reading body language and, unfortunately for Kelly, Barrett suspected it was the latter.

"Kelly, come sit down," Ariel said, patting the couch next to her. "You look exhausted."

No shit, Sherlock, Barrett thought. Where were you two hours ago?

Kelly practically fell onto the couch, the leather not making a sound. She kicked off her shoes and put her sock-clad feet on the table in front of her. Then she dropped her head back and let out a long sigh.

"I'm so glad you're home, Kel. I missed you so much." Ariel babbled on about nothing, and Barrett guessed that was what girlfriends did. She'd never had anyone close so really didn't know. But then Ariel said something that grabbed her attention.

"Going out just wasn't the same without you. We were always one short at bridge and an odd number when we rode the rides at the fair this year. David asked about you all the time." Barrett did recognize Ariel's tone. It was the one usually accompanied with a wink and a nod.

Barrett was floored. Kelly had just been released from being held hostage in an insect-infested jungle by a bunch of thugs, and her friend was telling her that some guy was asking about her? As in *asking* about her?

"Ariel, I appreciate the thought, but the last thing I can do is resume my life like I never left."

"We know that, Kel. We just think you need to get back on the horse, so to speak," Ariel said in all seriousness.

"And what horse is that? The one that attacked our clinic, shot and killed a dozen people just trying to help others? Or the horse that dragged me through the jungle by my hair? Maybe the one that beat me just because he was bored, or tied me to a dying man who'd just had his penis shredded because he dared to look at me—The Colonel's woman? Is that the one, Ariel? Or the one they called The

Colonel? He was the stallion of the herd and obviously as fertile. So forgive me, Ariel, if I can't quite figure out which one I'm supposed to get back on, as you so eloquently put it."

Barrett was stunned almost as much as Ariel was. It was all she could do to not shout, "You go, girl," and give Kelly a high five. Kelly's cheeks were flushed and her ears red with anger. If Barrett didn't know better she would swear steam was coming out of Kelly's ears. She couldn't even begin to describe Ariel's expression.

"Jesus Christ, Kel. You don't need to rip me a new asshole." Ariel sounded somewhat pissed. "I was only trying to help. And besides, we heard you were planning to get an abortion."

Kelly paled and Barrett held her breath.

"Where did you hear that?" Kelly asked calmly. Too calmly, Barrett thought.

"Your mother." Ariel was obviously clueless as to Kelly's state of mind. "When she called to tell me when you'd be home."

"What else did she say?"

"Just that they don't do abortions in Panama but that you were going to have one of the doctors at your hospital do it."

Ariel was either terribly naive, had an ulterior motive, or just a complete idiot, and the way Kelly was looking at her, she too was trying to figure which descriptor fit. Barrett watched as Kelly fought to maintain her composure. Why would her mother say such a thing? To force her into changing her mind? Kelly had told her about her conversation with her parents and how they hadn't let up on trying to get her to abort the baby. Barrett had been surprised. She never would have expected that type of behavior from the Mr. and Mrs. Ryan she'd met and that Kelly had talked about during their captivity. But then, what did she know about family dynamics?

"For the record, Ariel, I am not having an abortion, no matter how much my parents want me to. This is a child growing inside me, an innocent child, and I'm not combining one tragedy with another. I'm keeping this baby, and anyone who can only see her as a child of rape won't be in my life, no matter who they are."

"Of course, Kelly. You know I've always been pro-choice. Especially in a case like this."

Barrett winced. Could Ariel make this any worse? God, she hoped not, for Kelly's sake. Kelly stood, a look of hurt and disbelief on her face that Barrett had never seen.

"Good-bye Ariel," Kelly said, walking out of the room without looking back, and it was all Barrett could do to not hit Ariel's ass with the door on her way out.

Barrett found Kelly sitting on a bed in the master bedroom. Shades of blues filled the room dominated by a large king-size bed flanked by matching nightstands. A dresser on the adjacent wall and a rocker tucked into a corner nook completed the furnishings.

"This wasn't what I expected."

Kelly's voice was quiet and Barrett had to strain to hear her.

"These people were my friends, or at least I thought they were. These people…" She hesitated as if looking for the right adjective. "I don't know what they want from me. And my parents…"

Kelly's voice broke, and Barrett crossed the room and sat down beside her. She had no idea what to say or do to help her, and she said as much. "I'm so sorry, Kelly. I should have seen this coming."

"How were you supposed to know my parents would do this? Even I didn't think they would. I guess a lot of things have changed," she said, clearly dejected.

Another notch on the "should never have left her" stick Barrett beat herself up with. It was getting almost too big to handle. A few more occasions like this, and it would soon turn into a club.

"Thank you for bringing me home, Barrett," Kelly said. But Barrett heard the unspoken word "finally."

Numb was the first word Kelly could think of to describe how she felt. Hurt, shocked, disappointed, and betrayed were others that floated around her. Barrett had kept her word about everything, but then again she trusted Barrett. She wasn't responsible for this fiasco, and she shouldn't take it out on her. Trying to shake off her mood, Kelly stood.

"I'd ask you to stay for dinner, but I probably don't have anything edible in my kitchen. I need to get to the store and buy a few staples for the next few days," she said, starting to make a list in her head of what she'd need. Duh, how about absolutely everything from eggs to a new toothbrush.

She'd made Barrett stop at her bank to get some cash and a new debit and credit card. The debit card was no issue, but the credit card had been closed due to her overdue balance. Her credit must be in the toilet now. Barrett had said she'd have her attorney look into what she could do about any bad debt. Kelly had argued that she could do that, but Barrett had insisted, citing the numerous lawyers she had on her staff versus Kelly's none.

"You should have most of the staples and the ingredients to fix a few dinners. I found a service that'll shop and put stuff right in your fridge and cabinet," Barrett added, probably due to Kelly's expression. "Then tomorrow we'll get you a car."

"A car?" She must have misunderstood Barrett because surely she wasn't going to buy her a car? But then again she'd paid for her house, so what was a few ten thousand more?

"Yours was repossessed and I couldn't get it back."

Barrett's generosity was beginning to make her uncomfortable. She knew Barrett felt guilty about being forced to leave her behind, and it didn't take a PhD like Dr. Hinton to conclude that she was trying to make up for that fact. But the only person that blamed Barrett was Barrett. She, in turn, owed Barrett her life, and one way she could repay her was to graciously accept what Barrett thought she had to offer. God, it was confusing.

"I will buy my own car, Barrett. No." She put her hand up when Barrett started to object. "I will buy my own car." She emphasized every word. How she would pay for it was another matter altogether. Without proof of income she wouldn't be able to get a loan. She'd have to dip into her savings, which she didn't want to do but had no other choice.

"Okay," Barrett said. "Whatever you want."

Kelly heard the hurt in Barrett's voice. "I'm sorry." She laid her hand on Barrett's arm. "I didn't mean to sound so harsh. But this is something I have to do." That seemed to soften her harsh words, and Barrett nodded.

"I understand." Barrett stood and started toward the door. "You're probably exhausted. I should go."

Kelly didn't want Barrett to leave but needed some time to herself and to get reacquainted with her house, her things, herself. "Come for coffee in the morning?" Kelly asked, following Barrett down the hall toward the front door.

"Wouldn't miss it."

Butterflies danced in Kelly's stomach.

Barrett opened the front door to leave, and the late afternoon framed her in the doorway. The way the sun was angled made it look like every particle of the remaining sunlight was focused on Barrett's face. Barrett was absolutely stunning. Kelly's throat went dry and her knees suddenly felt weak. She'd never seen Barrett like this and certainly had never used that word to describe someone. Especially a woman. But it fit Barrett perfectly.

Kelly stepped forward, closed the distance between them, and hugged her. They'd gotten into the habit of hugging when they left each other. It had been a natural reaction for her to hug Barrett when she got off the plane in Panama, and Barrett had returned the gesture the first time she left her hospital room. Kelly never hugged her girlfriends when they parted, but it just felt natural with Barrett. And if the intensity of Barrett's hugs were any indication, she didn't seem to mind either.

She didn't want to let Barrett go. She would never grow tired of feeling her alive in her arms. After Barrett was rescued, Kelly had dreamed of the moment she saw Barrett again. When she stepped into her arms after getting off the plane she was lost in the sensation of overwhelming relief. Fortunately she got the opportunity to repeat it often. Reluctantly she pulled away.

"If you need anything, call me." They'd bought Kelly a cell phone, and Barrett's number was first on speed dial.

"I will."

Barrett clasped her hands and asked, "You sure you're going to be okay?"

"No, but I will be," she replied, clearly surprising Barrett by hugging her again. "Now go." Kelly turned her around so she faced the street. "Your work here is done. Breakfast is at eight. Don't be late or your eggs will get cold."

Kelly gave Barrett a slight push that got her moving down the sidewalk toward her car.

❖

Kelly closed the door before she could change her mind and ask Barrett to stay. Barrett made her feel safe, and she enjoyed her company. Now that they were out from under the constant eyes and scrutiny of their guards and were able to talk freely like normal people, she was getting a sense of Barrett's personality. She was intelligent but had a good dose of common sense. She was commanding and forceful but could be gentle and caring.

While in Panama waiting for her passport they'd gone for a walk and ended up in a nearby park. It was the middle of the day, and a few mothers were pushing toddlers on swings while an elderly man tossed a ball to his dog. They were sitting on one of the benches when the dog trotted over and dropped her soggy tennis ball in Barrett's lap.

"Hey, girl, what's this?" she asked, rubbing the Border collie on the top of her head and around her ears. "You wanna play? Is that it?" She stood and threw the ball, and the dog took off after it. She brought it back to Barrett and looked at her expectantly.

"Looks like you have a new friend."

"Yeah, she's a cutie," Barrett said, rubbing the dog behind the ears and throwing the ball again.

"You're a chick magnet. She came right up to you."

"Yeah, well, you know dogs and kids are a good judge of character." Barrett lobbed the ball to her left and the dog took off, but this time took it back to its owner. Barrett chuckled. "Obviously I've lost my animal magnetism."

"Oh, I doubt you'll ever lose it," Kelly said, enjoying herself for the first time in a very, very long time. Sitting on a park bench, the sun warming her face with a charming, intelligent woman was more than she'd ever imagined she would ever do again. But here she was sitting next to the woman who'd made it all possible. Overwhelming gratitude suddenly made her grab Barrett into a hug.

"Hey," Barrett said, obviously surprised. "Not that I'm complaining, but what's that for?"

"Because thank you just isn't enough."

Kelly closed the front door and her house was suddenly very empty. Of course it would be, she told herself. An hour ago thirty people were here, and now it was just her. She stopped. If she counted from the day she left for the medical mission, it had been more than two years since she'd been completely alone. The thought stunned her. She'd been with her medical team, then her guards, the hospital staff, and Barrett in the next room in the hotel in Panama.

Her steps echoed in her suddenly claustrophobic house. During one of their discussions Dr. Hinton had told her she'd more than likely have some difficulty transitioning back into her life. She might feel completely helpless or experience sensory overload and anything in between. She might feel numb or anxious. After having every minute of her life under the control of someone else without that direction, without being told what to do and when to do it, she might feel like she was drowning in emptiness.

Needle, she needed to get her dog Needle. Ariel had said she was at her house and she'd bring her over tomorrow. Brushing her anxiousness aside, Kelly wandered through her house. She had bought the single-story ranch as an investment when the housing market tanked several years ago. She felt guilty reaping the benefit of someone else's misfortune but eventually got over it. What was unfortunate was that before the previous owner left, he'd trashed the place. Every appliance was gone, every wall had at least three holes in the Sheetrock, and every faucet was broken. The toilets were clogged with God knew what, and the garage door was off the tracks. The yard was equally destroyed with weeds that grazed her butt as she walked by. But after several months, several thousands of dollars, and too many sore muscles and blisters to count, it was finally almost the way she wanted it. All that was left was the fourth bedroom currently serving as the proverbial junk room. Bedroom number two was the guest room, number three the office, but her pride and joy was her bedroom.

The large four-poster king-size bed sat in the middle of the large room. The bedspread had cost much more than she'd ever dreamed she would spend, but Kelly had fallen in love with it the minute she saw it. She'd painted the walls to bring out the various shades of blue, and the pillows completed the look. She wanted a warm, sensuous feeling in this room, a space she could go to nestle down, cuddle up, and make love. She could still see the imprint on the bed where Barrett had sat beside her. She hadn't said much, but it had comforted her just having Barrett here. She could get used to having Barrett around. It was easy to be with her. She didn't feel any pressure to be something she wasn't, a survivor of a horrible ordeal, a woman trying to get her life back. Barrett understood she was one of a handful of people that had shared that harrowing experience.

What would it have been like if she'd met Barrett under different circumstances? Fat chance they ever would have met. For crying out loud, they lived hundreds of miles apart. They didn't travel in the same business or social circles. She wondered what Barrett's friends were like. Were they successful business owners like her? Did they live near her or were they scattered around the world? Were they all lesbians or did she have straight friends? Those were just a few of the questions that drifted through her head as she washed a few loads of clothes and her dishes. She and Barrett had been together for months in the jungle, but when they were able to talk the subjects were more along the lines of survival—not last weekend's barbeque chatter.

The dryer buzzer shook her from her thoughts, and she loaded the basket with warm clothes. Returning to the couch she reached for the socks and started pairing them. Suddenly she dropped a pair like they were on fire, her hands shaking uncontrollably. Her heart raced and she couldn't breathe. She staggered to her feet, the basket of clothes falling to the floor. She grabbed the back of a nearby chair to stay on her feet. Instantly the room closed in. She had to get out.

❖

Barrett couldn't sleep. The hotel was nice, quiet, and a mirror image of any one of the hundreds she'd stayed in before. Different colors, different address, but one hotel room was about the same as any other. Sometimes she thought her bedroom at home was the strange place. So why couldn't she sleep?

A sliver of light from the parking lot broke through a gap in the drapes. She lay on her back with her hands behind her head. The ceiling fan was on low, its wide blades silently circling above her head. Kelly had a ceiling fan above her bed. Was she watching it spin around or was she sleeping? Had anyone else watched the blades spin in the dark? Anyone other than Kelly felt the cool breeze on their naked body? Who had lain under that fan and run their hands over her soft skin? Traced the curve of her breast, the arch of her back, the wet warmth of her? Who had kissed her senseless until she cried out their name in the dark. Who had taken her to the crest of passion and held her as she tumbled over and down into the haze of climax?

Sweet Jesus! Barrett threw off the sheet and practically jumped out of the bed. She opened the drapes wider, lighting the room enough to find the open bottle of Crown Royal on the minibar. Her hands shook slightly as she poured the contents into a glass and added a splash of Coke. Using her finger to stir the two together she looked out the window.

What in the hell was she doing having fantasies about Kelly? She was just beginning to recover and get her life back. And she was straight. Oh, and pregnant. She had absolutely no business thinking of her as anything other than a friend. What a pig. For God's sake. She needed her head examined if she were thinking about going there.

But what was she going to do now? She couldn't un-think something like that. Pretend she never thought about someone naked. How Kelly's skin would feel under her fingertips, her taste on her tongue, the little sounds she made, her moans of ecstasy, the sharp intake of breath at the first entry into very private places. Barrett couldn't not imagine the sound of Kelly's voice whispering her name, begging for release.

"Oh, God, what am I doing?" she asked the night. She repeated the question over and over as she paced the small room. "Get it together, Barrett," she said forcefully, changing her approach. "She doesn't need this from you." Actually she could name at least a dozen things she needed to do for Kelly.

Kelly was home and on her way to recovery. She had a safe place to live, food to eat, and tomorrow would have reliable transportation. She'd spoken with the head of nursing where Kelly worked before she was kidnapped, and the woman had guaranteed that Kelly would have a job to return to when she was ready. Barrett had asked to keep their discussion confidential, and the woman had easily agreed. Dr. Hinton's fees would be paid, and Barrett had taken care of the hospital bill before leaving Panama. Her attorney would handle any credit issues and overdue bills. What more was there to do for her?

She needed to get home and back to work. Debra had called several times with work-related items and each time tried to get Barrett to tell her where she was and what she was doing. When she'd received Trevor's call two weeks ago, she'd run out of the office with barely a second glance. Once she'd calmed down a bit, she'd called Debra to tell her she'd be out for a while.

"Out for what?" Debra asked in her not-so-subtle way.

"I have to do something."

"Like what?" When Barrett didn't answer she said, "What are you doing, Barrett? Where are you and who are you with? Are you shacking up with another redhead? God, I hope so. You need a good lay. You haven't been yourself since you got back. You space out in meetings, when you even bother to show up. I don't know how many times I've caught you staring into space. And quite frankly, you left your decision-making ability, sense of humor, and common

courtesy behind in that jungle. You've been a complete bitch, a pain in the ass, and a space cadet since you got back. Now, I don't begin to know what you went through while you were gone," Debra said, barely stopping to take a breath, "but a lot of people were affected by your kidnapping back here at home, and we deserve more than what you've been giving us."

Debra had been right. She was a completely different person than before. She had only been gone for seven months, but could that short time completely change a person? She hadn't expected it. Nothing really affected her or threw her. She was a pragmatist and, when faced with something ugly, simply addressed it and moved on. End of problem. She'd been proud of that descriptor, but had she left that behind in the jungle as well? She'd lost her edge and didn't care.

She called Debra and when she got to her room and, greeted with the same "where are you and what are you doing" questions, she finally told her.

"You did what?"

"I hired the same mercenaries that rescued me to go back and get the others."

"Jesus, Barrett, I had no idea. Why didn't you tell me?" Debra's voice had softened substantially.

"Because I could barely stand it myself. I couldn't deal with everyone asking me every day if I'd heard anything." That was the God's honest truth. Every time her phone would ring her heart had practically jumped out of her chest, and that was after she'd looked at it for hours begging it to ring.

"So how are they doing?"

Barrett filled her in on the four other hostages, saving Kelly for last. When she finished talking, she realized Debra was one of only a handful of people who knew what she'd done. But she wasn't in it for the glory or the notoriety. She was in it to get Kelly out.

So, now the mission was accomplished, what was next? She'd better figure that out pretty quickly because she was boring herself with the same question. Her life had always been about answering questions, solving difficult, complex problems, and turning chaos into order. Now Kelly was out and she could go back to her normal life. However, she was more unsettled than ever before.

❖

It was late when Kelly walked up the sidewalk to her front door. Her panic attack had driven her out of the house, in an overwhelming need to run. She knew what was happening and why, but was powerless to stop it. By the time she was at the end of the next block, it had started to subside. She'd never experienced anything like it, and she never wanted to again. It was unsettling to feel so out of herself like that. After everything she'd gone through at the camp, she'd never felt like she did an hour ago. Her hands still trembled slightly as she slid her key into the lock.

She hesitated before crossing the threshold, afraid if she went back in she'd have another attack. Panic attacks could be triggered by a situation, a thought, or for no reason at all. She couldn't live like this, in fear that something would throw her into fight-or-flight mode again. Mind over matter, her mother would say. She believed that you could think yourself sick and pray yourself to good health. Squaring her shoulders, Kelly took a deep breath and stepped inside.

As she turned off the light on the nightstand, Kelly remembered Barrett's comment about sleeping with the lights on. She settled into her bed, pulling the covers up under her chin. The sheets were soft and smelled fresh. After several minutes Kelly found the phrase "the silence was deafening" to be true. She hadn't tried to fall asleep in complete silence since before she left for Columbia. The jungle was always alive, even more so at night. During the day the monkeys' screams and chatter were her constant companion. At night, however, other creatures prowled unseen in the dark. On more than one night, growling and rustling leaves had kept her awake.

The numbers on the clock turned over to two thirty-three. What was Barrett doing? What a stupid question, she thought. Of course she'd be sleeping, just like she should be doing. She suspected Barrett slept naked, the image of Barrett's bare chest under her head in the hotel in Panama coming to mind. She didn't know how long she'd been in Barrett's arms, but she hadn't been in any hurry to move. Barrett was warm, the even rise and fall of her breasts drawing her attention. Kelly wondered if they were as soft as they looked. She remembered how Barrett's nipple had hardened when her breath accidently blew over the peak. Was that all it took?

Her nipples were sensitive too. At least they used to be. Hesitantly she cupped her breasts. Since she'd lost so much weight they were much smaller, easily filling her hands. Her thumbs grazed her nipples and nothing happened. She felt nothing. No familiar tingling between her legs, no tightening of her groin, no tension starting to build. "Fuck," she said, dropping her hands onto the bed. What was she doing? Her first night home and she was…what? What was she doing? Seeing if she could still feel anything? If she could make herself…? Did Barrett…?

Why was she thinking about Barrett this way? She wasn't a lesbian. She'd never been attracted to women. She wasn't afraid to shower in the gym and didn't think every lesbian wanted to hit on her. Too bad she couldn't say the same for the men she met.

What was it like making love to a woman? It would have to be pretty awesome, if that's what turned you on. Everyone was different, but a woman knew a woman's body. What felt good, how much, how hard, and for how long. What was Barrett like as a lover? Was she a romantic? Did she get straight to the point or leisurely enjoy the experience? Was she one-and-done or a multiple girl? Did she go first? On top? She didn't have any direct experience but could imagine what lesbians did under the sheets. The tools were different but the fundamentals were basically the same.

A flush of warmth coursed through her body, settling in the pit of her stomach. She took a deep breath and fanned herself with her hands to cool off. When she did, her T-shirt moved over her nipples.

They were hard, the familiar feeling faint. It was too much. She couldn't deal with this right now.

She couldn't even begin to think about sex. Why was she even wasting time on such thoughts? She'd been beaten, starved, isolated, and brutalized. She was overwhelmed with the events of the past two weeks. She was completely out of her life. She was here but felt like an observer in her own life. In Maslow's hierarchy of needs she was definitely at the bottom. She needed food, water, safety, security, shelter, and freedom from fear. Was Barrett her safety, security and freedom from fear? Was she the chicken or the egg? Did Barrett give her what she needed? She was certainly responsible for putting her in the position to get it.

"Ugh," she said out loud. "I can't deal with this." God, that was a phrase she'd used dozens of times in the last few days. She knew she had to, but when would she be ready? Would she ever be ready to deal with anything?

CHAPTER EIGHTEEN

K elly held true to her word the next day and negotiated her own deal for a car. Barrett tried on several occasions to help, but Kelly had insisted. She did, however, let her buy lunch.

Kelly gave her directions, and in fifteen minutes they were looking for a parking space near a quaint little walking mall.

"There's this fabulous little sandwich shop that makes their own bread," Kelly said, getting out of the car. She pointed to the sidewalk across the street. "They have this honey-grain bread that's delicious. Ariel and I would come here on Saturday if I wasn't working, have lunch and sit and watch people for hours. We'd drink coffee and find a solution for world peace or plot how to find a date for that night."

"Must have been for her. I can't imagine you had any difficulty getting a date for any reason," Barrett said as they started walking toward the mall, Kelly on her left.

"Most of the time it was for her. But not because of the reason you said. I didn't date much, but if you asked Ariel she'd say I didn't date at all."

"Why would she say that?" Barrett asked, stepping to her right and off the sidewalk to allow a woman with a walker to pass between them. Even though there was plenty of room on the sidewalk for the woman and Kelly, Kelly quickly moved so that Barrett was between her and the woman. She didn't answer until the woman passed, and even then she looked over her shoulder at her.

"I worked a lot, volunteered, and worked on my house. I preferred to stay home alone than try to make stupid small talk with some guy who was boring as hell. I'd rather do myself than do that."

Barrett stumbled and caught herself before she made a complete fool of herself. Did Kelly say what she thought she had? Did she mean it the way it came out?

"You okay?" Kelly asked, as she grabbed Barrett's arm.

Not in a million years. "Yeah, just not watching where I'm going." Lie number two.

An approaching car slowed and Kelly froze. Barrett moved Kelly to her left so her body was between Kelly and the car. She put her arm around Kelly's shoulders. "It's okay. They're just turning."

They started walking again and Kelly was silent. Barrett knew Kelly's reaction was normal, but it still hurt her nonetheless. She dropped her arm from Kelly's shoulder and wrapped it through her elbow instead.

"I think you mentioned once that you'd been married." Lie number three. Kelly had never mentioned it, but Barrett was trying to get her mind off her fear of the street.

"Yes, a long time ago."

"What happened?" When Aaron had told Barrett about Kelly's failed marriage right after Barrett had been rescued, he hadn't provided any details. She was curious and wanted a distraction for Kelly.

"I don't know. It just wasn't working. I think I got married because it was the thing to do. You know, go to school, grow up, get married, live happily ever after. I even had a white picket fence."

Barrett saw Kelly start to relax and even smile.

"Max was good to me, but after a few months I started to realize he wasn't for me. I spent the next few months really trying to make it work, but we finally decided to call it quits. He and I are still close. Do you think that's weird?" she asked, looking at Barrett seriously.

"I suppose it depends on why you got divorced and how it all ended between you. But what do I know? I do know, however, that you can never have too many friends." She didn't, but it sounded like the right thing to say.

"I suppose." Kelly didn't sound like she was sure herself. "Ariel thinks it's just weird, like I still have a torch for him."

"Do you?" Barrett asked, even though in the pit of her stomach she didn't want to know the answer.

"No, not in the slightest. We make better friends than we did lovers."

Barrett definitely didn't want to even think about Kelly making love, even if it was with her husband. "He wasn't at your homecoming."

"He has better sense than that," Kelly answered, real affection in her voice.

"I think I like him already." Little lie number four.

"Oh, no." Kelly stopped abruptly.

"What?" Barrett asked, looking around to see if she could locate the source of the frown that had replaced Kelly's smile. Nothing looked amiss, but then again, how would she know? She'd never been here in her life.

"It's gone." Kelly sounded heartbroken.

"What's gone?"

"The restaurant I was taking you to." Her shoulders slumped. "I guess a lot of things changed while I wasn't here."

Barrett didn't know what to do. And she had absolutely no idea what to say, but she had to say something. "Maybe they moved." God, that sounded lame.

"Maybe," Kelly replied, but not too confidently.

"We can go in and ask." Barrett had to make this right for Kelly. "They may know where they went." She still didn't know which store was the one in question. Kelly would have to lead.

The manager of the new deli had no idea if or where the other shop was now, and it wasn't listed in any app on her phone.

"Forget it," Kelly said, obviously trying not to show her disappointment. "I know a dozen other places we can go to. That is if they're still here," she added. "Come on." She took Barrett's hand and pulled her across the street.

"So what do you think about my foray into married life?" Kelly asked, after the waiter took their order. They'd ended up in a diner not far from their original destination.

"That's not what I dreamed about when I was a little girl."
Kelly's eyes lit up, and Barrett knew she shouldn't have said that.
She wasn't sure she wanted to have this conversation.

"What do little lesbian girls dream about when they're young?"

Barrett was speechless. It was the first time Kelly had referenced
the fact that she was a lesbian. She knew, of course, but it had never
been a topic of conversation. But then again, when would it have
been?

"Well, I can't speak for all little lesbian girls," she answered,
uncomfortable. "I suppose some did, but I think for the most part
they didn't think it was even a possibility to walk down the aisle and
marry Ms. Right."

"How sad."

"Maybe. Some probably dreamt of being strong and successful."

"Like you?" Barrett had told Kelly the story of the proof-of-life
question the negotiator had asked her about pretending she was an
executive.

"Maybe," she repeated.

"Don't you and your girlfriends ever talk about that kind of
stuff, or is that just reserved for straight women?"

Barrett wasn't sure if Kelly's question was serious or teasing.
"I don't usually talk about those kinds of things," she answered
carefully. This was starting to go somewhere Barrett didn't want it
to go, but she didn't know how to stop it.

"Why not? What do lesbian girlfriends talk about? Wait a
minute," Kelly said, obviously just realizing something. "Can I even
use that term, girlfriend? That has more than one meaning. I mean
when I say girlfriend it means my girl friend, but when lesbians say
it does it mean the equivalent of boyfriend?" Kelly sat back in her
chair. "God, this is confusing."

Barrett had to laugh, some of the tension subsiding. "It can be,"
she said, nodding. "I suppose when lesbian friends get together they
talk about the same things non-lesbians do, at least to a point."

"What point?"

"Well, I suppose some lesbians worry about their hair and their
next date and if this outfit makes them look fat—"

"Hey. Isn't that stereotyping straight women?" Kelly pretended to be mad but was having a hard time keeping the smile off her face.

"I suppose. Not any different than every straight woman thinking every lesbian wants to get them naked."

"Do you want to get me naked?"

Water spewed out of Barrett's mouth and across the table, almost hitting Kelly. WTF? No, no, no!

"Well, do you?" Kelly asked after Barrett was finally able to stop choking on the water that had managed to go down the wrong pipe.

Barrett felt like a fish trying to get air. Her mouth was opening and closing, but no words could come out. Her brain had completely shut down. She looked around for an escape.

Barrett laughed. "That's a no-win question. If I say yes, then I'm a letch. If I say no, then that might be even worse. Let's just say I don't think that way. So see, I guess we both don't fit our respective stereotype."

Thankfully Barrett was spared any further conversation on this topic when the waiter served their lunch.

"You look a little tired," Kelly said a few minutes later.

She hadn't slept well last night, especially after wondering who had been in Kelly's bed. And between their pre-lunch conversation and watching Kelly's tongue dart out just before the spoon disappeared into Kelly's mouth, she was a complete basket case.

"Just a little, I guess," she answered vaguely.

"What did you do last night?"

"A little work." Lie number five was okay. No way was she going to say she sat in front of the window and thought about her. How even though Kelly was home, she was still almost completely consumed with guilt that Kelly had to deal with everything. And my God, she was pregnant too.

Dr. Hinton had spoken to her before they left Panama and cautioned Barrett again not to assume responsibility for Kelly's situation. She'd reiterated that the circumstances of her own rescue were completely out of her control. Barrett saw her lips move and heard sound, but the words had never penetrated. She wouldn't let them.

"How about you?"

"It was kind of weird. I knew I was home, but it didn't really feel like home. I did a few loads of laundry, took a shower, and went to bed. You know, normal stuff. I was in familiar surroundings, but it felt anything but normal. I felt a little disjointed, like I had one foot here and the other back there."

Kelly didn't need to define "back there." "I remember the first night back in my own bed," Barrett said. "It was the weirdest feeling sleeping in a bed again. I really had a hard time. Don't tell anyone, but I even spent a few nights on the floor." Kelly laughed, an absolutely wonderful sound.

"I won't tell if you don't," Kelly said, her smile a little brighter than the day before and the day before that. It was a small sign she was recovering. She made a zipper movement across her lips with her fingertips. "Your secret is safe with me."

Barrett suddenly wanted Kelly to know all her secrets.

Kelly didn't have to ask twice for Barrett to go shopping with her later that afternoon. She'd lost over sixty pounds during her captivity, and not only did nothing in her closet fit, but she also needed maternity clothes.

When shopping, Barrett always knew exactly what she needed and where to go, and when she found it she bought it. That is, if she was unable to buy it online or have someone else buy it for her. She'd never shopped with girlfriends as a teenager, and since she didn't have girlfriends as an adult she'd spent very little time doing it. She hated shopping for anything, had her groceries delivered, and sent Lori out for obligatory gifts.

Barrett sensed Kelly's growing tension as they approached the shopping mall. She wanted to turn around and take Kelly back to her house, where she felt safe, and never let her be afraid again.

"You sure you're up to this?" she asked carefully. She didn't want Kelly to feel embarrassed. "You've had a long day already."

"I've got to get at least a few things."

Barrett heard the trepidation in Kelly's voice. Besides, she ignored the question.

"Okay, but if you start to get too tired, just say the word and we'll go." Barrett was more than ever determined to keep a close eye on Kelly but didn't think it would be a problem. What was a problem, however, was the look they received from the sales clerk when they both stepped into the small dressing room in one of the stores. Like they were going to fuck in the dressing room of Mommie and Me.

Kelly was obviously petrified to be in the Saturday-afternoon crowds. She stayed so close to Barrett that more than once they tripped over each other, and Kelly had a death grip on her arm. Guilt tore into Barrett to see Kelly in such a state, and after only two stores she convinced Kelly to go back to her house and shop online.

Barrett was startled when Kelly dropped her fork and it rattled on her dinner plate. After carrying in her packages, Kelly had asked Barrett to stay for dinner. Her heart jumped when Kelly grabbed her stomach, her eyes wide.

"What is it? Kelly, are you okay? Is it the baby?" Barrett fired off the questions without giving Kelly a chance to answer. In her haste to get to Kelly she knocked over her chair, which clattered on the floor. She hurried over to Kelly and knelt beside her. Her pulse raced and she was scared. Kelly had been through so much; she didn't need anything else. Kelly's expression turned from shock and surprise to wonder. "Kelly?" Barrett had no idea what was going on.

"She kicked."

"What?"

"The baby. She kicked. Just now," Kelly said, watching her hands move slowly over her growing stomach. She gasped and her hands stopped moving. "Oh, my God, this is amazing."

She grabbed Barrett's hand and placed it on her stomach, pushing her palm flat against it. Barrett involuntarily jerked her hand away when she felt a fluttering under her fingers. "Was that her?" Barrett looked at her hand. She'd never felt anything so light yet firm at the same time. It scared the shit out of her, and she wasn't the one with the little creature inside her.

"Yes, it was."

"Is this the first time you've felt it?"

"Yes." Her voice was quiet, almost reverent.

Kelly raised her head, and their eyes met. Barrett had never seen such indescribable joy, awe, and wonder. Kelly's eyes sparkled and her face glowed. It was a stunning combination. She was absolutely beautiful. It took her breath away.

"Oh, there she is again." Kelly broke into a huge smile and slid Barrett's hand higher on her stomach, stopping just under her breast.

The top of Barrett's fingers lightly brushed against Kelly's breasts, and she didn't know if the experience of Kelly's baby moving or Kelly herself made her so light-headed. Both were the most intimate experiences of her life.

"There, did you feel it?" Kelly asked breathlessly.

Oh I felt it all right. She nodded instead.

"It's amazing. My baby. I'm actually having a baby. I never really thought about it before now. I know it doesn't make any sense, but it was never really real until just now. I'm going to have a baby," she repeated.

Yes. You are, and if I hadn't left you behind you wouldn't be.

"I guess I'd better start thinking about a name."

"You have some time. My admin Lori said you have to try the name out for a few months. See how it sounds. She said it has to be screamable—I think was the phrase she used. You know, how it sounds when you're calling her to dinner or when you've got your mom thing going on. She'll know she's in trouble when you pull out the big guns of the first, middle, and last name."

Kelly laughed, her breasts making contact with Barrett's fingers. Between that sensation, Kelly's smile, and the joy in her laugh, Barrett was completely fucked.

Chapter Nineteen

Saying good-bye to Kelly this time was different. Barrett wasn't leaving to come back later or even tomorrow to check up on how she was doing or if she needed anything. She was saying good-bye here at the airport. She was flying back to San Francisco—to her job, her responsibilities, her life. And it didn't include Kelly.

She'd stayed in Denver, near Kelly, for three more weeks. She'd seen improvement in Kelly and knew she was talking with Dr. Hinton every day. She was still afraid and on guard when around people, when they were in crowds, and she refused to go to a movie. Her friends visited or called, and Kelly had agreed to meet them for dinner a few times.

But Barrett had to get back to the office. Debra was calling every day, and when asking Barrett to come back didn't work, she tried threats and even a thorough dose of guilt.

"Barrett, you have got to get back here and start dealing with your own things. I understand your tie to Kelly, but you have responsibility for thousands of other people as well. Business is suffering. Clients are asking where you are and worried that Digital won't be able to continue to support them. They're no longer buying the 'she's out of town' line. Rumors are circulating about your psychological state and the financial stability of the company. Some are dropping not-so-subtle hints that if they don't see you soon, they'll take their business elsewhere."

"Debra—"

"No, Barrett. Get your shit together and get your ass back here. I expect to see you Monday morning at eight. If not, I'll go to court and take control of Digital, and don't think I won't. I don't need this job, but I will not let you ruin the lives of every employee in this company. I mean it, Barrett. Monday eight sharp." Barrett had never heard that tone in Debra's voice before.

Kelly trembled in her arms, a horn honking somewhere around them, and Barrett knew Kelly was doing her best to be strong. Anyone else looking at them would simply see the emotional reaction of two friends saying good-bye. But Barrett knew Kelly better than that. She was still scared, anxious, and too cautious. But as much as she wanted to stay by her side forever, she knew it wasn't good for her or Kelly. This would be a major turning point in Kelly's recovery.

"You're going to be okay," Barrett said into Kelly's strawberry-scented hair as they hugged. Kelly had insisted on driving her to the airport, and they were standing on the sidewalk below the departure sign for US Air.

"I'll call you tonight, after I get home," Barrett said. "You know you can call me anytime, day or night. Doesn't matter if you want to ask my opinion on paper or plastic or if you just want to gab." She was trying to turn the scene from sad to lighthearted, but when Kelly tightened her arms she knew she wouldn't succeed.

God, she wanted to stay here exactly like this forever. Well, maybe not exactly like this, in the hustle and bustle of the airport departure area, but in Kelly's life, keeping her safe and giving her everything she needed. If she was honest with herself, she'd also add staying in her arms. It was Kelly that finally pulled away.

"Okay, that's enough. You're going to miss your flight if you stay here any longer."

Kelly wasn't even trying to hide the tears cascading down her cheeks. Barrett suddenly felt sick.

Kelly's hands shook as she pulled out a tissue and wiped her cheeks. "I knew this would happen and I came prepared."

Barrett saw the effort it took for Kelly to try to smile, and if she didn't leave this very instant she never would, business and her life be damned. Then Kelly completely surprised her and kissed her on the lips.

"I can't even begin to express what you mean to me, so I won't even try. *Thank you* and *I love you* seem so inadequate, but that's all I've got. Now go before I drag you back into my new car, and we'll both regret it."

Kelly kissed her one more time, turned her around, and lightly pushed her toward the automatic doors leading into the airport. Barrett didn't look back as she heard Kelly's car start and pull away.

❖

It was later than usual when Barrett pulled into her reserved parking space. She looked at it for a moment, not having really seen it before. Parking in the space had become more of a habit than anything else, and for the first time she felt a little uneasy because of its prime location.

Why did she get to park by the front door? Did it mean she worked harder than any other employee? It clearly meant that with rank comes privilege. But today it seemed to say that the big boss gets to park up front and everyone else didn't.

Barrett took her briefcase out of the backseat and walked the short distance to the front doors. The building wasn't the most ostentatious in the complex, nor was it the most humble. It was, however, environmentally friendly, near where she lived and big enough to symbolize the importance of Global Digital.

She walked inside with several other employees who were talking to each other, overhearing snippets of conversation about the football game last night, the number of tourists on the beach this weekend, and Suzanne's wedding. Barrett had no idea about any of the three topics. She couldn't be expected to know the personal lives of every employee. At one time she did. Now that was completely impractical, Digital's employment numbers approaching three thousand.

She had no idea who'd played football yesterday, and other than the view of the beach from her back patio, she couldn't remember the last time she'd been to one. That troubled her.

Once she'd spent a lot of time, as the song said, ass in the sand, toes in the water, before she had her own private beach. She'd go to the public beach on the Pacific Highway with her lawn chair, a notebook, two pens, sunscreen, and a large thermos of coffee. That was where she'd envisioned and sketched out what Global Digital could be. Where she'd plotted the roadmap and the strategy and the timeline to get to where she was today.

Actually what she'd written on those cheap pieces of paper in her forty-nine-cent theme book was nowhere near what Global had actually achieved. How did that happen? When had her vision gone from several dozen employees where she knew everyone's name and personal events to today? When did she become a target for a fifty-two-million-dollar ransom?

"Good morning, Ms. Taylor," the receptionist said, with a tentative smile.

Barrett studied her as she walked by. Was she new? Had she been there before she left five weeks ago to get Kelly? Had she been there a year? Five years? Barrett was ashamed that she didn't know.

More people were waiting in the elevator lobby, and they too chatted about their weekend with friends and family. One even talked about the volunteer day that Global had sponsored on Saturday. From what she could gather, employees had selected four different elementary schools, and with donations from the local hardware store and the generous donation of playground equipment from Global Digital, they'd built new playgrounds that hundreds of children would enjoy, beginning this morning.

"Ms. Taylor?" said one of the young men brave enough to speak with her. "I'd like to thank you for sponsoring the Build a Playground project this weekend. Without the generosity of Global we wouldn't have been able to make it happen."

Barrett literally didn't know what to say. Employees rarely spoke to her, and certainly not like this. When did she become so unapproachable? However, what came out of her mouth was her much-practiced, smooth corporate-speak. "Global has an obligation to our community to give back. This was just one of the many things we do," she said, without even thinking, the words tumbling out of her mouth on autopilot. This time, however, they sounded shallow.

"Well, thank you again," the young man said as he looked her directly in the eye.

He triggered something in Barrett and she held out her hand. "And you are?"

"Jonathon Trace," the man said a little hesitantly but didn't break eye contact.

"Well, Jonathon, thank *you* for spending your free time helping those kids. Have a good day." Barrett released his hand as the elevator doors opened on the young man's floor.

"Yes, ma'am. You too."

The doors closed behind him, and the remaining employees didn't look at her but were all looking at her. Barrett couldn't remember feeling so uncomfortable and under a microscope.

One by one the employees got off on their floors until she was riding the remaining two floors to the executive suites. The door slid open and Barrett saw, with absolute clarity, the way the vestibule in front of her was furnished. In stark contrast to the other floors, which featured tile, Sheetrock, and pale colors, here she saw plush carpet, mahogany-paneled walls, and subdued lighting.

Frowning, she walked down the corridor to the suite of offices where she, Debra, and her executive team were located and approached the receptionist's desk. She knew this woman's name and how long she'd been here, but little else. Contrary to the receptionist on the first floor, this one looked her directly in the eye as she spoke.

"Good morning, Ms. Taylor. Welcome back."

"Thank you, Caroline," she said to the woman, continuing through the double doors that the woman had unlocked with a remote under the desk.

A chorus of "good morning" from the other administrative assistants of her staff greeted her as she passed, and she acknowledged them similarly to her comment to Caroline a few moments ago.

Sharon, who sat at the workstation next to Lori's, jumped up quickly, hurrying over to the open space.

"Good morning, Ms. Taylor. Lori just went to the coffee room. Can I get you anything?"

"No, thank you, Sharon. I'm fine. Lori can come in whenever she's ready and bombard me with the stack of papers I know she has stacked up."

Barrett opened the largest door in the area with a soft metallic click. She stopped just inside and closed the door behind her. Her office was large, measuring twenty-seven feet by twenty-three. She remembered when her architect had showed her the plans for her office, and she remembered the exact measurements. Obviously it had been important to her then.

Her large, custom-made desk faced the door, a bank of windows spanning the entire length of the room behind it. On the credenza behind the desk were numerous awards from various civic groups to which Global either donated or sponsored their cause. The wood was polished to a high shine, and with the reflection of the early morning sun, not a speck of dust was visible.

To her right sat a leather loveseat, two antique Elizabethan side chairs, and a coffee table made by the same popular craftsman that had made her desk. Across the room from the casual seating area was a conference table with seating for six and leather coasters with the Global Digital insignia stacked neatly in the center. Heaven forbid that anyone might mar the surface of the table with their coffee-cup ring or the sweat from their glass.

The walls were adorned with framed pictures, where either she or Global was featured on the cover. Everything except the signed Georgia O'Keeffe she had mortgaged her first house to buy, everything was all about her. Words like *ego*, *narcissistic*, and *self-absorbed* came to mind. She felt sick. The door opened behind her, bumping her in the back. She took a few steps forward and turned around.

"Oh, sorry, Barrett. I didn't know you were standing there. Is everything okay?" Concern hardened Lori's soft features.

Lori had been her assistant since the day she could afford one, and that was years after she needed one. Barrett knew more about Lori than any other employee she'd encountered this morning, and that was only because Lori insisted on sharing her life with her. Barrett rarely asked, but that didn't stop Lori.

"Yes, I'm fine." Barrett chose not to answer all her questions. Lori was sharp and picked up on her reluctance immediately but knew better than to ask again.

"Sharon said you were here. I brought you some coffee,"

"Thanks," Barrett said automatically. Striding across the office, she set her briefcase on her desk.

"How was your trip? Get everything accomplished? Get any new deals? Make a boatload of money?" Lori asked jokingly.

Barrett studied her a moment, deciding which approach to take. She could say the customary yes, had a good trip, made good contacts, and sold a few things, or she could share her experience with Lori. Barrett never talked about personal things in the office. Business was business and pleasure was pleasure, and the two rarely met. How would Lori react if she did?

What if she said, *Actually it was a very stressful five weeks. I hired the same mercenaries that rescued me to go back into the jungle and rescue the other captives, one of which was a woman who, because I didn't get it done in time, came back pregnant. I paid off the woman's house so it didn't go into foreclosure and tried to buy her a car. She refused but did allow me to buy her some new clothes, some of which were maternity, due to what happened to her in captivity after I left, and let me do some other things in my miniscule, pathetic attempt to make up for leaving her. No, I didn't make any money, no, I didn't shake any hands, but I did have by far the most productive and insightful five weeks of my life.*

But if she said all that she'd be forced to call 911 because Lori would drop dead right in front of her seventeen-thousand-dollar desk. Of course all these thoughts came to her in a nanosecond, along with the decision that had driven her all of her life.

"It was good. What do you have for me," Barrett said instead, shifting into boss mode and effectively shutting down any further conversation. This time, however, Barrett felt the burning need to say more. But she didn't, and that both comforted and disturbed her.

❖

It was well past nine when Barrett walked out of the building. Everyone in executive row had gone. They all had lives they were eager to get home to. Only Lori and Debra had commented that Barrett had replaced the expensive artwork, magazine covers, and awards that had covered her office walls with framed prints. She was alone in the elevator, which didn't stop on any of the seventeen floors below hers. The unknown receptionist in the lobby had been replaced with an equally generic security guard, who barely looked up as she passed.

She exited the building into the cool summer night. The halogen lights in the parking lot provided enough light for her to be safe and secure, yet were designed to be energy efficient, aka cost-effective. Her car was the only one left in the parking lot. When looking at this same scene she used to think, Yeah, I'm the big boss. I'm here later than any of you. I work harder than any of you. I deserve that parking space, the furnishings on my floor, and the view over my shoulder. Now all these things made her feel lonely and shallow.

The chirp of the security alarm on her car sounded as expensive as it was. Other vehicles emitted a honk, a series of chirps, or a variety of other obnoxious sounds to indicate that their car was secure from riff-raff, as her Uncle Al used to call it. Riff-raff—the folks that would rather steal than work.

She opened the car door, the subdued overhead lighting reflecting the rich, smooth leather seats and wood-grained interior. She buckled her seat belt and a soft European voice greeted her. "Good evening, Barrett. What is your destination?"

The salesman at the dealership had been very eager to show her the personalized navigation system. The owner could program the greeting and simply state a series of instructions or choices that would, in turn, activate the GPS so she wouldn't end up somewhere else. Barrett's company had designed the interactive system that knew if it was morning, afternoon, or evening, depending on the time on the quartz digital clock on the dash. She'd waited for him to finish his pitch before asking to speak to his manager.

She asked the manager to tell her what he knew about the system, and after he finished, she asked to speak to his manager. Finally she got to the manager of the dealership and informed him of her experience. She then went on to tell all of them exactly what her system did and did not do and that her VP of product development would be in the owner's office first thing Monday morning to ensure that their customers would not be misled in the future. She made a mental note to send some employees as secret shoppers to the other BMW dealerships to determine if similar misinformation was being communicated. She didn't tolerate incompetence when it came to a product with her company's name on it.

Barrett put the car in drive, ignoring the question. She must have driven home on autopilot because she didn't remember any of it. Usually she was on the phone with overseas clients or suppliers or simply dictating a reminder note, memo, or letter for Lori to pick up in the morning. Often times she wondered, if she needed to react to avoid an accident, could she?

Stepping through the door that led into the house from the garage, Barrett keyed in the security code on the alarm-system keypad. The beeping sound stopped, and the only other sound was the heels of her loafers clicking on the tile floor.

The smell of glass cleaner and furniture polish wasn't as strong today as it was yesterday when she'd arrived home from the airport. She'd called her housekeeper a few days before she left Denver, and the woman had made a special trip to, what she called it, freshen up the house.

She rummaged in the refrigerator for something palatable but wasn't really hungry. She hadn't eaten any breakfast and had just moved the food around on her plate during lunch with a client. She needed to eat something but couldn't bring herself to do anything other than open a bottle of beer. She kicked off her shoes and sat down on the couch, lifting her feet to the coffee table in front of her. She leaned her head back and closed her eyes, suddenly very tired.

Sleep had eluded her last night and the night before, her last night in Denver. She and Kelly had eaten dinner at a small Italian restaurant not far from Kelly's house. They'd shared a bottle of alcohol-free wine, three breadsticks, and a pizza. They were both subdued, the conversation was strained, and they'd passed on dessert and gone to bed early.

Somehow Barrett had made it through today. She'd felt completely disconnected from what was going on and attributed it to the fact that she rarely took time off, and never this long. She couldn't focus or keep her attention on the topic of conversation. Several times she'd asked for something to be repeated, and once she saw two employees exchange glances. The phrase "she's just not herself" had certainly been true today. She almost felt like she didn't belong anymore.

❖

The ringing of the phone jolted Barrett awake. Calls in the middle of the night were never good news.

"Hello," she mumbled, not even bothering to sound awake.

"Oh, I woke you. I'm sorry."

Kelly's voice on the other end of the line was apologetic. "I never should have called. I don't know what I was thinking. Go back to sleep."

Barrett sat up. "No, no, Kelly. It's not a problem." She glanced at the clock. It was 2:42. She thought she'd finally fallen asleep sometime after midnight. "What's up?"

"Uh…"

"Couldn't sleep." Barrett suspected what Kelly wanted to say but couldn't.

"Yeah."

"I get it." She plumped the pillow behind her after turning on the light beside the bed. "Remember back in the hospital you asked me what made me change my mind and talk to Dr. Hinton? Remember what I said?"

"Um…"

Barrett imagined Kelly's face scrunching, as was her habit when she was thinking. "I said nightmares, flashbacks, and that I slept with the light on. It took awhile before I could sleep through the night," which was a minor lie. She had yet to sleep through the night, but Kelly didn't need to know that. "I didn't expect to have that problem. I thought that now that I was home and safe, I'd sleep like a baby, as the saying goes. I did fall asleep, but I woke up so many times with dreams that after a while I was afraid to go to sleep. Afraid that if I went to sleep I'd have nightmares and wake up kicking and screaming in the dark."

"What did you do? I mean what made it—"

"Time." Kelly was having a difficult time asking questions, so Barrett volunteered the information instead. "Also talking to Dr. Hinton, sleeping pills, and complete exhaustion. Not necessarily in that order. But it does get better."

"So why is all this happening now? I mean when I was in the jungle I didn't have any trouble sleeping. If anything, I should have, never knowing what was going to happen one minute to the next."

"Because you're safe here," Barrett replied softly, practically mimicking Dr. Hinton when she'd asked the same question. "You're safe, and you know it, but your subconscious just hasn't quite got there yet."

"I suppose so,"

"What did Dr. Hinton say?"

"Same thing you did."

"Well, that's good," Barrett said, attempting to ease some of the tension she could feel even over the phone line. "So what did you do today?"

"I know what you're doing."

"Oh my God," Barrett said with fake surprise. "Do you have a camera in my bedroom? I'd better put some clothes on."

"You're trying to change the subject so I won't think about it."

"No, I'm changing the subject because I want to know what you did today." Since Barrett had returned home, they'd talked every day. Barrett often called Kelly as she drove home from work, and at times their conversation continued well into the evening. They talked about everything and nothing at all. They laughed at each other's childhood antics and cringed at each "first-time" story.

"Some friends came by." Kelly's voice was flat.

"And how was it?"

"It was a little…tense. They skirted the issues and pretended it hadn't happened."

"That's to be expected. You know it's either going to be that way or just the opposite, where they want to know every gory detail. They obviously care about you, Kelly. They just don't want to say anything to upset you."

"Well, they need to say something. I'm pregnant. I'm so god damn skinny it looks like I have a basketball under my shirt. It's kind of hard to ignore." Kelly was laughing.

"And how is baby Ryan?"

"She doesn't want to sleep at night either."

"She's getting used to being up in the middle of the night."

"I've always heard that you're supposed to get as much sleep as possible before you have a baby because you don't get any after."

"I've heard that too."

"Well, somebody needs to tell her that, because she didn't get the memo."

It was Barrett's turn to laugh. "She's the new generation, Kelly. They don't do memos. They text, do Instagram, Snap Chat, Kik, and Twitter, and as a last resort, Facebook."

"So I should, what, put my phone on my stomach?"

"That's an idea." Barrett heard muffling and scratching sounds on the phone before Kelly spoke again.

"Okay, go ahead."

Kelly had put her on speaker. "What are you doing?" she asked.

"I have the phone on my stomach. Go ahead. Talk to her, because she sure as hell isn't listening to me."

Barrett laughed, enjoying Kelly's sardonic sense of humor. "Again, she's preparing you for motherhood. She's a girl. She'll never listen to you."

"Then if she's not going to listen to me she needs to listen to Aunt Barrett."

Barrett's pulse skipped several beats. Aunt Barrett?

"Just talk to her."

"Um, hey, baby girl Ryan. This is your Aunt Barrett. I understand that…you're…um…kicking around in there. You practicing for the soccer team? Maybe football? You know by the time you're old enough they may be allowing women to play football. I can see the headlines now. Baby girl Ryan, first female quarterback in the NFL, leads her team to a Super Bowl victory. And what does she say directly into the camera after the game-winning touchdown? 'I'm taking my wonderful mom to Disneyland.'"

Kelly laughed, and Barrett's initial unease shifted to the point that she began enjoying herself. She felt like a complete idiot, but grown men, bigger and tougher than her, did the required baby talk. She was just doing it a little early.

"What if she wants to be a figure skater?" Kelly asked, laughter clearly in her voice.

"Then she'll say it on the gold-medal stand at the 2030 Olympics, which will probably be held someplace no one has ever heard of."

"And what if she wants to follow in your footsteps?"

That was something Barrett definitely didn't expect. Follow in her footsteps? She knew she was tired, but did the honorary Aunt Barrett and the footsteps comment mean that Kelly wanted her to be a part of her baby's life? Holy crap. She didn't have any idea what to do with kids. She'd never really been around them.

"Barrett? Did you fall asleep on me?"

"I'm still here," Barrett said over the butterflies in her stomach. "You know if she's going to follow in my footsteps and be a wildly successful business executive, you need to be sure to give her an appropriate name."

"Really?"

"Yes, really. I can't tell you how many women I've met whose name completely contradicts their position or the position they're trying to get."

"Give me an example."

"Well, I don't remember when, but I met this woman, the head of a major organization, who made a jillion dollars a year, had thousands of people working for her, and her name was Bambi Anderson. Can you imagine that on a gold-embossed business card? Can you image what it looks like in a room full of shareholders or the media when her name is flashed across a fifty-foot screen? All you see is Bambi, and like it or not, we all have an idea of what a Bambi is. Now I don't mean to be judgmental, but come on."

"Good point, Kelly replied, her laughter tickling Barrett's ear. "So what do you suggest?"

Barrett hesitated a minute. "I don't know. I haven't thought about it. It's your baby."

"Yeah, but you have a different perspective."

"Okay, uh, how about Leigh or Dylan? Maybe something like Elliott or Lane. You know, powerful and strong, or even something like—"

Kelly jumped in. "Barrett Elizabeth Taylor."

Barrett didn't know what to say. How had Kelly learned her middle name? She never disclosed it. She thought her name was powerful and strong? She wouldn't seriously name her baby after her, would she? Would she? "My mother loved Elizabeth Taylor. Besides, I think that name's already taken," she said shakily.

"Good point," Kelly replied.

"And you need to watch out for initials too. You don't want to name her Ann Suzanne Stevens or Barbara Francis Davis."

Kelly laughed and Barrett joined in, feeling a little less rattled. "You have to look ahead and at the practical side of things."

They chatted for the next ten minutes or so, sharing stories and laughing at each other's sense of humor until Kelly asked, "What are you doing?"

"Getting dressed."

"At this hour?"

"Unless you want me going to the airport in my jammies, it would be a good idea."

"Where are you going?"

"Colorado," Barrett answered vaguely.

"Where in Colorado?"

Barrett knew she was busted. "Denver."

"Barrett."

"Kelly."

"Barrett Elizabeth, do not come here."

"See what I mean, about the name thing? You sound a lot more scary than if you'd said Bambi Jane." Barrett tried to steer the conversation in the right direction, but Kelly wouldn't let her.

"I'm fine. I'm just having a rough night. There's no need for you to come here."

"Maybe I want to," Barrett replied, her voice quiet and a bit seductive, if she heard herself correctly.

"I don't need you here."

"Liar." There was silence on the line. "I can come," Barrett said quietly, grimacing as if she were expecting to be hit over the head. As if someone could knock some sense into her.

"I appreciate that, but I don't need you to."

"Maybe I need to."

"I need to get through this. Having you come to my rescue every time doesn't do me or you any good."

"I'm just trying to help."

"Just the fact that for the past twenty minutes you've talked to me when you could have been sleeping tells me…I know you care, Barrett. I know you want to help. But I'm fine, really. Talking with you helped me put things into perspective."

"All right then," Barrett said after a long pause. "What are you planning to do tomorrow? Or should I say today?"

"I'm going to hang up, pull the covers up to my chin, and go back to sleep. Something you need to do as well. I don't know what I'm going to do the rest of the day. I'll play it by ear. What about you?"

"Well, as much as I'd like nothing better to do than play it by ear, I have a boatload of work on my desk. And I didn't say that to make you feel bad about waking me up," she added quickly. "Seriously, Kelly, you can call me anytime. I'll always answer. I'll always have time for you."

"Good night, Barrett," Kelly said just before she pushed the end button on the face of her phone. She knew Barrett would never hang up so she did.

Why did she feel like she'd severed more than just the telephone connection? She'd been completely panicked, and the instant she heard Barrett's voice coming through the phone she began to calm down. Barrett had a way of talking to her. It didn't matter what she said. It was the sound of her voice, the cadence of the words, the mere fact that she was talking to her. Barrett understood what she was going through and knew when to use her sense of humor to break the tension without embarrassing her.

Once fiercely independent and emotionally strong, she was now suspicious of everything and everyone around her. The woman who returned from the jungle wasn't the woman who entered it. Once outgoing and trusting, she was now serious and cautious. Her goals in life used to be to provide care to the unfortunate, but now it was all she could do to get through every day.

Kelly got up, walked to the kitchen, and got a bottle of water from the fridge. On her way back, she started to turn off the lights that she'd turned on earlier but stopped. She thought about what Barrett had said about sleeping with the lights on and decided to give it a try. Who knew? Maybe that would work. Barrett said she was no longer afraid of the dark. That day couldn't come soon enough for her.

She got back into bed, pulled the covers up, and closed her eyes. The sense of dread and panic earlier when she woke started in the pit of her chest and threatened to consume her again. "Stop it," she said out loud. Instead of counting sheep to fall asleep, she thought of Barrett.

She thought of how wonderful she looked waiting for her at the airport, how ragged she looked after several days at the hospital, how she looked exhausted from being by her side the entire time. How she looked standing in the doorway of her hotel room and when she held her in her arms after her first nightmare. The curve of her breast was inches from her mouth, her nipple within touching distance.

Kelly sat up and tossed off the covers, suddenly hot. "What in the hell am I thinking?" she asked, fanning herself. *Jesus, Kelly, get a grip. There was nothing sexual about our physical proximity to each other so why am I thinking there was? Barrett was always...had never...had never even tried...*She stumbled to find the right words. She lay back down and stared at the ceiling.

"God. I'm even more messed up than I thought I was."

CHAPTER TWENTY

"The hospital called and asked me to come in to talk about my job."

"And how did that go?" Dr. Hinton asked, her voice noncommittal yet encouraging. Kelly had been seeing her twice a week through Skype since she came home and felt ready to decrease the frequency of their sessions. This was the first time she'd talked with her in over a week.

"It was good actually. They said that my failure to return to work," Kelly emphasized the phrase with air quotes, "wasn't my fault and because of that they'd reinstate me when I was ready to come back."

"And how do you feel about that?"

"Relieved."

"But..."

"But I don't know if I can."

"How so?"

"I don't know how to explain it."

"Try. You don't have to come up with the perfect words. Just say what you think, what's on your mind. We'll figure out the right phrasing."

"It sounds kind of silly." Dr. Hinton looked at her with an expression Kelly had come to know quite well: that nothing, no feeling was silly, no comment stupid if it was hers.

"Sorry," she said, "wrong choice of words. I don't want to be the subject of everybody's comments, whispers, and pointing. I don't want people to look at me and say that's the nurse that was kidnapped and held in the jungle for two years and came out with a baby. I don't want to have to deal with their looks of pity and condemnation."

"Why do you use the word condemnation?"

"Because how stupid of me was it to go to a place where I put my life in danger? I mean I could have gone and helped in any inner-city clinic."

"And wouldn't your life be in danger there?" Dr. Hinton asked.

"Not nearly as much as where I went."

"And what about the level of care you provide in the inner city versus what you did in Columbia?"

"Drastically different."

"And do you think those people you're concerned with having that viewpoint of you and your actions…do any of those people participate or volunteer for your kind of medical mission?"

"Probably not."

"Do they have any idea what your patients need and what you give them that no one else will?"

"No." Kelly was starting to understand where Dr. Hinton was going with this and told her so. "That these people…that they haven't walked a mile in my shoes, so who are they to judge."

"Actually, I was thinking more along the lines that they haven't even put their foot in your shoes."

"You're right." She liked Dr. Hinton's view.

"Okay. We can come back to that. "Why else do you think you're not ready?"

"My entire perspective of the world has changed. I'm a very different person than I was before."

"In what way?"

They'd talked about this particular viewpoint often during their discussions, and each time Kelly came away with more clarity.

"I see the world differently. What I think is important is different. I'm far less tolerant of crap and bullshit that's really not a big deal. I'm afraid that attitude will come across to my patients."

"It might. But then again, do you think that gives you a different perspective on their care. What they're going through? What their families are going through?"

"I suppose."

"You don't sound very sure."

"I'm not. I just don't know if it would translate into my actions."

"And if it did?"

"It would make me a better nurse. I'd be more caring and compassionate toward everyone."

"And if it didn't?"

"It would make me a terrible nurse, because I wouldn't care. I might treat someone coming in to the ER because they did something stupid, disregarded some safety or just common-sense thing differently than if they'd come in as a victim."

"Possibly," Dr. Hinton said. "And if you turned out to be that type of nurse, the nurse you don't want to be, what would you do?"

"I'd quit. I'd find something else."

"But if you didn't?"

"Then I'd continue to do what I love."

"The choice is yours, Kelly. We've always talked about that. You've said before that it's important to you that you regain control of your life. If you assume you'll be a bad nurse and don't do anything to either prove it or disprove it, is that taking control?"

"No." It was abdicating control.

"So you're not sure if you want to return to work because of people who have no reference point to your life and because you're afraid you might have lost your compassion. What else?"

"I'll have a child now, or I will soon. I think it's important that I bond with her."

"Are you afraid you won't?" She held her hand up to stop Kelly from answering. "Before you answer that, don't lie to yourself."

"Yes, I am. I'm afraid that every time I look at her I'll see The Colonel, the brutality, the pain."

"That's understandable. Look at yourself, right now this instant. Look at your hands." Even though their appointment was through Skype, their cameras were placed so they could see each other's full body.

Kelly glanced down and saw that her hands were on her stomach, almost forming a protective cocoon around her baby.

"That's right," Dr Hinton said. "You're protecting your baby right now. If you didn't want this child, if you didn't love this child you wouldn't be doing that. You refer to her as if she was a person, not as an 'it' when you talk about her. So we'll come back to that too. Have you heard from Barrett?"

Just the mere mention of her name made Kelly's pulse spike. "No, I haven't." They'd agreed not to talk everyday, at Kelly's request.

"At the risk of sounding like a shrink, how does that make you feel?"

Kelly chuckled. Dr. Hinton always laid it out on the table. She called it what it was, and Kelly didn't have to think about the underlying meaning in her words or her questions.

"I think it sucks. I miss her. I miss talking to her. I miss her sense of humor, her pragmatism. The way she approaches a problem and diagrams a solution. The way she thinks. I miss knowing what's going on in her life, what she's done every day."

Her answers didn't seem to surprise Dr. Hinton. Actually, she thought she detected a slight nod and she said, "And…"

"And I miss talking to her about what I did that day. How I was able to go to the grocery store and only freak out three times instead of five. How *almost* every light in the house is on when I go to bed and not *every* one. How I had a terrible craving for chocolate-chip ice cream after dark, and I was actually able to get up and go to the Quick Mart and get some." Kelly remembered the incident clearly and was proud of herself for what she'd accomplished. Prior to that she wouldn't go anywhere after the sun went down.

"And why do you want to share it with her?"

"Because she understands. She knows what it's like. She knows that minor accomplishments that other people would think are ridiculous are major steps in my recovery. She doesn't judge me or make me feel ridiculous because I was finally able to make eye contact with a complete stranger. Because I just want to," she added, almost wistfully.

"How about your friends? What's been happening with them since we spoke last?"

"About the same. One of them even went so far as to ask me if it was too late to have an abortion. My God, I'm seven months pregnant. What a stupid question. This baby is real. She moves and reacts to what I react to. She lets me know what she likes and what she doesn't. She lets me know when she's ready to get up and when she's not ready to go to sleep. She can't see past the fact that this child was conceived in rape, in a horrible, horrible way. I know she cares for me and wants the best for me, but what she thinks is best for me isn't. And I can't get her to understand that."

"So what did you do?"

"I finally had to tell her to just shut up about it. I didn't want to hear any comments or suggestions, and to just shut up."

"And what did she say to that?"

"Exactly what I expected. She got angry. Something along the lines of so you want me to just pretend this baby doesn't exist? I said no, that's not what I want you to do. This baby exists. This is my daughter and we're a package deal. If you can't accept her and look at her and be happy for me and treat her like any other child you see or any child I may have conceived in the conventional sense of the word, then I don't want you in my life. And I certainly don't want you in my daughter's life."

Dr. Hinton was smiling and nodding by the time Kelly finished describing her conversation with one of her now ex-friends. She realized how adamant, strong, and forceful she was in her conversations with her friend. She'd meant every word.

"So think about that, Kelly. This was a friend of yours? Someone you were pretty close to?"

"Yes. We've known each other since nursing school."

"And I'm going to paraphrase here, so basically you told her to deal with it or get the fuck out of your life."

Kelly laughed a deep, full laugh.

"Am I right, or did I misinterpret what you said?"

"No, Dr. Hinton. You're spot on."

"And what you said to her—what's her name by the way?"

"Suzanne."

"So what you said to Suzanne, is that any different than what you'd say to the people back at work that are thinking the same thing? Other than the fact that you don't know what they're thinking and therefore you can't tell them."

"I guess it's really not any different."

The expression on Dr. Hinton's face clearly said, *BINGO, you got it*. Kelly nodded. "I get it."

Dr. Hinton was an excellent therapist in that she didn't "tell" Kelly things. She helped her draw her own conclusions.

"Let's circle back around to Barrett. You want her to share her life with you, and again I'm paraphrasing here. You want her to share her life with you, and you want to share your life with her."

"Yes."

"You know we've talked a bit about your sense of obligation to Barrett because she saved your life. And because she saved your life you feel the need to accept what she offers you." She waited for Kelly to nod. "Even though in our last few discussions we came to the conclusion that Barrett is probably dealing with her own set of guilt and obligation because she feels she left you behind."

"Is that what she said to you?"

"I haven't spoken to Barrett since you came home."

That was Dr. Hinton's way of telling Kelly she wasn't going to tell her even if she had seen Barrett.

"So tie those threads together for me. The fact that you feel obligated to accept what she offers and you want to be part of her life and you want to share your life with her. How do those fit together?"

Kelly sat back and thought for several minutes, the silence between them not uncomfortable. "I don't think there is one."

Dr. Hinton waved her hand as if to say, *More…*

"If I felt obligated to accept her actions I wouldn't want to share my life with her. I wouldn't want to tell her what I've been able to do."

"And why is that?"

"Because that would only make her feel guiltier. She'd continue to think she was responsible for me not being able to go to the grocery store, or the bank, or anywhere where there was more than one person without looking over my shoulder. That would only make her feel guiltier and increase her actions to try to assuage the guilt." Kelly sat back against the couch and rubbed her face with both hands. "God, what a fucking vicious circle," she concluded.

"Yes, it can be. Emotions like guilt and obligation and responsibility can drive us into behaviors that may or may not be good for us. May or may not be good for the person with whom you feel you need to make amends to. The more you do it, the guiltier you feel because you can never make up for what you think you did wrong. There's never enough. And until you realize that and forgive yourself…"

"Then I'll continue the behavior," Kelly said. "So how do I get Barrett to forgive herself?"

"You don't. You can't. You can't do anything. Whatever you'd try would be just as ineffective as what she's trying to do. They don't work. On the contrary, they feed on each other."

"So then what do I do?"

"I don't think you can do anything other than graciously accept. It's a fine line between gushing over what's been given to you and ignoring it, acting like it's not a big deal."

"And only I can figure that out."

"I'm afraid so."

❖

"I don't care."

"What do you mean you don't care?"

"Listen to me, Debra. Read my lips if you have to. I said I don't care." They were in her office and had been arguing for the last ten minutes, and Barrett wasn't sure she even knew what the subject was anymore.

Barrett was determined to appear like she'd readjusted and was getting back into the swing of her life. On the inside, however, she was anxious and unsettled. She hadn't spoken to Kelly in four days and was desperate to hear her voice.

In the past several weeks since Kelly had called in the middle of the night, she'd gone from bad to worse. She'd snapped at everyone, didn't return calls, and had cancelled several meetings with prospective clients.

"What's going on with you, Barrett?" Debra's voice was calmer than it had been a moment ago. "And please don't tell me nothing. I know you better than that. Actually, I probably know you better than you know yourself."

"There's nothing to talk about. I mean it," she added when Debra looked at her skeptically. She didn't want to admit to herself that she just flat-out missed Kelly. She certainly wasn't going to admit it to anyone else.

What was Kelly doing? Did she go back to work? Had she reconnected with her friends? Her parents? How was baby girl Ryan? Did she need anything? Because she couldn't help Kelly, Barrett felt completely empty, like she was wandering around in an open field with no direction or purpose. She was looking for a guidepost she couldn't find.

"Please, Debra," she said. Barrett didn't care if it sounded like she was pleading. She didn't care about anything anymore. "I don't want to talk about it."

Debra looked at her, obviously deciding whether to push Barrett or just let it go. The longer she waited, the more uncomfortable Barrett became. This was new to her too. She often used silence as an effective negotiating tactic, but now it was against her. Finally Debra spoke.

"I never thought I'd say this, Barrett, but you're in some deep shit over this woman."

"What are you talking about? What woman?" God, that was lame, she thought, and she'd just made a complete ass of herself by asking such asinine questions. Debra looked at her with that you-know-exactly-what-and-who-I'm-talking-about look.

"Okay." She acquiesced. "I admit I'm worried about how Kelly's doing, but I wouldn't say it's anywhere near deep shit."

"Uh-huh."

"No, really, she's been through a lot." God damn, she wished Debra would say something. She was feeling more and more like an idiot every second. "She's straight, Debra." Fuck. That sealed it. She was a complete idiot.

CHAPTER TWENTY-ONE

I can't do that," Kelly said emphatically. Bed rest for the next six weeks was out of the question. She had things to do. She had to get her job back, buy baby furniture, and at least ten dozen other things.

"Kelly, listen to me," her obstetrician, Dr. Reed, had said patiently during an emergency visit. She had been spotting off and on for several days. Kelly liked Dr. Reed. She'd been recommended by one of her friends who wasn't subtly or in some cases not so subtly pushing her to give her daughter up for adoption. They, however, didn't call it her daughter or the baby. She guessed if they called her baby "it," it wouldn't seem like a real person.

She'd talked with Dr. Hinton about her friends' reactions many times. The conversations about her parents were even more numerous. Everyone had their opinion and views about abortion and adoption, but Kelly had known from the beginning that she'd be the one to live with the consequences. It would be her face in the mirror every morning, her hopes and dreams that would be affected. This was the most personal decision possible. She'd made hers and never looked back.

"Kelly, you're a nurse, and I don't need to tell you this, but I will," Dr. Reed had said. "You're in danger of delivering early, and your baby isn't ready. Her lungs aren't developed enough and she'll have trouble breathing. She might have to be on a ventilator. She may have jaundice, bleeding in her brain, an immature gastrointestinal and digestive tract, and not be able to maintain her body heat."

If Dr. Reed had been trying to scare her, it was mission accomplished. If she'd lost the baby early on it might have been for the best, but this was her child, her daughter, and she loved her more than she could ever imagine.

Kelly gathered her laptop, large bottle of water, and the telephone before she parked her butt on the couch. Dr. Reed had given her specific instructions to do nothing more strenuous than going to the bathroom or making a sandwich. No serious cooking, no running to the store or the mailbox. She couldn't be on her feet for more than a few minutes, and absolutely no lifting.

Her laptop no longer fit on her lap, so she put the breakfast tray over her legs instead. She needed to buy a few things for the baby and had better get on the stick and get it done. She was running out of time. Her friends had offered to give her a baby shower, but she'd declined. The last thing she needed was a bunch of women stumbling all over themselves not to say the wrong thing. It only made sense to her, but her baby and everything surrounding it was private.

Her daughter was due in four weeks, and she hadn't settled on a name, didn't have a stitch of furniture, and had only begun to pick up baby clothes here and there. She needed diapers and blankets, and her baby couldn't come home unless she was securely strapped in a car seat.

She was reading consumer reviews about strollers when the phone rang. Butterflies scampered around in her stomach when her favorite picture of Barrett popped up on the caller ID.

"Hey, stranger. How's your trip?" Barrett had been in Hong Kong for a week, and with the time difference they'd only been able to talk a few times.

"Long and over," Barrett replied.

God, it was good to hear her voice. "Are you at home?" Kelly looked at the clock on the wall over the TV.

"No."

"Barrett, it's eight thirty. I hope you're not still at the office. You work too much." Kelly knew Barrett often stayed late at the office.

"I'm not at the office."

Something in Barrett's tone made her stomach flutter. It wasn't the baby. She was long past the flutter stage and was well into serious, breath-stopping kicks. "Where are you then?"

"At your front door."

❖

"What?" Just then Kelly's doorbell rang. She started to jump up, but the baby wouldn't let her. She scooted forward on the couch cushion and managed to stand without knocking over her water or her laptop. She hurried to the door and pulled it open.

Barrett stood there looking even better than Kelly remembered. It had been six weeks since their emotional good-bye at the airport, and seeing her made Kelly realize just how much she missed her.

"Hi," Barrett said, her smile beaming in the porch light. "I took a big chance in stopping by, but I wanted to see you."

Barrett spoke fast, her words clipped, and Kelly realized she was nervous. Her smile started to fade.

"Is this a bad time?"

"Oh, my God, Barrett. You're actually here," Kelly sputtered out, still shocked over her sudden appearance. She practically jumped into Barrett's arms, at least as much as baby girl Ryan allowed.

Barrett's arms around her felt wonderful. They were like a shield protecting her from anything that could harm her.

"Hey, I missed you too. Maybe we better go inside. What are your neighbors going to think?"

"That you came back to me," she said without thinking. "God, it's good to see you. I've missed you so much." She stepped back and kissed Barrett on the mouth, then felt Barrett stiffen and drop her arms. Kelly pulled away and looked at Barrett's odd expression.

"Come on in, come in." Kelly took Barrett's hand and pulled her through the door. "What are you doing here? I can't believe you're really here." She hugged Barrett again. "How did you get here? I thought you were in Hong Kong?" Question after question tumbled out of her mouth so quickly she didn't give Barrett a chance to answer any of them.

They sat on the couch facing each other, both not saying anything. She couldn't believe Barrett was in her living room sitting right next to her. Barrett looked wonderful and she couldn't stop touching her. She hadn't let go of Barrett's hand since she'd grabbed it and pulled her inside. But her other hand kept straying to their hands, her arm, and finally her cheek.

Barrett's eyes darkened and her expression changed. Concerned she'd done something wrong, Kelly began to pull her hand away when Barrett trapped it against her cheek. This time something flashed in her eyes. Kelly suddenly found it hard to breathe. After what felt like both an instant and forever, Barrett turned her head and lightly kissed her palm.

Barrett's eyes burned brighter and Kelly had an overwhelming need to kiss her. Not a chaste welcome-home kiss like the one they'd shared at the door, but an honest-to-goodness kiss. A kiss that made her toes curl and her brain shut down. Where she couldn't think, only feel. A kiss that led to that place where she'd never be the same again. And Kelly wanted to go there. She needed to go there. It'd been so long since she'd felt like this. It'd been so long since she'd felt anything. She leaned forward.

Slowly she closed the distance between her lips and Barrett's. Her mind was screaming at her to stop, but she couldn't. She didn't want to. She wanted this kiss more than she'd wanted anything in her life. It was right. After so much in her life that was wrong, this was right. Absolutely right.

Barrett moved toward her a fraction of an inch and Kelly's pulse skyrocketed. Barrett wanted this too! She wanted to kiss her. This was a game changer. Kelly kissed her.

It was soft and gentle at first, not unlike others they'd shared in greeting or leaving. But it quickly turned into something else. Barrett's lips were warm and soft and tentative, but Kelly wanted more. She moved slightly, sliding her hand behind Barrett's head, and Barrett immediately responded.

Kelly was rocked to her soul and completely lost any sense of time and space. She was floating on a sensation unlike anything she'd ever experienced, transported to a place she never wanted to leave. She deepened the kiss. No longer were they simply comrades in a battle for survival, an experience that would tie them together forever. No, they'd crossed the line, and Kelly never wanted to go back. Barrett reached for her.

❖

A sudden pain ripped through Kelly. She wrenched away, grabbing her stomach and breathing in short, sharp gasps. The pain was piercing.

"Kelly! What is it? Is it the baby? Is something wrong?"

No, not now. Please not now, you're not ready, she pleaded silently to her baby. She held her hand up as the pain subsided. Thankfully Barrett stopped asking questions as she tried to catch her breath. At last she could talk.

"She's been a little temperamental these last few weeks," she replied, finally able to take a deep breath.

"What does that mean?" Barrett's voice was filled with concern. "*Exactly* what does that mean?"

"She wants to come out and join the world, but she's not ready. Dr. Reed put me on bed rest until my due date."

"And you didn't tell me!" Barrett demanded, anger replacing concern. "When did this happen?"

"Two weeks ago." Kelly waited for Barrett's reaction, but it wasn't at all what she expected. She was angry, almost furious.

"Two weeks?" Barrett's eyebrows rose skeptically. How could the fire in her eyes one minute ago now mean something altogether different? Kelly nodded. Barrett's jaw clenched.

"Were you going to tell me?" She hesitated, and Barrett didn't give her a chance to continue. "You weren't, were you?"

"Of course I was."

"When? *After* the baby was born? Were you even going to tell me you had the baby?"

Barrett's tone was icy. Her daughter didn't like it either and kicked her disapproval. "Barrett. You were out of town and I didn't want to bother you."

"And your doctor putting you on bed rest wasn't important enough to call?" Barrett got up and started pacing the room. "Didn't want to…do you think so little of me to believe something like this wouldn't bother me? Jesus, Kelly." Barrett ran her hands through her hair, obviously perplexed and something else, but Kelly had no idea what.

"What would you have done, Barrett? Charter another private jet and fly here to take care of me?" Now she was angry. Why was she getting shit? This was her life, her baby. She was perfectly capable of taking care of both. "I am not believing this is happening," she said, disgusted with this entire scene. She started to get up.

"Sit down," Barrett barked.

"Excuse me?" Kelly made it clear that no one would speak to her like this. Never again.

Barrett lowered her voice. "Please sit down. Whatever you need, I'll get it. You shouldn't get upset."

"You should have thought of that before you reamed me out for not calling you," Kelly shot back.

"Look," Barrett said. "Can we start over? You threw me for a loop, and you surprised me with the news about the baby. I reacted badly. I apologize." Barrett actually looked contrite, standing there in her wrinkled khakis.

Kelly bit back a retort. Her hormones had her emotions strapped in a roller-coaster seat lately. They wouldn't get anywhere bickering back and forth.

"I'm glad to see you." Actually she was ecstatic, but she was wary of putting her feelings out on the table again.

"It's good to see you too," Barrett replied, sounding equally cool. "I missed you, so I arranged to land here in Denver instead of in San Francisco. I wanted to see you." Barrett's voice warmed as she spoke.

"I'm glad you did. I missed you too. Please sit down. You're making me nervous." Kelly patted the couch beside her, where

Barrett had sat when they kissed. *Oh my God, when we kissed.* She inhaled sharply, her hand instinctively going to her mouth as she remembered the taste and feel of Barrett's lips. Barrett couldn't miss her reaction and her eyes were piercing.

"Kelly," Barrett said, and Kelly knew she was going to talk about what had happened. She didn't want to talk about it. She wanted to pretend it had never happened and wanted it to happen again. Jesus, this was all she needed now. Baby girl kept insisting on having a birthday, she was running low on funds, and she'd kissed a woman. No, she'd kissed Barrett. *Must be the hormones. Please, God, let it be the hormones.*

Kelly was definitely trying to change the subject. She asked about her trip, Hong Kong, and anything else she could think of except the kiss. The shock-of-her-life-that-blew-the-top-off-her-head kiss. If Kelly didn't want to talk about it, she'd let it go. Barrett had read that the hormones of women sometimes went completely haywire when they were pregnant. Actually she'd read everything she could get her hands on about pregnancy to better understand what Kelly was going through. Most of it was fascinating, some made her nauseous, and some scared the hell out of her.

Barrett hadn't seen it on the horizon, not in the slightest. She'd come here because she couldn't wait another minute to see Kelly. She thought about Kelly constantly, reliving every conversation and minute they'd been together. She worried about Kelly more now that she was further along in her pregnancy and, after the bombshell of mandatory bed rest, rightfully so.

She wanted to kiss Kelly, had dreamt about it. How her lips would feel as they moved under hers. How she would taste. Would she be aggressive or let Barrett take the lead? Would she want more? Would she slap her face? Would she lose her forever? There were a lot of things Barrett didn't know, but she did know that she would never, ever make a move.

"Wow. BGR is getting big," she said, sitting back down on the couch and framing Kelly's stomach with her hands. She didn't dare touch her.

"BGR?"

"Yeah, BGR. Baby girl Ryan. Unless you've picked a name." The baby must have kicked, because Kelly grimaced and grabbed her stomach. Kelly held up her hand.

"It's just a kick. I don't know if that means she likes it or not, and no, I'm still deciding."

Barrett's fear dropped a notch. "How's she doing? What does the doctor say? I mean besides the bed rest."

"That everything's looking good." Kelly moved her hands under her stomach as if she could hold her baby in a few weeks longer.

"Are you scared?" I'm petrified, she thought.

"A little. I've never had a baby before," Kelly said wryly. "I don't know what to expect. I've seen babies born and I know there are good drugs, but still…that big thing coming out of that little thing is a bit daunting."

Kelly's comment diffused some of the tension, and Barrett breathed a little easier. "Are you ready? Got lots of little pink onesies and blankets folded in her dresser?"

"Onesies?"

"Yeah. You know the little one-piece things they practically live in for the first few months," she said, feeling a little awkward even saying the word.

"I know what a onesie is. How do you know about them?"

"How do I know?" Barrett faked indignation. "Need I remind you my undergraduate degree is in information technology and my graduate degree is in electrical engineering and I have an MBA from The Wharton School of Business."

"Yeah, and you're the owner of a very successful software-development company, all of which validates my original question." Kelly was smiling now, relaxed and enjoying the banter.

"I read."

"You read?"

"Yes." Kelly looked at her, obviously waiting for her to continue. *"Parents, Motherhood, Baby Life."* Barrett named a few other magazines she'd subscribed to. "Not only do I know about onesies, but I know what type of diaper genie got the best rating from new mothers, ointment or cream for diaper rash, how to say no to the constant stream of visitors when the baby comes home, and the pros and cons of breast or bottle feeding."

"Wow, I'm impressed," Kelly said, smiling. "And for the record, I'm breast feeding."

"Good choice." Barrett gave Kelly a thumbs-up. "An unlimited supply, very cost-effective, no getting up in the middle of the night to warm a bottle, and my favorite, no dishes." Barrett didn't move when Kelly touched her arm as she laughed. She didn't want to lose the sensation, but even more she didn't want Kelly to feel self-conscious.

"Now about those onesies," Barrett said, bringing the topic back around. "Are you ready?"

"Almost."

Kelly's answer was vague. "How most is almost? Kelly?" she said, when Kelly didn't immediately answer. "Where's her room?" She got up and pointed in the direction of the bedrooms.

"Next to mine."

Barrett knew Kelly was hiding something, and as she turned the corner and entered the baby's room she knew exactly what it was. Nothing. Absolutely nothing. She turned and retraced her steps.

"I thought I had lots of time." Kelly spoke before she could say anything. "I *had* a lot of time until this bed-rest thing happened. I was about to shop online when you called. Here, look," Kelly said, handing her laptop to her.

Barrett touched the keyboard, waking up the page of a familiar baby-supply store. That wasn't what they called them, but the baby store just didn't sound right, like the hardware store or the grocery store.

"All right, let's start with the basics." Barrett sat down beside her and entered a few keystrokes into the search bar.

An hour and ten minutes later a crib, changing table, matching dresser and toy box, as well as eight-dozen diapers, six receiving blankets, three nursing bras, and a diaper genie were on the way. They would be delivered in the next three to five days, free shipping included.

Barrett was exhausted. Between her sleepless nights, her worry over Kelly, and a severe case of jet lag, she was practically dead on her feet. Kelly offered her guest room, and Barrett accepted without objection. She did insist on making the bed herself and informed Kelly she'd cook breakfast in the morning.

But morning was a long way off as she lay in the bedroom just down the hall from Kelly. She'd helped her lock up and get into her own bed. Barrett wanted to give her a kiss on the forehead and tell her sweet dreams but didn't dare. Instead, she'd said she'd leave her door open and for Kelly to call if she needed anything during the night.

Now it was her turn to go to sleep, which eluded her like cool water through her fingers. Every time she closed her eyes she saw Kelly moving toward her, her lips open and inviting. Every time she turned over she remembered how Kelly's hand felt brushing her leg, her arm, caressing her cheek. Every time she exhaled she felt Kelly's soft breath on her face just before she kissed her. It certainly didn't help the situation that when she groaned, it sounded just like Kelly had when she deepened the kiss.

Barrett was in serious trouble. No way could she mess up Kelly's life any more than she already had. She owed it to Kelly to keep her hands to herself. She'd do everything she could to keep Kelly from being hurt again, and getting involved with Barrett was definitely not in that category.

Giving up on sleep, Barrett slid out of bed and grabbed her iPad from her briefcase. Maybe a few chapters of the latest Eve Dallas case would settle her enough that she could fall asleep. She left the door cracked and turned on the lamp beside the bed. It wasn't bright and softened the harsh light of the iPad screen. Forty-two pages later she stumbled into bed and fell asleep.

❖

The very fact that Barrett was lying in a bed ten feet down the hall was doing nothing for Kelly's orders to rest. After the baby had interrupted their kiss, both she and Barrett avoided the topic. She didn't know about Barrett, but as far as she was concerned it had become something they really couldn't ignore.

She tried to put it out of her mind as they talked about names, looked at furniture, and selected bibs and blankets, but it was always right there under the surface. Her attraction to Barrett was confusing. She'd had many, many girlfriends in her life, some closer than others but had never even had a glancing desire to kiss them, even as a teenager when they were learning about the complicated matters of life, the drama of going steady and sex. Some of her friends had experimented with other girls, though Kelly never did. The only thing she'd done was kiss Cindy Baker and a few other girls while playing spin the bottle at a birthday slumber party when she was fourteen, but she certainly hadn't been attracted to her.

She'd had butterflies just out of curiosity when one of the girls had suggested the traditional boy-girl game, but it was more about walking on the edge than actual curiosity about kissing a girl. When the bottle had stopped spinning and pointed at her, she and her partner had gone into the hall, like the four girls before them. She was more uncomfortable than nervous or excited, and it took several minutes before they decided whose head was going in which direction before they did it. It wasn't unpleasant, but she didn't feel any of the bells and whistles and butterflies and giddiness she had when she'd kissed Jeff Stevens the week before. A couple more turns in the hall and Kelly knew for certain girls were not her thing.

So why was she feeling like this toward Barrett? Why had she kissed her? Why did she still want to kiss her? She'd have to talk to Dr. Hinton about this and thought about what the good doctor would say. For certain it would be, "And what do you think this means, Kelly?" She would stammer and stumble over some words and ultimately come up with a few that wouldn't even begin to describe her confusion over what she was experiencing.

Did she feel like this toward Barrett because of what they'd been through together? Yes, that was a bond that could never be broken, but was she mistaking gratitude toward Barrett for getting her out of that hellhole and saving her and her baby's life with something more? Gratitude and need could often be confused with desire. Was that what was happening here?

Could someone all of a sudden turn gay? She laughed at her own phrase—turn gay. How ridiculous did that sound? People didn't turn gay. They either were or they weren't. But was it that simple? Were you born gay, or did you fall in love with someone, and if they happened to be the same sex, then you became gay? She hadn't thought about that. But she was certainly thinking about it now when she should be resting.

The baby moved and Kelly realized it might be pointless to even try to go to sleep because her daughter obviously had other plans. Barrett had asked if she'd settled on a name yet. She needed to. Dr. Reed had scared her into realizing that this baby could come any day, whether she was ready or not. She had a name in mind and was trying it out, but she wasn't to the point of selecting it. She wanted to get Barrett's opinion, and she smiled when she thought about all the pieces of paper she'd thrown away with various names on them in the shape of a business card. That had been Barrett's suggestion. At first she'd thought it was silly, but the more she went through the names, the more she changed her mind.

Barrett's viewpoint and what she might think of something was in the forefront of her mind more every day. In the beginning it had bothered her. She'd been single for so long and had made her own decisions very early on, rarely second-guessing herself. Now she was almost the complete opposite. She wondered if Barrett would think these colors went together, or if she should paint the baby's room pink or a neutral color, or if she should hire a nanny.

At first she considered it a sign of weakness that she was afraid to make a decision. When she was first kidnapped, if she did anything without asking or being told, she was severely punished. Because the mind is a wonderful thing and a complicated thing, it didn't take her long to change her pattern of behavior in order to survive. When she was rescued and came home, she had to unlearn that behavior. But she had, or at least she thought she had until she started considering Barrett's opinion more and more often. Now she was comfortable that she simply wanted to know what Barrett thought. She didn't base her decisions on what Barrett said, but she did consider it. This evening was an excellent example.

When they were scrolling through the various options for cribs, high chairs, and car seats, she listened to Barrett's opinion and recommendation on style or color. At times they made sense, but at other times she had her own opinion and chose what she wanted.

Now she wanted to know what Barrett thought of their kiss, or more precisely when *she* kissed *her*. She knew it wasn't until the last split second before Barrett had realized she was going to kiss her, and it'd taken her several seconds before she kissed her back.

But what did Barrett think about it? Was she lying in her bed, wide-awake, trying to figure out what had happened and what to do next? Kelly had no freaking clue.

Chapter Twenty-two

Two days later, Barrett opened the door to the UPS girl and signed for eight boxes. The next day and the day after that, the woman in brown returned. On the fourth day the woman had written her name and a phone number on a yellow Post-it Note in the center of the signature box. In her previous life Barrett would have invited her to stop by after work. Today Kelly and her baby were her sole focus. She signed the pad, her bold signature skirting around the note. Barrett saw the look of disappointment in the woman's eyes, but the next day when she delivered the box containing the stroller she was nothing but business.

After Kelly's bombshell about bed rest, Barrett refused to leave and had set up shop in Kelly's spare bedroom. Global Digital was a virtual company, so holding meetings via Skype or conference calls was nothing new. Lori had fussed at her continually, and Debra started and ended almost every conversation with a not-so-subtle shake of her head and an accompanying *tsk, tsk.*

The furniture was due to arrive in two days, and Barrett was putting the finishing touches on the trim in the baby's room. Kelly was in the recliner in the living room supervising her painting via the baby-cam Barrett had purchased the day before.

Barrett had come home from the paint store with squares the size of her palm in various colors, as well as two books with wallpaper samples. Over dinner Kelly had agreed on the color for the walls, a border to encircle the room at eye level, and trim for the window frame. She set to work the next day, forbidding Kelly to set foot in the room, afraid the paint fumes would harm the baby.

"I could get used to having you around." Kelly's amused voice came over the speaker, which made Barrett smile. She was already used to being around.

"You just like that I cook for you," she said, dipping the narrow brush into the paint can. Kelly's laugh was full, and warmth filled her. They'd both avoided talking about the kiss they'd shared the evening she'd arrived. The first day was awkward, but they quickly fell back into the comfort level they'd shared before. At least that's what Barrett kept telling herself.

"Your idea of cooking is picking up the phone."

"So? There are all different kinds of cooking. Creole, Cajun, Mexican, barbeque—"

"And takeout," Kelly said.

"Yes, and takeout. And your point is?" She wiped her hands on an old T-shirt Kelly had transformed into a paint rag.

"My point is to keep you humble."

"Humble? Why would I want to be humble?"

"Because you look so cute with paint on your cheek."

Barrett hesitated mid-stroke after hearing Kelly's comment. Cute? Did she really think she was cute? Couldn't be. She had to be teasing. Neither one of them had approached the topic of their kiss eight days ago, both seeming to silently agree that if they didn't talk about it, it hadn't really happened.

At night when it was dark and quiet, Barrett relived every second of it. But she never did anything else. She didn't want Kelly to feel uncomfortable or embarrassed so she left it alone. That surprised her because she always faced things head-on, especially if they were difficult. But this was different. This was Kelly, and the last thing Kelly needed at this point was another uncomfortable, awkward situation.

"What's the matter, Rembrandt? Cat got your tongue?" Kelly said, bringing Barrett's thoughts back to the present.

She couldn't have been standing there more than a moment or two, dripping paint on the drop cloth like a goofball. Her back to the camera, she blinked a few times and quietly cleared her throat.

"Don't you have something to do, like fold receiving blankets or match baby socks?" Her paintbrush shook a little as she dipped the brush back in the can. She heard Kelly chuckle and then the sound of the evening news come through the speaker.

Barrett stepped back and inspected her progress on the windowsill. She'd have to re-do it because she'd done such a crappy job after Kelly had made her comment. It was getting late and she was losing the light so she decided to clean up and finish the job tomorrow. It was going to be another long night.

❖

The next morning Barrett walked into the baby's room, fully intending to correct the mess she'd made yesterday. She heard Kelly's voice over the monitor, and Barrett realized she'd forgotten to turn off the monitor when she left the room last night. Kelly was talking with Dr. Hinton, which was why she'd chosen this time to finish the painting. As she walked across the room to turn it off, Kelly spoke again.

"I told her she was cute, but what I really wanted to tell her was that she was the sexiest thing I'd ever seen."

Barrett froze, her fingers on the off switch.

Kelly spoke again. "Yes. Yes, I did. No, I have no idea."

As much as she wanted to continue to listen, Kelly deserved her privacy, so Barrett turned the knob to the off position. She would have heard only Kelly's side of the conversation, which might or might not have given her any additional insight. No matter how much she wanted to know, she refused to violate Kelly's trust. She was folding the drop cloth when she heard the doorbell ring.

"Furniture's here," Kelly said from the other room.

❖

Barrett leaned in closer. She didn't blink, and she wasn't even sure she was breathing. "Is that her?"

Dr. Reed moved the wand a little and pushed a few buttons. "Yep, there she is."

Barrett had driven Kelly to her checkup, and Dr. Reed was doing another sonogram. Barrett was standing beside Kelly as the baby came into focus. "Oh my God, Kelly. She's beautiful."

"Barrett, she's waving at you," Kelly said.

"No, she isn't," Barrett said. Or was she? "Oh, man, she's moving. Look at her. It's like she's floating." Barrett had never seen anything as breathtaking as this. Kelly took her hand, and Barrett dragged her eyes away from the baby and looked at her. She didn't know which was more beautiful, the sight of Kelly's baby growing inside her or what she saw in Kelly's eyes. They were filled with tears threatening to overflow.

"Kelly? Honey, what is it?" She turned to Dr. Reed, her heart crowding her throat. "Is something wrong with the baby? Is something wrong with Kelly?"

"No, no, not at all," Kelly said quickly. "I'm fine and the baby's fine. I'm just so happy you're here. With me and my baby."

Barrett's relief was so overwhelming she had to sit down. She was actually shaking. She'd thought she might lose Kelly, and she was still trying to breathe normally.

"Oh, Barrett, I'm so sorry. I didn't mean to frighten you."

"Frighten me? You scared the ever-living holy shit out of me. God, Kelly if anything happened to you…" Her own tears were choking her.

"Nothing's going to happen to either one of them, if I have anything to say about it," Dr. Reed said. Barrett had forgotten she was even in the room and had to pull herself together. She was teetering on the edge of—what? She had no idea, but she didn't like it.

"How does that thing work?" Barrett asked the doctor, trying to get her legs back under her. Technology, that's what she knew and that's what grounded her.

"The gel is a conductor for the sound waves. The transducer," the doctor waved the wand in the air, "produces sound waves into the uterus. The sound waves bounce off bones and tissue, returning to the transducer to generate black-and-white images of the fetus."

"Wow," Barrett said, more impressed with what the technology was showing than the actual technology itself. That was amazing and another thing about herself that Barrett didn't recognize.

The doctor had given Barrett a copy of the sonogram, and Barrett still hadn't taken her eyes off it even after they got home.

❖

"Thank you for taking me today," Kelly said later that evening, her feet propped up on two pillows at the end of the couch.

"Thank you for letting me." Barrett was still a little choked up over the entire experience, and Kelly suddenly seemed on the verge of crying. "Kelly, what is it?" She moved closer and sat precariously on the edge of the couch. If she wasn't careful she'd end up on her butt or in Kelly's lap, or what was left of it.

When Kelly tried to answer only her mouth moved. Barrett's pulse rocketed again.

"Kelly, honey, you can talk to me. Tell me." Barrett was almost pleading, but she had to find out what was wrong.

"I'm afraid I won't love her."

What? Who? She won't love who? Oh my God, she's afraid she won't love the baby. Barrett fought to maintain control over her facial expressions as she worked through what to say. "Kelly—"

"Don't give me a bunch of platitudes. I've already said them to myself a hundred times. 'Of course you'll love her, she's your daughter,' or 'you're just scared, all first-time mothers are.'"

"I wasn't going to say that. I was going to say that what you're feeling is probably perfectly normal in your situation. I'd be scared too if I were in your shoes. But you're a woman full of life and full of love and caring, and that will transfer to your baby. You'll be a fabulous mother." Somehow Barrett knew that was true.

"I'm afraid," Kelly said, just before she started to cry.

Barrett gathered her in her arms. "I know. I know." She pulled Kelly onto her lap. "I'm here for you."

"You're the only one." Kelly had a handful of her shirt and her faced was pressed tight against it.

"The only one what?" God, she hated it when a woman cried, and it was especially hard because it was Kelly.

"There's no one…nobody that I…" The rest was muffled in her shirt.

Barrett finally got it. She was the only one Kelly was sharing this with. Her parents, her friends, maybe even a husband should be with her, reveling in the joy of Kelly having a baby, becoming a mother. Helping her through the swollen ankles, mood swings, and insecurities.

"I'm afraid she'll look like…"

Barrett put her finger under Kelly's chin and lifted it so that their eyes met. She shook her head. "No. She'll have dark hair and big brown eyes that look at the world with wonder and curiosity. She'll have dimples and a smile that'll take your breath away. She'll be smart and inquisitive, strong and gentle. She'll be kind and thoughtful, always thinking of others." Barrett caressed Kelly's cheek with the back of her hand. "She'll be beautiful, just like her mother."

❖

Kelly fell into the depths of Barrett's words. She knew Barrett and was certain she'd meant every word. She could see it in her eyes when she looked at her and in her expression when she saw the baby for the first time this afternoon. The way she helped her in and out of the car and the bathroom revealed Barrett's sincerity.

She had to find a way to tell Barrett how she felt, how much she meant to her. What a wonderful woman she was and how lucky she was to have her in her life. But that wasn't quite it either. There was more to it than that, but Kelly didn't know what it was or how to convey it. She was grasping for words when she pulled Barrett to her and kissed her.

It was soft and gentle, tentative and exploring, and Barrett let her lead. She was inundated with sensations she'd never experienced. She longed for Barrett to wrap her strong arms around her. She craved her touch, needed her strong body next to her, beside her, under her, on top of her. Lightning shot through her when she realized she wanted Barrett—wanted her, needed her. Desired her.

"Barrett, please," she said against Barrett's mouth. God, she was driving herself crazy, and Barrett's restraint wasn't helping. Kelly reached around and wrapped her arms around Barrett, running her hands up and down her back. She felt Barrett struggle for control and reveled in the thought that she could make this strong, wonderful woman lose it. She felt powerful yet humble, desired yet unsure, reckless yet cautious. And it was all because of Barrett. She hadn't fallen for a woman; she had fallen for Barrett.

Her knowledge gave her power, and she accepted it. She took Barrett without hesitation, kissing her more deeply, sliding her hands under her shirt. Oh, God, her skin was soft and hot, and Kelly had never felt anything so perfect. It quivered under her tentative touch, arched under the exploring fingers, responded to her bold moves.

Barrett's breasts were as soft as she'd imagined they would be those months ago in that dark hotel room in Panama. She was frightened then, but now, in Barrett's arms, she was fearless. Kelly needed more. She needed to taste every inch of this wonderful woman, feel her naked skin against hers. She pushed Barrett's shirt up and started with the tip of the breast that haunted her dreams.

When she kissed it lightly it swelled against her lips. Barrett groaned and grabbed the back of her head, pulling her closer. Words couldn't describe the rush of joy that cascaded through her body at Barrett's reaction. She had the power to make her vulnerable, and she would never, ever abuse it.

Suddenly Barrett pulled away, struggling to dislodge herself from Kelly's embrace. She was flushed, breathing quickly, and dragged her shaking hands through her short hair, yanking her shirt down.

"We can't do this."

"What?" Kelly asked, confused. This was the last thing she'd expected.

"We can't do this, Kelly," Barrett repeated, not making eye contact with her.

"Why not?" When Barrett didn't answer she repeated the question. "Why not, Barrett?"

"Because…because you…and I…" She waved her hands in the air as if trying to pull words down and into her mouth.

"Because I what? I'm ugly? Pregnant? Straight? Damaged?" She almost choked on the last word.

"What? No, no," Barrett said quickly. "No, I mean yes, but no."

If this moment wasn't so awkward it would be funny. "Which is it, Barrett?"

Barrett closed her eyes and took a deep breath, then opened them again. "No, it's not because you're pregnant. I think you're beautiful, and never, ever refer to yourself as damaged again." Barrett's voice got stronger as she answered Kelly's questions. But she'd only answered two of them.

"Then what is it, Barrett? It can't be because I'm straight. No straight woman would kiss you like that, no matter how attractive you are."

Barrett paced the room. "Kelly, you don't understand," she said, then seemed to run out of steam.

"Then make me," she shot back. Barrett was infuriating, and Kelly was beginning to lose what little control she'd regained after touching Barrett's body.

Barrett stumbled over her words, none of which made any sense. Finally Kelly said, "Barrett, sometimes you think too much. You might not think you want to continue what happened here on this couch, but your body told me otherwise. And if I can figure it out, you can too. I can't wait around all day for you to sort it all out. I'm about to get really busy here, and you can either get on this little yellow school bus or get on your Learjet and fly out of town. I care for you, Barrett. More than I ever thought I would, and in a way that I never thought I could."

"Do you think you're feeling this because of what happened in Columbia?" Barrett finally said.

"What do you mean?"

"Because of The Colonel and what he—"

"So because I was raped I now desire women?"

"It's been known to happen," Barrett said carefully.

"Well, that's not what happened to me."

Barrett nodded. "It's been known to happen," Barrett said again.

"Stop saying that! Sure it can happen, but I don't understand that. If I was a lesbian and raped by a woman, then that's going to make me straight? That argument is fundamentally flawed."

"Kelly—"

"No, Barrett, you listen to me. Why are you making all these excuses for me? Yeah, I've never desired a woman before, but up until last week I never ate Brussels sprouts either, and I thought they were pretty damn good. So just because I haven't ever, doesn't mean I'm not."

Barrett was at a loss for words. She was trying to figure out how to explain to Kelly what she was going through. She tried a different approach. "Have you heard of transference?"

Kelly cocked her head, a look on her face that said you've got to be fucking kidding me, which she quickly verbalized by saying exactly that. "I know what transference is. And so what you're saying is that because I'm grateful that you saved my life I'm transferring those feelings to you? That I'll have sex with you because you want to and I feel obligated because you saved my life? That I've fallen for you? I desire you? I want to have sex with you? Make love with you? Put my mouth on you? How does that work? Because I don't think that argument holds any more water than your other one does. You are so full of shit you don't know just how full of shit you are."

"I get it now," Kelly said, suddenly enlightened. "You don't want me. You don't want me and my baby. So why don't you just dyke up and say so."

"Kelly, that's not—"

"Yes, it is. You seem to think you know what I'm thinking and feeling. Then I'll mirror that. Let me tell you something, Barrett, that no one probably has the guts to tell you, the great and powerful Barrett Taylor." Kelly pointed at her. "You are fucking wrong. Flat-out fucking wrong. You need to open your eyes to what's right in front of you, because if you don't," Kelly said calmly, "you're going to miss the best thing that ever happened to you." With that she got off the couch and walked out of the room.

Barrett was stunned. If she hadn't known what to say before, she definitely didn't know what to say now. She'd completely underestimated Kelly. She'd continued to view her as a victim when Kelly certainly no longer viewed herself that way, if she ever had.

CHAPTER TWENTY-THREE

B arrett."
    Kelly's whisper was soft and warm, her touch on her arm arousing.

"Barrett."

"I love the sound of your voice saying my name." She arched to where the sound was coming from, wanting for the sound to caress her body.

"Barrett, honey, I need you to wake up."

Barrett opened her eyes and saw Kelly's beautiful face right in front of her. Even in the shadows of the night she could see Kelly's eyes clearly. They were dark and burning. She reached up and slid her hand behind Kelly's neck and pulled her into a kiss. Rockets danced behind her eyelids. The kiss they'd shared yesterday was almost chaste in comparison to this one. It was bold and sensuous, with the promise of more to come. Tongues battling for control, both of them gasping for breath, Barrett pulled Kelly fully into an embrace, her body warm and compliant. Suddenly Kelly broke away with a gasp that brought Barrett out of her bliss.

"Ugh," Kelly said, grabbing her stomach and panting in short, quick breaths—obviously in pain instead of passion.

"Kelly, my God, what is it?" Barrett shook the last of the sleep from her brain. She had no idea what was going on. One minute Kelly was waking her with kisses, the next…oh, fuck!

Barrett scampered to a sitting position, turning on the light beside the bed. Kelly was doubled over, her face twisted in agony. "My God, Kelly, is it the baby?"

"Yes," she said through clenched teeth. "I've already called the doctor. We've got to go. She wants me at the hospital."

At that point the full reality of what was going on hit her. Kelly was having the baby. She scrambled out of bed, almost knocking Kelly to the floor, then grabbed her with both hands and set her gently back on the bed. "Jesus, Kelly, I'm sorry. Are you all right?"

Kelly's breathing was beginning to return to normal. "At this very moment, yes." Kelly looked at her. "But I suggest you get dressed, *now*."

Barrett glanced down and saw that she was completely naked. She hustled into the heap of clothes she'd dumped in a pile on the floor, slipped on her shoes, and grabbed her wallet and phone off the nightstand.

She helped Kelly into the car, and they were speeding down the expressway before her brain started working again. "When did you start having contractions?"

"I woke up about one thirty and felt, I don't know, odd. The first one hit a few minutes after two. It didn't feel like the ones I'd had before, so I called Dr. Reed. While I was waiting for the answering service to put me through, my water broke. So ready or not, this little girl is on her way."

Kelly grimaced again, panting again. "Jesus," Barrett said, and stomped on the gas, throwing both of them against the back of the seats. It seemed like forever until the grip of the contraction started to let loose. "How far apart are they?" She remembered reading that the closer the contractions the closer the baby's head. No way was she going to let Kelly give birth in the backseat of her car.

"How do women do this?" she asked. "Having something moving around inside you, kicking and making it hard to breathe and leaning against your bladder so you have to pee all the time. And to get it out through…" Barrett couldn't even imagine. "No offense, but this doesn't look like a good time." She wasn't even sure it was the right time to be asking these stupid questions, but she was more nervous than she'd been in her entire life.

Kelly didn't have to answer; the blinking red sign of the emergency room came into view. She pulled into the circle drive and jumped out almost before she turned off the car. She grabbed one of the empty wheelchairs lined up like toy soldiers waiting for their battle assignments. She helped Kelly into the wide chair and shut the door harder than she meant to, adrenaline racing through her. She approached the double doors and they automatically opened.

The lights were bright, the smell identical to that of any other hospital she'd been in. Flashbacks of when she was wheeled into the emergency room in Panama tickled the edge of her consciousness. She pushed them back. This wasn't about her; this was about Kelly.

She wheeled Kelly inside and glanced around. The requisite black plastic chairs were scattered around the waiting room, two or three of them filled with people who appeared to be napping. She hurried to the receptionist sitting behind bulletproof glass. Bulletproof glass? This was an emergency room, not a battle zone, she thought just before the young woman looked up.

"Dr. Reed told us to come in," Barrett said, somehow taking control. "Kelly Ryan, having a baby."

"Yes, Miss Ryan, we've been expecting you. Congratulations. Come right through." The woman pointed to a set of green double doors that immediately swung open. Barrett started through when a nurse in purple scrubs stepped forward.

"I'll take her now," she said, reaching for the handles of the chair. "You need to wait here until we get her all settled."

"No," Barrett and Kelly said in unison, obviously too forceful if the nurse's reaction was any indication.

"Please," Kelly said. "I need her with me."

The nurse looked at Barrett as if deciding whether she was worth breaking the rules for. Before she had a chance to decide, another nurse came hurrying down the hall.

"It's okay, Tammy," she said to the nurse who was obviously perturbed at the bending of the rules. "Dr. Reed left orders that Ms. Taylor can stay the entire time."

Kelly visibly relaxed, and Barrett traded the handle of the wheelchair for Kelly's hand as they walked down the hall.

The nurses expertly shifted Kelly from the wheelchair to the bed in the labor and delivery room. A new set of nurses came in, each one repeating the same actions and questions as the previous two, one starting an IV in her left hand, the other attaching a fetal monitor around Kelly's stomach. Kelly had another contraction, and as she squeezed her hand Barrett watched the monitor on the screen over her head. It was similar to the monitor in the hospital in Panama, except in place of a bouncing yellow line, it was green. The nurse made a few notes on her chart, and the door opened. Dr. Reed finally came in.

"Well, Kelly, it looks like this little girl is tired of waiting. Barrett, it's good to see you again," she said, shaking Barrett's hand. "Relax." Dr. Reed had a kind smile. "She's going to be fine. Women have been giving birth for thousands of years."

Barrett didn't find that very comforting, because none of them had been Kelly. She didn't say anything, just smiled back and nodded.

"Let's see where this little girl is." Dr. Reed lifted the sheet covering Kelly's knees, and one gloved hand disappeared under the sheet, the other moving around on the top of Kelly's stomach. Dr. Reed's head turned to the side, a look of concentration on her face as if she was imagining the position of the baby.

"Okay, she said, pulling her hands back and tossing her gloves in the hazmat trash. "You're doing good, Kelly. You're about six centimeters, which means it'll be a little bit longer." Barrett must have moaned because she smiled and said, "You'll be fine too." She turned back to Kelly. "However, she's breech. I'll be back in about ten minutes and we'll see if we can get her turned to the south. If not—"

"I'll need a C-section."

Dr. Reed patted Kelly on the leg. "Let's cross that bridge if we get there, okay? I'll be right back."

"Do you want me to call your parents?" Barrett asked after Dr. Reed left he room.

"No." Kelly's decision was firm and not open for discussion. "Ariel?"

Kelly shook her head this time.

"Okay. Anybody you want me to call?"

"No," Kelly said quietly.

"Okay, can I get you anything?" Barrett wasn't sure what she was supposed to be doing, if anything. It seemed a little odd for her to just sit there and wait when Kelly was doing all the work.

"Just don't leave me."

"Never." Kelly had another contraction. She grabbed Barrett's hand and grimaced in pain, and it was all Barrett could do not to fall to her knees and beg Kelly for forgiveness.

CHAPTER TWENTY-FOUR

I told you she'd be beautiful," Barrett said, handing the baby to Kelly in the delivery room. Holding something so tiny made her nervous. It didn't make sense. Her briefcase often weighed twice as much as this five-pound, tightly wrapped, pink-faced bundle, but Barrett was afraid she'd drop her anyway.

Alexandra McKayla Ryan had made her entrance screaming bloody murder just before lunch. Kelly had insisted Barrett cut the cord, and every minute of the entire experience had fascinated her. With Alexandra in the nursery and Kelly in her room for some much-needed rest, Barrett collapsed on the hard plastic chair in the cafeteria. A plate of spaghetti sat in front of her, and she held a steaming cup of coffee.

She hadn't had a minute to think since Kelly woke her less than twelve hours ago. Watching Kelly suffer and strain were the longest hours of her life. Fear, joy, panic, terror, anxiety, and elation fought for space in her brain, heart, and stomach. She was alternately bursting with joy then overcome with nausea. Her brain froze, yet she captured every second as if it were recorded on video. The miracle of childbirth didn't even begin to describe what she'd experienced.

How had she never given any thought to what it took to have a child? She'd been buried in her job and her life and had completely disregarded anything and everything else. Barrett pushed the plate away and dropped her head on the table, ashamed of how shallow she'd been.

"May I join you?"

Barrett lifted her head and looked up at a white lab coat, past a tray containing a salad and a carton of milk, and into the inquiring face of Dr. Reed. Barrett sat up and slid her tray to the other side of the table, making room for the doctor's.

"So, how are you holding up?" Dr. Reed asked, using her teeth to open the salad-dressing package.

"Why ask me? I didn't do all the work. I didn't do anything but stand there and hold her hand." And it was the best job she'd ever had. Dr. Reed chuckled.

"You've got a point there," she said. "Sometimes it's harder on the one who has to watch. It's difficult watching someone you love in pain. Even if she's having your child." The crisp lettuce snapped as she stuck her fork in a piece.

"It's not my child and I'm not in love with Kelly," Barrett said, her gut full of knots. Actually, Barrett thought, it was her child. Her fault the child was here in the first place.

"That's not what I see."

"No offense, Doctor, but maybe you need to clean your glasses." Dr. Reed chuckled even louder.

"Forgive me," she said, between laughing and taking a bite of her lunch, "if I overstep, but I've found life's too short."

"Too short for what?"

"Denial."

"I beg your pardon?" This conversation was completely confusing Barrett. "I'm sorry. I know I'm tired, but what are you talking about?" Barrett had no clue why they were discussing this. She'd met Dr. Reed exactly three times when she took Kelly in for her weekly checkups. It wasn't as if they were the best of friends or even knew each other slightly. She was Kelly's doctor, for God's sake, not hers.

"You and Kelly."

"There is no me and Kelly." However, Kelly's kiss last night—jeez, was it only last night—might say otherwise.

"If you say so." Dr. Reed wiped her mouth and drank a few swallows of her milk.

"Yes, I do." Barrett was adamant that there would be no "me and Kelly." Kelly had recently come home and had just had a baby, for crying out loud. She needed to take a lesbian lover like she needed another six months in hell.

Dr. Reed finished her breadstick. "I checked on Kelly and the baby before I came down."

Barrett's heart jumped into her throat and stayed there. "Is something wrong?"

Dr. Reed smiled yet again and looked at Barrett. "No, nothing at all. Just routine. Alexandra is a beautiful name. Does it have any special significance?"

"Not that I know of. I didn't know Kelly had settled on one." And why had it been a secret?

Dr. Reed glanced at her watch. "I'm sorry, I've got to run. Kelly will be here another day or two, and if there are no complications, which I don't anticipate, then she and the baby can go home."

"Thank you, Dr. Reed."

Before she stood Dr. Reed said, "You've got a beautiful woman and a beautiful, healthy child. Don't let them slip away, Barrett."

Shit. That was twice in less than twenty-four hours she'd been told not to let Kelly slip through her fingers. Was everybody insane? Instead of the flu, they'd caught the love bug. *Give me a break.* The only way she was keeping Kelly was out of a sense of obligation and responsibility for her. No way was she going to further complicate Kelly's life. And she certainly wasn't going to fuck it up either.

Alexandra had other ideas than sleeping on the way home. She cried the entire way, and Barrett had to pull over so Kelly could nurse her for a few minutes. It still embarrassed her when Kelly lifted her shirt and pulled Alexandra to her breast. Breast-feeding was perfectly natural, but she felt like a prude if she turned away and a pervert because she didn't want to.

Kelly's breast had gone from being sexual to functional. What happened when women who breast-fed had sex? Did her partner get a mouthful of milk? Did her body know it was time to shut down the milk factory? Did new mothers even have sex? She'd learned from one of the many magazines she'd read that between breast-feeding, laundry, and sleeping only a few hours at a time, if they were lucky, new mothers were completely exhausted. She wondered if there really was a physical reason for the no-sex-for-six-weeks rule or if the new mother just needed rest.

Good God, why was she thinking about these things? When had her life gone from mergers and acquisitions to diapers and baby wipes? It had happened the minute she left Kelly behind.

"Barrett? Kelly said, touching Barrett's arm. "We're here."

Barrett jumped as if Kelly's hand was a hot poker. She was strung pretty tight today. "Oh, yeah, right," she said, pulling into the drive and turning off the car. She jumped out of the car and hurried over to the passenger side to help Kelly out. She was still a little wobbly and in pain. She hadn't needed a C-section, but Alexandra had needed some help.

Grabbing Kelly in one arm and the baby in the other, Barrett walked toward her front door. She felt like she was looking down, an observer on the scene, and she didn't recognize herself. She was being kind and gentle only because Kelly needed her to be, not because it would get her something. They looked like any other young couple bringing home their baby for the first time. A new life beginning for all of them. She could see herself in this role for a while. She was uncomfortable yet somehow it just felt right. Her view from above was certainly different than the view on the ground.

Chapter Twenty-five

A re we going to talk about it?"

The *it* had been hovering around them for weeks. The *it* was the direction her life would go. The *it* was the direction Kelly's life would turn. The *it* was life-defining. *It* was the biggest, most important decision in her life.

"Kelly, I..." Barrett began before Kelly raised her hand. Barrett's stomach was in knots and her hands started shaking so bad she thought she might drop the baby. If she wasn't already sitting down her knees would probably be shaking too. As it was, she rocked a little faster. She had no idea what Kelly was going to say, and as she watched her sit calmly on the couch she tensed.

"If you're going to stick with your position that I don't know what I'm doing, that it's transference or hormones, you're an idiot and you can just leave. If you don't want the responsibility of this—" Kelly waved her hands around the room. The stack of diapers had tipped over, the pile of baby clothes on the couch needed to be folded, and a blanket with spit-up on the corner lay in a heap on the floor, "then leave. If you can only see me as a victim for whom you owe something, then just leave. I don't want or need your pity or your ridiculous sense of obligation.

"Yes, I've been through a lot. I've been through hell and I have a child. But I am well on my way out the other side and I'll come out stronger because of you. If you think you're to blame for all of this, then yes, you are. Because of you I was able to find the strength to go on. Because of you I found the courage to face the past and embrace the future. Because of you I have a life I never expected. Because of you, Barrett. But if you leave I'll still be like this. I'll still be strong. If you leave I'll be fine, Alexandra and I will be fine. Will I love another woman? I don't know. I didn't fall in love with a woman, Barrett. I fell in love with you. It's your decision. I've already made mine."

Barrett could only sit, stunned as Kelly crossed to her. She didn't make eye contact or even touch her as she lifted Alexandra from her arms and left the room. She didn't know what to do, how to act, what to say. She had no point of reference for this. These feelings, this desire, this want was something she had never experienced. She wanted Kelly, that was a given, but she wanted her in her life, not only in her bed, and she wanted it every day.

Could she live up to Kelly's expectations? Could she live up to her own? Would she be a good mother? What would happen with her company? Did she sell it to Debra or telecommute? How could she leave Kelly and the baby for weeks at a time like her job currently demanded? Would Kelly move to San Francisco? Would she move to Denver? Could she be faithful to one woman? Did she know how?

If Kelly was willing to try, so was she. Barrett scrambled out of the chair and followed her.

Kelly was covering Alexandra with a light blanket, and Barrett hovered just outside the door. "Is she asleep?" Her voice sounded odd, a mixture of nerves and hesitation.

"Yes," Kelly replied looking at her watch. She turned on the baby monitor next to Alexandra's bed. "She should sleep several hours." Alexandra had been home for three weeks and had quickly adapted to an easy routine.

"She's a good baby," Barrett said. Kelly looked at her as if she had just claimed to have found the way to ensure world peace. "I mean that she's a good sleeper." She was going from bad to worse fast. Kelly pulled Alexandra's bedroom door almost closed and walked into her bedroom. Barrett wasn't sure if she should follow Kelly but instinctively knew she had to do something. She was stalling and stammering like a virgin. But then again, wasn't that what she was in an ironic sort of way. She had never made love to a woman she loved, and the pressure to please Kelly was daunting.

"What are you doing, Barrett?" Kelly asked, turning to look at her where she stood in the doorway.

"Excuse me?"

"I asked what you were doing. Are you going to stand there and look at me, or do you have something to say? Because I've got things to do."

Kelly stood next to the bed, a pillow in her hand. The warm afternoon sun scissored through the half-opened blinds on either side of the large unmade bed.

"Kelly, I…" Barrett stopped mid-sentence. Not because she didn't know what to say but because Kelly was the most beautiful woman she had ever seen and she couldn't speak. Words almost seemed inadequate to describe the strength, wisdom, kindness, and sheer inner beauty embodied in front of her.

All the pieces fell into place, pieces she hadn't even realized had been missing in her life. She loved Kelly. She had nothing in her life to compare it to, but she knew without a doubt that she loved her.

Kelly's eyes darkened as Barrett approached her. She stopped so close to Kelly, their breasts were almost touching. Speckles of green and brown she'd never noticed before danced in Kelly's eyes and something else. Something familiar, yet very, very new. Desire.

Her hands shook as she cupped Kelly's face and slowly pulled her lips closer. The lips, the ones that made her pulse race and her brain stop with just one kiss. The lips that she desperately wanted to feel on hers again, on her nipple, on her everywhere.

"Kelly…"

"No more excuses, Barrett. Either take me now or leave." Kelly's voice was barely above a whisper.

"You didn't give me a chance to finish." Barrett traced the outline of Kelly's lips with the tip of her thumb. "Kelly, I love you, and I love your daughter. Nothing would make me happier than to change diapers, clean up barf, and raise Alexandra as ours for the rest of my life."

Barrett watched as understanding and joy filled Kelly's face. Finally, after so many nights alone, so many days empty of what truly mattered, she felt like she had truly come home. And as Alexandra slept through the night for the first time, they didn't.

The End

About the Author

Julie Cannon is a corporate suit, a partner, mom, sister, friend, and writer. Julie and Laura, her partner of twenty-one years, have lived in at least a half a dozen states, and have an unending supply of dedicated friends.

Julie has eleven books published by Bold Strokes Books. Her first novel, *Come and Get Me*, was a finalist for the Golden Crown Literary Society's Best Lesbian Romance and Debut Author Awards, and in 2014 *I Remember* was a winner for Best Lesbian Romance. In 2012 her ninth novel, *Rescue Me*, was a finalist as Best Lesbian Romance from the prestigious Lambda Literary Society. Julie has also published five short stories in Bold Strokes anthologies.

Books Available from Bold Strokes Books

Because of You by Julie Cannon. What would you do for the woman you were forced to leave behind? (978-1-62639-199-4)

The Job by Jove Belle. Sera always dreamed that she would one day reunite with Tor. She just didn't think it would involve terrorists, firearms, and hostages. (978-1-62639-200-7)

Making Time by C.J. Harte. Two women going in different directions meet after fifteen years and struggle to reconnect in spite of the past that separated them. (978-1-62639-201-4)

Once The Clouds Have Gone by KE Payne. Overwhelmed by the dark clouds of her past, Tag Grainger is lost until the intriguing and spirited Freddie Metcalfe unexpectedly forces her to reevaluate her life. (978-1-62639-202-1)

The Acquittal by Anne Laughlin. Chicago private investigator Josie Harper searches for the real killer of a woman whose lover has been acquitted of the crime. (978-1-62639-203-8)

An American Queer: The Amazon Trail by Lee Lynch. Lee Lynch's heartening and heart-rending history of gay life from the turbulence of the late 1900s to the triumphs of the early 2000s are recorded in this selection of her columns. (978-1-62639-204-5)

Stick McLaughlin: The Prohibition Years by CF Frizzell. Corruption in 1918 cost Stick her lover, her freedom, and her identity, but a very special flapper and the family bond of her own gang could help win them back—even if it means outwitting the Boston Mob. (978-1-62639-205-2)

Edge of Awareness by C.A. Popovich. When Maria, a woman in the middle of her third divorce, meets Dana, an out lesbian, awareness of her feelings bring up reservations about the teachings of her church. (978-1-62639-188-8)

Taken by Storm by Kim Baldwin. Lives depend on two women when a train derails high in the remote Alps, but an unforgiving mountain, avalanches, crevasses, and other perils stand between them and safety. (978-1-62639-189-5)

The Common Thread by Jaime Maddox. Dr. Nicole Coussart's life is falling apart, but fortunately, DEA Attorney Rae Rhodes is there to pick up the pieces and help Nic put them back together. (978-1-62639-190-1)

Jolt by Kris Bryant. Mystery writer Bethany Lange wasn't prepared for the twisting emotions that left her breathless the moment she laid eyes on folk singer sensation Ali Hart. (978-1-62639-191-8)

Searching For Forever by Emily Smith. Dr. Natalie Jenner's life has always been about saving others, until young paramedic Charlie Thompson comes along and shows her maybe she's the one who needs saving. (978-1-62639-186-4)

A Queer Sort of Justice: Prison Tales Across Time by Rebecca S. Buck. When liberty is only a memory, and all seems lost, what freedoms and hopes can be found within us? (978-1-62639-195-6E)

Blue Water Dreams by Dena Hankins. Lania Marchiol keeps her wary sailor's gaze trained on the horizon until Oly Rassmussen, a wickedly handsome trans man, sends her trusty compass spinning off course. (978-1-62639-192-5)

Rest Home Runaways by Clifford Henderson. Baby boomer Morgan Ronzio's troubled marriage is the least of her worries when she gets the call that her addled, eighty-six-year-old, half-blind dad has escaped the rest home. (978-1-62639-169-7)

Charm City by Mason Dixon. Raq Overstreet's loyalty to her drug kingpin boss is put to the test when she begins to fall for Bathsheba Morris, the undercover cop assigned to bring him down. (978-1-62639-198-7)

Let the Lover Be by Sheree Greer. Kiana Lewis, a functional alcoholic on the verge of destruction, finally faces the demons of her past while finding love and earning redemption in New Orleans. (978-1-62639-077-5)

Blindsided by Karis Walsh. Blindsided by love, guide dog trainer Lenae McIntyre and media personality Cara Bradley learn to trust what they see with their hearts. (978-1-62639-078-2)

About Face by VK Powell. Forensic artist Macy Sheridan and Detective Leigh Monroe work on a case that has troubled them both for years, but they're hampered by the past and their unlikely yet undeniable attraction. (978-1-62639-079-9)

Blackstone by Shea Godfrey. For Darry and Jessa, their chance at a life of freedom is stolen by the arrival of war and an ancient prophecy that just might destroy their love. (978-1-62639-080-5)

Out of This World by Maggie Morton. Iris decided to cross an ocean to get over her ex. But instead, she ends up traveling much farther, all the way to another world. Once there, only a mysterious, sexy, and magical woman can help her return home. (978-1-62639-083-6)

Kiss The Girl by Melissa Brayden. Sleeping with the enemy has never been so complicated. Brooklyn Campbell and Jessica Lennox face off in love and advertising in fast-paced New York City. (978-1-62639-071-3)

Taking Fire: A First Responders Novel by Radclyffe. Hunted by extremists and under siege by nature's most virulent weapons, Navy medic Max de Milles and Red Cross worker Rachel Winslow join forces to survive and discover something far more lasting. (978-1-62639-072-0)

First Tango in Paris by Shelley Thrasher. When French law student Eva Laroche meets American call girl Brigitte Green in 1970s Paris, they have no idea how their pasts and futures will intersect. (978-1-62639-073-7)

The War Within by Yolanda Wallace. Army nurse Meredith Moser went to Vietnam in 1967 looking to help those in need; she didn't expect to meet the love of her life along the way. (978-1-62639-074-4)

Escapades by MJ Williamz. Two women, afraid to love again, must overcome their fears to find the happiness that awaits them. (978-1-62639-182-6)

Desire at Dawn by Fiona Zedde. For Kylie, love had always come armed with sharp teeth and claws. But with the human, Olivia, she bares her vampire heart for the very first time, sharing passion, lust, and a tenderness she'd never dared dream of before. (978-1-62639-064-5)

Visions by Larkin Rose. Sometimes the mysteries of love reveal themselves when you least expect it. Other times they hide behind a black satin mask. Can Paige unveil her masked stranger this time? (978-1-62639-065-2)

All In by Nell Stark. Internet poker champion Annie Navarro loses everything when the Feds shut down online gambling, and she turns to experienced casino host Vesper Blake for advice—but can Nova convince Vesper to take a gamble on romance? (978-1-62639-066-9)

Vermilion Justice by Sheri Lewis Wohl. What's a vampire to do when Dracula is no longer just a character in a novel? (978-1-62639-067-6)

Switchblade by Carsen Taite. Lines were meant to be crossed. Γ in the Luca Bennett Bounty Hunter Series. (978-1-62639-058-4)

Nightingale by Andrea Bramhall. Culture, faith, and duty conspire to tear two young lovers apart, yet fate seems to have different plans for them both. (978-1-62639-059-1)

No Boundaries by Donna K. Ford. A chance meeting and a nightmare from the past threaten more than Andi Massey's solitude as she and Gwen Palmer struggle to understand the complexity of love without boundaries. (978-1-62639-060-7)

Timeless by Rachel Spangler. When Stevie Geller returns to her hometown, will she do things differently the second time around or will she be in such a hurry to leave her past that she misses out on a better future? (978-1-62639-050-8)

Second to None by L.T. Marie. Can a physical therapist and a custom motorcycle designer conquer their pasts and build a future with one another? (978-1-62639-051-5)

Seneca Falls by Jesse Thoma. Together, two women discover love truly can conquer all evil. (978-1-62639-052-2)

A Kingdom Lost by Barbara Ann Wright. Without knowing each other's fates, Princess Katya and her consort Starbride seek to reclaim their kingdom from the magic-wielding madman who seized the throne and is murdering their people. (978-1-62639-053-9)

Season of the Wolf by Robin Summers. Two women running from their pasts are thrust together by an unimaginable evil. Can they overcome the horrors that haunt them in time to save each other? (978-1-62639-043-0)

The Heat of Angels by Lisa Girolami. Fires burn in more than one place in Los Angeles. (978-1-62639-042-3)

Desperate Measures by P. J. Trebelhorn. Homicide detective Kay Griffith and contractor Brenda Jansen meet amidst turmoil neither of them is aware of until murder suspect Tommy Rayne makes his move to exact revenge on Kay. (978-1-62639-044-7)

The Magic Hunt by L.L. Raand. With her Pack being hunted by human extremists and beset by enemies masquerading as friends, can Sylvan protect them and her mate, or will she succumb to the feral rage that threatens to turn her rogue, destroying them all? A Midnight Hunters novel. (978-1-62639-045-4)